MERLIN'S SECRET

The Truth Revealed

LORD MALCOLM JOHN BAKER

ISBN 978-1-955156-65-3 (paperback)
ISBN 978-1-955156-66-0 (hardcover)
ISBN 978-1-955156-67-7 (digital)

Rushmore Press LLC
1 800 460 9188
www.rushmorepress.com

Printed in the United States of America

Other books by Lord Malcolm John Baker

Revenge Is Mine
From a Jack to a King
Daylight Robbery
Which is the Clone?
Annabelle
The African Duke

Merlin Series.
Merlin's Secret
Merlin's Shakespeare Encounter
Merlin's French Encounter
Merlin's American Encounter

Coming soon.
The Key

Malcolm's websites are.
WWW.malcolmjohnbaker.us
www. malcolmjohnbaker.com
email m-baker12@sky.com

CHAPTER ONE

570 AD

In a small corner of Avalon lived a community of witches, amid a secluded wooded glade hewn out by a glacier as the ice age had ended. The glacier also left behind several caves, ideal accommodation for the witches. In one of them lived a witch named Beverley with her five-year-daughter, Viviane, and two other ladies. It was a chilly January morning, and though there had been an overnight dusting of snow, it had cleared quickly in the sunshine. But the dew in the air was freezing and sparkled like diamonds.

Thinking it best to let her daughter keep warm and sleep in while she goes about collecting herbs and grasses for her potions, Beverley left Viviane inside the cave, behind the fire she'd lit at the entrance – a large fire of timber collected from the surrounding woods. The sparks she'd watched rising from the two-foot-high flames had reminded her of the day the late king's father had been burned at his pyre all those years ago, before Uther had taken Camelot's throne, when she'd thought the flashing sparks had looked like leaping fairies.

Income was scarce to come by for the witches, and some in the community – which had grown considerably in recent years – had turned to black magic, making spells to enable the men of the kingdom to control their women. As a result, the community had gained a bad name, especially since some of the king's subjects had grown mad or murderous under the influence of those black spells. This had led the council of knights to force a decree from King Uther Pendragon demanding that the practice of witchcraft be outlawed and that all witches be executed.

Uther's problem was that one witch had helped him a while ago in getting an heir to his throne. Uther and his wife hadn't been able to have children no matter how hard they'd tried, Uther's wife was barren, but then he'd turned to Beverley, and she'd cast a spell, and magically, they'd had a strong son. Arthur was now five years old and would inherit Camelot's throne on Uther's death; the lineage was now established. Uther could rest in peace knowing he had done his duty for the nation.

This morning, Uther sent out a detachment of thirty soldiers to destroy the enclave and the witches within it. However, he ordered that one witch, Beverley, be saved at all costs. The soldiers approached the enclave not expecting any trouble; the hamlet was situated in the dugout surrounded by thirty-foot rock cliffs with several tree-lined paths leading down.

The captain and his men, who were dressed in leather armor comprising a head cap, vest, and a Celtic-type kilt to keep the cold out were spaced around the top of the cliffs. Their swords were raised high, the sunlight glinting on the polished metal, but evil shone in their eyes that day. The witches saw the sun's beams reflecting on the swords, and it momentarily blinded them. The soldiers on the high ground openly picked out their prey from those in the enclave below.

A particularly ferocious, well-built soldier said to his colleague, "I'll take the blonde one there if you take the redhead." He fondled his groin in anticipation, and his kilt was now projecting. *Wait till she feels this*, he thought.

"Yes, I like the look of the redhead," was the response.

The captain said to his men, "I want those blades covered in blood by the end of the day."

The witches were a peaceful, isolated people and did not move; they believed the Woodsman, god of the forest, would protect them. Several uttered vicious curses, all to no avail; the soldiers were adamant.

The captain yelled the order: "Charge, but it is imperative, on peril your own life, to save the witch Beverley. You all heard the king's order."

Vengeance on their minds, thirty bloodthirsty soldiers descended on the camp, swords held high, and they yelled the battle cry: "Death to the witches."

Like many soldiers at war, they intended to take their pleasures from the young witches. The hags would be left to die by the sword, but the young ones would be raped first.

A massacre happened that day. Women and children were raped and slaughtered, and bodies, covered in blood and mutilated, littered the ground. Beverley had a knife in a scabbard under her dress. As a soldier attacked her, lifting her skirt – she was one of the pretty ones – she managed to get the knife out of its scabbard. The soldier raised his kilt to reveal his erection. Beverley raised her knife, and with one quick slash, his penis fell to the ground. Blood squirted out of the wound, covering her. The soldier screamed in pain as she plunged the knife between his ribs and into his heart. The screaming stopped as the soldier fell on top of her.

She feigned death, and when she thought the coast was clear, she heaved the soldier off and ran to the cave where her daughter was still asleep. She comforted the waking child, telling her to keep quiet. The encampment had been razed to the ground; soldiers were laughing at what they had done. A soldier walked past the entrance to Beverley's cave but did not go in.

Inside, Beverley was ready with her knife. "I'll kill any bastard who comes in here," she whispered to herself.

Half an hour later, it was quiet outside, and Beverley ventured gingerly out, telling Viviane to stay inside.

Everywhere was carnage; the ground was littered with dead bodies of women, many naked and covered in wet blood. Wooden huts were burning, and children lay mutilated. Beverley vomited at the devastating sight.

She cried out, with tears running down her face, "How could the king do this to us? You are supposed to be a fair man, Uther." Several dead soldiers lay nearby, but one, the captain, was still barely alive. Beverley went to him; she felt compassion as she raised her knife, intending to kill him, but then she asked herself, *Why?*

The captain managed to mutter, "What's your name?"

"Beverley."

"Good, I have obeyed my instructions, then. King Uther said you were to be saved."

"Did he now?" said Beverley as she plunged her knife into the captain's chest. Maybe Uther was more grateful than she had thought.

King Uther had issued the decree under pressure; he was a gentle man, really.

Five years passed, and Viviane was now ten years old. Beverley had given up casting spells after the carnage all those years ago and taken on a low profile. Witchcraft is like a gift, though, or a curse: once received, it never goes away. Beverley had been ill for some months now. She knew she was dying; her body seemed to be eating itself away. She could not cast a spell to stop that, but on her deathbed, she cast one more spell on her daughter.

Beverley had always been grateful to the king for allowing her to live, so she charged Viviane to look after the Pendragon name and to promote the formation of one country that would one day exceed the might of the Roman Empire. She put a spell on Viviane that she would always be a spirit after her death and thus able to carry out this charge.

The years passed, and by 590 AD, the beautiful and feisty girl Viviane had grown into a desirable twenty-five-year-old. She had many of the local boys seeking her as a bride, but she was true to only one.

Her long blonde hair, which was usually down to her shoulders, was almost horizontal in the wind, but it showed off her bright blue eyes. On this day, she was standing at the edge of the lake at Camelot with her boyfriend. She was very impish, and she knew it.

Viviane challenged her boyfriend to a swimming contest, saying that he could not swim the lake as fast as her. The challenge was taken up, and despite the threat of encroaching severe weather, they decide to go ahead. "We are not cowards," Viviane said, although her boyfriend wasn't so sure. He was not prepared to let Viviane best him, though.

Taking off their clothes, they stood at the edge of the lake; Viviane thought it should take about ten minutes to swim across. They dove into the rough water, and as soon as they set off, the weather deteriorated even further, and the lake turned into a raging torrent. The wind picked up, and the water was like a sea: waves showed white horses, and the spray blew in their faces. Lightning flashed from cloud to cloud, followed by roars of thunder. Viviane's boyfriend was way out in front, but sadly, she was overcome by the foaming current.

The water entered her mouth, and she started choking on it. Her boyfriend was well ahead of her now, so he didn't hear her calls. Viviane panicked, and though she managed to come up for air one more time, eventually, she sank for good.

It was midday, and a large barn owl was sleeping on the top branch of an oak tree on the edge of the lake. It suddenly woke up and flew over the lake, descending to where Viviane was drowning. Then, while flying in a circle, it dropped a twig on the spot where the young woman was sinking. Behind the owl, in the distance, could be seen twenty-four white doves flying in line to the spot where Viviane was going down.

When they reached the oak twig, they circled over the spot while the barn owl flew back to its tree to resume its sleep. Viviane's boyfriend could not see her, but he saw the doves circling. At that moment, a ghostly hand appeared from the lake, and then another, followed by the spirit of Viviane's body. The lightning was now coming down to the ground, great bolts of jagged blades followed by explosions of thunder. A bolt hit Viviane's spirit, and she lit up as she ascended to the sky. She turned to her boyfriend, who was still swimming, and blew him a kiss, the last one she would make, and then she flew up into the heavens.

Viviane drowned that day, sinking to the bottom of the lake, but her spirit lived on. Her boyfriend never forgave himself for not hearing and rescuing her. Viviane's body was never recovered despite her boyfriend making many dives, and she was missed in Avalon, but her spirit returned when it was needed, as her mother had decreed. Although her mother's charge was to transform Avalon into the British Empire, Viviane had her own goal: to help misguided youths on their way to adulthood.

CHAPTER TWO

2019 AD

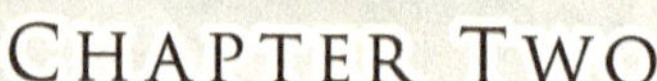

℟obert ℌunt was meeting some acquaintances – they could not be classed as friends – on a surprisingly warm March evening. They met at a local bar in Bromley, a small town on the outskirts of South London in the United Kingdom. For Robert, the New Year had started out just the same as the old one that had left, except that it was now 2019.

He had become involved with a group of petty criminals. It had not been his intention; it had just happened. Robert was like that: things just happened to him, and he went along with them. He knew he was drifting, but he didn't know what to do about it. He was limited educationally, financially, and socially.

The group wanted to move up the ladder into big-time crime and money. They planned to carry out a bank raid. This was not what Robert wanted at all, and he told them so, but like so many young people in his circumstances, he was dragged into it. On the way to the bar where the meeting was to be held to finalize the arrangements, he thought, *How the hell did I get involved in this escapade? What would my parents have thought?* He knew he was letting them down and wanted to leave the gang, but he didn't have the guts to do so; he had nothing else to do anyway.

Robert was twenty years old. He'd tragically lost both his parents in a car crash when he was ten. It had devastated him, and he had never gotten over it. How could the Almighty have been so cruel? An only child, he had been brought up by his grandmother, but he missed his parents so much. He had only just gotten to know them when they'd died. *How could this have happened to me?* he'd often thought when he'd watched his friends enjoying family life. *It's just not fair.*

His grandmother had been very strict with him, but she knew Robert needed a male role model, and he would have loved a father to play games with. He had rebelled and left home at the age of eighteen; he'd concluded it was not fair for a lady in her eighties to bring up a child. Robert had wanted to share a flat with a chum called Alan; they'd been at school together. Alan was slimmer than Robert. He liked the gym; he always said it kept him fit. Robert thought that one day, he would have to go to the gym, but that was as far as it got.

Alan was in a situation similar to Robert's, and the two just gravitated together. It was more a friendship of convenience than anything else. Robert desperately wanted to be part of a real family; he'd always wished his parents had had more children. Alan was the closest he had to a brother, but a real brother or sister was what he wanted most of all.

Robert had found a flat to rent on the internet; it was over the butcher's shop on High Street: a small unit with two bedrooms, a good-sized lounge and kitchen, and a small bathroom. At the flat, he and Alan met the landlord, who thought they would make good tenants and gave them a reasonable rent. The agreement was signed, and they had scrimped together the first month's rent and deposit, so they handed it over, and the flat was theirs.

The next day, neither of them was working, and Alan had arranged for his brother and family to come to afternoon tea to see the flat. Robert was inwardly jealous and felt very depressed. He knew he shouldn't be, but he had no family to show off the apartment to. He so desperately needed a family and to be wanted.

He said to Alan, "I'll go to the movies this afternoon. That will give you more room in the flat for your family."

"Don't be silly. There's plenty of room for all of us," said Alan, but he understood Robert's viewpoint; they had discussed it before. Robert went to the movie theater to see the latest version of *Beauty and the Beast*.

He chose a quiet part of the theater to sit in. There was no one else in his row; he didn't want any company that day. He entered the row, moving along until he came to the middle, and then he lowered the seat and sat down. The film had just started when the seat next to him came down as though someone had sat on it, but there was no one there. At one point, he thought he could hear a quiet giggle, and then he thought he could feel someone touch his arm, but he decided he had imagined it.

When the film had finished, he decided he had enjoyed it; he got up to leave, at which time his seat reverted upright to its vertical position. So did the seat next to him, which had been down all through the film. *That's weird,* he thought. While walking out of the cinema, all he could think about were the families he had seen at the front. They had all looked so happy. He returned to his flat at seven in the evening, depressed. Alan's family had gone, and they'd cleaned up the flat.

"I understand how you feel about the lack of a family. I discussed it with my brother, and he said you must look to him as your family as well," said Alan

"That's very kind of him," said Robert, knowing that was not the same. *Maybe one day I'll marry and have my own family*, he thought.

Robert's pride and joy was his small moped, which he kept spick and span. It was the only real possession he had. He would spend hours polishing it until it gleamed. His real goal was to have a proper motorbike, but there was no way he could afford one. He could, however, window shop at the local bike shop, which he did almost daily. Gazing through the window at the row of Harley-Davidsons lining the back wall, he thought, *One day, I'll have one.* He would have taken any of them, but he really liked the look of the Road King Special.

Robert was intrinsically a good lad; he had been brought up to obey the law, to be courteous, and to help others when he could. He was well behaved at school, unusual for this day and age. It was only since leaving school that things had started to go wrong. He was fairly intelligent, but he did not make it into university, not that he could have afforded it in any case. He wanted to become someone of note, though, and leave his name on this earth. He had read the James Bond books and thought, *Maybe I'll be like that and one day and become a hero for the country.* It was n different than every boyhood dream, although he was old enough to realize it probably would never happen in his mundane life.

Although he had fallen out with his grandmother two years ago, he still went back to see her regularly. She was the only family he had, after all, but tragedy had struck last month when she had suddenly died. Now he had no one left and felt desperately alone in the big wide world.

The only friend he had was his flatmate, Alan. He'd had a girlfriend when he was sixteen, but that had only lasted a few months. She'd said he was wimpish, and he hadn't had another since. He so wanted to have his own family, but if he couldn't get a girlfriend, how could that happen?

Robert and Alan were servers at the Piano Bar on High Street. Robert was a very tall guy, six foot three. He had chestnut-brown hair with a natural curl. He thought he was attractive, but clearly, the girls weren't so sure. He had to admit that his nose was turned up, and he was somewhat overweight at two hundred pounds. He tried to overcome these problems by dressing as well as he could afford, which had its limitations. He didn't earn much and relied on tips, and people in England don't tip much.

Robert and Alan had become involved with four other guys who frequented the Piano Bar most nights. Edward Brice led the group, and they had higher ideas of grandeur. Edward was a domineering type, well dressed but without the grace to pull it off. *At least he can afford the clothes*, thought Robert. He knew Edward would become a hardened criminal; he had that thug appearance, a greasy face with a scar down the left side. It had come from a fight at school when an older boy had slashed his face, but no one else knew this; all the gang was too scared to ask.

Edward wanted to carry out his first bank raid and get rich quick. He had chosen a bank at the far end of town and had researched it for weeks. He'd found the best means of entry would be through the roof via an old iron fire escape at the rear.

The building was old, dating back to Victorian days, and had a slate roof. Edward had calculated that they could remove enough slates to make a hole large enough for them to get in. They didn't want to be seen from the street below, although the job would be done at night, when this quiet town would certainly be asleep.

Edward's daytime job is in the burglar alarm business, which is handy as one of his clients was the bank they were planning to rob. He knew that only the exterior doors and windows had alarms.

Edward said, "Once we get in through the roof, we are free to walk around inside the building without concern."

Once inside, they would go down to the basement, where the safety deposit boxes were housed. Edward had acquired explosives to blow the locks on the safes. The plan was to take as many valuables as they could and leave as soon as possible, no more than fifteen minutes after they arrived. That was the time Edward calculated would be the minimum for the police to arrive. They realized that once the locks were blown, further alarms might be sparked off or heard by neighbors.

So, they met at the bar two days earlier than the date chosen to finalize last-minute details. Robert just sat and listened; he would do as he was told. He knew they only wanted him for his muscle. He was a strong lad, capable of looking after himself, but he knew he was not Edward's favorite, and the feeling was mutual. They chose Sunday at eleven in the evening to carry out their raid, the day after tomorrow.

Sitting in the chair behind the group was a manifestation, and her head was turning from side to side in disbelief. She said aloud, though no one could hear, "What is wrong with the youth of today? It was not like this in my time." Although Robert heard nothing, he did get a sense of a presence, and a shiver went up his spine.

Robert thought he would go to the bank to get the ambiance of the building and check it out. He always thought he was a little psychic and believed in the vibes that came from buildings, especially old ones that had a history. He stood outside, looking at the building on Saturday morning at eleven o'clock. Next to him, but unseen, was a beautiful girl. She was looking around, taking in the ambiance as well. Robert thought he could feel someone breathing on his neck, but when he turned around, there was no one there. He shuddered, and another reaction shot up his spine.

The bank was certainly a timeworn, spooky building, one of the few Victorian properties left in the area, built in the mid-1850s, with large stone cladding; he thought it looked creepy. The doorman peered at Robert as though he was a burglar. *He can't possibly know that*, thought Robert, and shrugged he it off.

Robert entered through the revolving doors, which carried on revolving after he had gone through as though there was someone behind him. He then walked around the banking hall, which was still in its original design. He didn't like the feeling he was getting, but he persevered. He imagined ghosts coming out of those grotesque marble statues that lined the walls. Unbeknownst to Robert, a real ghost was standing behind one. He could feel the hairs on the back of his neck stand on end, and another shiver shot up his spine. After ten minutes, he had more than he could take and left the building, not feeling good about this whole experience. The ghost smiled, thinking, *He's just what I need.*

The time arrived the next day for the operation to begin, and Robert was at the meeting point at eleven o'clock that night. It was a mile away from the bank, in an empty plot. Edward had provided a truck to drive the rest of the way.

They needed it to load all the money, Edward had said, but Robert wondered whether there would be that much. He was now so afraid that he was shaking; his whole body was telling him to get out of here.

Access to the roof at the rear of the building was on a rickety, old iron fire escape stairway. It dropped down to the ground; it must have been original as it was rusting away, but it was just barely usable. *What a stupid thing to leave around in a bank*, thought Robert. *The owners are asking for a burglary. Why is it there in any event? The flats above the bank are no longer in use.*

They climbed the staircase and onto the roof one at a time. One step simply broke away from Robert's weight on his way up, so the others had to climb two at that point. Having made it to the top, they removed about twenty slates to make a five-foot square hole, which they clambered through one at a time.

One slate suddenly slid down the roof and over the end gutter and smashed on the pavement below. "Careful!" Edward called to Robert, the last person to enter.

Robert said, "It wasn't me," but he could hear a girl's voice say, "Oops."

"Who else, then, you imbecile?" said Edward.

Robert had no idea, and he shrugged. About five minutes had elapsed, but their stopwatch wouldn't start until they blew the safe boxes. Once in the roof space, they knew they had to move fast; no one wanted to hang around longer than was necessary. They cut a hole in the ceiling big enough to squeeze through, and they all dropped to the floor below.

Edward had made preliminary investigations before the raid in case the bank had gone to a different security firm, but they hadn't. There were no internal alarm sensors in the rooms, or so he thought.

As quietly as they could, they crept down to the basement, where the personal deposit boxes were. Robert thought, *I don't know why we are creeping. No one can hear us,* but he was feeling anxious, depressed, and scared. Having got down the stairs and into the basement, they were in a reception area. During office hours, a receptionist would sit behind her desk, and customers would sign in to get access to their boxes. The deposit boxes lined the whole wall in the adjoining room. Each client had their one key, and the bank receptionist held the second key, and they opened the safe together.

"Oh, shit!" yelled Edward as he looked at the doorway into the safe area. "The buggers have installed lasers across the doorway. When the hell did they do that?"

Sure enough, at two-foot-high intervals, there were four laser beams.

"That's going to make life difficult. We'll need to step over the lower ray while bending down under the second, but it's doable. Is everyone happy with that?" said Edward.

Most nodded but Robert, who wished he had been to the gym, said, "You must be joking. I'm much too large to manage that."

"Yes, I suppose you are. I don't know why you are here. Well, you need to stay on this side, and we will push the contents of the boxes out to you under the lowest beam," said Edward, who thought that it had been a mistake to bring this fat slob with him.

"That's great. I can cope with that," said Robert. All the others just sniggered.

So, the other five all took off their trousers to give them more flexibility. They were less likely to touch the rays. One at a time, they then did their contortion act, stepping over the lowest beam with one leg while bending down and under the higher one. Then brought the other leg over, all without touching either beam. Slowly, they managed it, and after ten minutes, they all were on the other side. Robert thought, *It's lucky they are all athletic types; I could never have done that.*

While they were doing their gymnastics, Robert was looking around the room. It was a typical bank vault, solid, unadorned walls in the basement. He checked out the wooden desk, which looked as though it had seen better days; all the drawers were locked, and one of its legs had an extra screw where it had broken at some point. There wasn't much else in the room other than a built-in cupboard and three pictures on the walls. He lifted the pictures – one was of a ghost rising out of a lake – but there was nothing behind them. What had he expected? The other two were prints of country scenes, nothing spectacular.

He then nervously opened the door to the cupboard. Why he did it so slowly, even he didn't know. Maybe he was expecting a jack-in-box fist to come out and punch him, but he was shocked to find there was absolutely nothing inside. How strange to have an empty cupboard like that. He went around the walls inside, banging them to see if they were hollow. Someone was looking over his shoulder, smiling, but he had no idea.

The walls were solid and lined expensively in veneered wood to a high standard. In the middle, at head height, engraved in wood was the name "Viviane." The face behind him smiled again. *How strange.* He rubbed his hand over the name, and he thought he saw sparkling gold dust appear around it, but it disappeared as quickly as it had come. It frightened him; why on earth would such an elaborate cupboard be in this bank unused, and who was Viviane?

Robert had his mobile phone with him, and although the signal was not good in the basement, the bank did have Wi-Fi, so while waiting for some action, he logged into the internet. He searched the name Viviane, but all he could come up with that could remotely connect was a reference to the Lady of the Lake from the King Arthur legend.

By this time, the others had gotten over the beams and were ready to start putting explosives on the safes, so Robert left the cupboard quickly and didn't bother to close the door. He was now in a rush to get to his position, crouching under the desk in case the ceiling caved in. He felt like a small child while waiting for the first explosion. He put his phone on top of the desk and was feeling more relaxed now, although he still wished he hadn't gotten involved with this gang.

Edward chose twelve of the largest boxes and applied tiny amounts of explosive putty over the locks. There was a whoosh of air that went past Robert; he had no idea where it came from. The detonators were all linked to a single plunger. Edward told the others to look the other way, and once they did, he pushed the plunger down. They all had their fingers in their ears, expecting a bombshell blast. There was a series of explosions that blew the doors off with little more noise than a deep puff. Edward was pleased with himself.

"That's the first time I've done that," he said. The others thought, *Some explosion!*

They immediately started emptying the boxes. There was a lot of cash, which they collected in one of the sacks. There were ten small bars of gold, which was unexpected but welcome. There was some jewelry, which also went into the cash bag. There was much paperwork, which they ignored. They knew they had to be quick now before the police arrived; the stopwatch had now started, and they had fifteen minutes.

Edward was also concerned that the newly installed lasers might also have an alarm to pick up any blast.

Edward slid the gold bars one at a time under the beams to Robert, followed by the sack of cash, saying, "Slide back another sack." Robert did, and they repeated the exercise three more times. Finally, they had a collection of four sacks of cash and ten bars of gold.

Edward said, "I think we've got enough. It has now been fifteen minutes since the explosions. It's time to go just in case the police arrive. We have a good haul."

Now they needed to repeat the exercise of evading the lasers. Edward sent the others out one at a time, each one putting their trousers back on once they were through the beams. Soon, it was just Edward to go through; the others had started to move upstairs, each taking a sack. That just left the ten gold bars for Robert and Edward to carry, five each. They were only small ingots, and although they were still heavy, they could manage them all right, thought Robert.

Edward got his first leg over the beam and bent under the higher one. As he brought his second leg over, he just caught the laser with his shoe. All hell broke loose: alarm bells were going off all over the bank. The door behind them slammed closed with a sound that was louder than Edward's explosions, and they could hear other doors in the building shutting. Edward put on his pants, and after picking up two bars of gold, he was upstairs and off in a trice.

Robert went into a deep trance. *What the hell do I do now?* He slapped his face and pulled himself together. Time was moving on; he knew the police would be on the way by now; they only had fifteen minutes at the most to get away. All that was going through his mind was to get outside of the building. He rushed past the pile of gold bars; one seemed to jump from the pile into his hand, and it gave him a start. He had to have something to show from this exploit, although disaster would be a better word.

Outside the bank, the police had arrived in record time, and a small crowd was building up in response to the blue flashing lights and sirens of the police cars. The police quickly laid out blue tape across the road to warn neighbors not to cross.

Edward was well gone by now – he had managed to get outside before the police arrived – but Robert was still rushing upstairs. On his way, he heard a gunshot and breaking glass. *Oh my God, what was that?* He was now on the ground floor in the main banking hall. Some of the other members of the team had managed to smash the front door. He realized that someone had brought a gun, and he panicked more now. Armed robbery, that was something else, a long jail sentence, and the others seemed to have gotten away.

The crowd was growing in size by the minute. Everyone was attracted by a police presence, and they were being pushed back by the police officers. Everyone ducked down for cover at the sound of a shot. Minutes passed, and no more shots were heard, and the crowd started to rise again and break into chatter.

"What is happening?"

"That was a shot, wasn't it?"

"Can you see anyone?"

"Is that one of them over there?"

"Why don't the police go in?"

The police commenced pushing the crowd further back and out of their way. They needed a clear area for their attack into the building. Inside the bank, Robert was on his own; he had no idea where anyone else was. He could hear the screaming sirens screaming of at least three police cars. The reflection of the blue flashing lights lit the room; it was the only light as the building was now in darkness. More police officers arrived and filed out of their cars. Twelve officers ran around the building, but they were not entering the building until the outside was secured.

The police cars were parked at ten-foot intervals. Hearing the gunshot, the police supervisor called for more armed reinforcements. The policemen switched off their sirens but left on the blue lights. They also had a small searchlight on the roof of each car, which they trained on the building. One focused on the staircase Robert had used to enter the bank. The sirens of more police cars approaching could be heard in the distance. Up above, a helicopter was circling, its powerful light moving across the ground. Caution was now the name of the game for the police as a gun had been fired.

Robert didn't know what to do. He was aware that it was no good going up to the roof, where they had come in; that would now be under surveillance. He could see through the front door that two of the gang members were now under arrest. Handcuffed, they were being led into the police cars. One of them was Alan, Robert's roommate.

There was no sign of Edward, who had caused the mess.

The police inspector in charge said through a megaphone, "The building is surrounded. If there is anyone still inside, come out now with your hands up. Leave your gun inside."

Robert felt like crying, but he knew there was no point, and no tears came. He was alone, so he got on his knees and prayed. "Please help me, Lord, and I will never do anything like this again, I promise, if you get me out." *I wonder how many times God has heard that before*, thought Robert, *but I mean it.*

He did the only thing he could think of, and that was to go back downstairs to wait for his arrest. At least there was solitude and peace downstairs. He walked down despondently. Sitting on the desk, watching Robert, was the ghost, still invisible. The police had not entered the building yet; they wanted to make sure it was safe first.

Outside, Edward, who had managed to get out before the main contingent of police cars arrived, was hiding in the old basement storage shelter of the adjoining building. He knew he was going to have to make a dash for it soon, before the police carried out inspections of the neighboring buildings.

Although the police cars were shining their lights on the bank, the adjoining building where Edward was hiding was still in darkness. He crept up the stairs to ground level and walked away from the bank, trying to settle into the crowd of watchers so as not to be noticed.

Unluckily for him, he had put the gold bars in his pocket, but one was hanging out. As he walked, it slipped and landed on the pavement with a clang. Immediately, the police turned to the sound, saw Edward, and chased after him. There were three of them; one picked up the gold bar, and the other two chased Edward, who was not as fit as he thought. One of the officers made a flying rugby tackle, wrapping his arms around Edward's legs, and brought him down.

"I believe you dropped this, sir," said the officer with the gold bar said sarcastically.

"You're nicked," said another officer, who then read him his rights.

Edward was handcuffed and brought back to the main contingent. The inspector questioned him "How many of you are there?"

Edward, who was a coward, said, "Six."

The inspector did a quick count. Including Edward, they had five in custody. That meant one was still at large; that is, if he could believe Edward. The inspector thought there had been only one gunshot, and that had been at least ten minutes ago now, so he said to his men, "It's time to go in. There's one more inside."

The police officers entered the bank gingerly. Two officers went upstairs, searched the rooms, and shouted down the staircase, "All clear up here."

At the same time, two officers searched the ground floor; they too said, "All clear." That just left the basement. Two more officers slowly descended the stairs to where Robert was hiding.

Robert was now in the office he had so recently left; the remainder of the gold bars were still there. The cupboard door was still open wide. He could see the legs of the police officers coming down the stairs. He knew there was nowhere to go, but he edged as far away as he could out of instinct, his heart racing and his head throbbing.

He was by the open door of the cupboard. The ghost thought, *Time I moved into position at the back of the cupboard.* The officers were now downstairs, their flashlights shining the way. They saw Robert, but not knowing whether he was the one with the gun, one said, "Okay, son, the games up. Come quietly. Don't do anything silly. It will be in your best interest. It's only robbery at this time."

Suddenly, an immense white light shone from the cupboard. The light hadn't been there the last time Robert had been in the room. It seemed to be pulling him in, but how was that possible?

He didn't care; it might be a way out of this mess. He moved to the cupboard in shock. He didn't know why, but mentally, he was being drawn into it. It was sucking him in like a magnet. In front of him was an apparition: a ghostly-looking lady, her blonde hair blowing out backward as though there was a wind. She was smiling and looked as though she meant to comfort him, her arms outstretched.

"Come to me. I will save you," the ghost said. She was now fully visible.

At first, Robert was scared. She looked friendly, but was she? She could have been from *The Shining.* She looked young, a little older than himself. He could feel his heart starting to race even faster. Should he go to her or face certain imprisonment for the armed robbery he had just committed. He chose instantaneously to go for the spirit.

The police officers who were watching all this stopped still. They turned to each other in amazement, uttering the words: "Oh Christ, what is happening?"

Robert couldn't stop himself and didn't want to anymore; he had decided. He kept walking straight into the cupboard, and as he entered the apparition, he was out of control, flying straight through the back of the cupboard, which was no longer there. He was scared, and his mind was reeling, but it was all over in seconds.

The light was gone now, and the police officers checked the cupboard, but it was empty. They went to upstairs to explain to their boss what had happened. It was lucky there was two of them! The inspector didn't believe them, so he went downstairs to see for himself. No one was there. He said, "I think there must have been only five crooks here," not wanting to look a fool.

CHAPTER THREE

$\mathfrak{T}$here **was no going back now**; the light had gone, and Robert found himself outside in open countryside. He had landed with a bump and was sitting on a grassy knoll. It was a beautiful day, and the sun was shining brightly. He was fully conscious, which surprised him, having pinched himself to make sure he wasn't dreaming. His heart was still thumping fast, and he was breathing heavily. *Where the hell am I?* he thought. This was certainly not Bromley; he knew that much. The area here was green and fertile; on a childhood picnic, he would have loved this place, but now he was panicked.

Large trees were growing all around, deciduous trees, oaks, beeches, and sycamores, trees that he knew, but these didn't look quite the same as the ones he knew, although he couldn't quite put his finger on why that was.

He stopped and looked in amazement; the landscape was lush with grass. It was very peaceful, and birds and butterflies were fluttering over the grass, looking for bugs. The countryside was undulating and hilly, but what was he thinking? He was in the South of England, so why were there no buildings?

The most surprising thing was the smell: a freshness he had never smelled in London before, no dusty smog, no smell of rubbish or traffic. In fact, there was no smell of anything other than grass and the distant smell of saltwater. *I must be near the sea*, he thought, although he couldn't see it.

His savior was watching him, but Robert can't see her now. She thought, *I'll let him settle down for a while.*

Robert's mind was boggling; he couldn't take it all in, and he was petrified. He had goosebumps all up his arms, and he was panting. What had just happened? He sat down for ten minutes just to clear his mind. He knew he had to slow down his pulse and breathing. He breathed in deeply and exhaled slowly, trying to relax, but he could still hear his heart thumping. No one else had come through the cupboard. Then it hit him. *What cupboard? Where is it?* He turned a full circle, but there was nothing that looked remotely like a door or a cupboard. He walked around, punching the air just in case it was invisible. It was not there, and he was undoubtedly stuck here, wherever here was.

"I must have been transported, but to where?" he said aloud, praying that someone would hear. "Oh my God." Then he heard a voice coming from nowhere.

"Fear not, Robert. I am Viviane, the Lady of the Lake. You needed to get out of a tight corner. I know you are not really a bad boy. I have been watching you for some time, and that's why I chose you. You are only a few years younger than I was when I died; I was selected to promote the formation of the British Empire. That is a long way off, but you are at the start of things to come. You said you wanted to make a name for yourself, and I am going to make that happen.

You have been brought back to early Britain after the Romans have left. You are to formulate the legend of King

Arthur and the start of the British Empire. I will be watching you all the time. If you need me, I will be there. In doing so, you will develop your own character. Take strength from what you know; that's the secret. You come from an advanced culture, so help these people develop. Good luck."

He listened to all that without saying a thing; he was too much in shock. Now she was gone, but it was no good staying where he was and feeling sorry for himself. Did he believe her anyway? But there was that name again, Viviane, as written on the back of the cupboard. If she was genuine, the cupboard must have been her portal.

Was he sorry in any event? He didn't like his life in 2019. He had no real prospects; perhaps he could do better here, in whatever year this was. He had, after all, gotten clear of a bank raid without the police catching him. The others didn't have that good fortune. That made him feel somewhat better. *I must look on the bright side. Perhaps I do have a guardian angel after all. Viviane said she would help me when I need her. Maybe she can get me back, but will I want to go?*

Robert took a few minutes to rest. The stress was getting to him. He breathed deeply to get his heart rate down, and as he relaxed, he drifted into sleep. After an hour, he woke up, got to his feet, and started to walk; he had no idea which direction he was going. He reflected on Viviane. *I wonder who she really is. I may find out.* He then realized he had left his mobile in the bank, and he laughed realizing there would be no signal here in any case. He felt pleased he could still laugh; it made him feel better.

He forgot about Viviane for the time being. The sky, at least, looked the same; there was only one sun, after all. It was shining brightly just like the one he had left in Bromley. He scoured his surroundings as he walked. It was mainly open countryside; there were no paved roads. He did come across tracks, which were wider where people and animals must have trodden down the grass and foliage.

At one point, he came across a wider track that looked as though cattle had been driven along it; he could see the hoof prints. That encouraged him to think there must be some civilization here. He did wonder whether little green men might suddenly appear, whatever the ghost had said. He wasn't sure he believed her. He had never believed in ghosts anyway.

His heart was beating regularly now; he could no longer feel it thumping. He realized he still had the bar of gold in his pocket. Hopefully, gold was valuable here. Feeling hungry, he managed to find some berries growing in the bushes at the side of the path. They looked almost like the raspberries and blackberries he knew of, so he took the chance and ate some. They were good, and after an hour, still being alive, he decided that they were not poisonous.

He now had time to think more clearly. Would he be up to this task that this Viviane had set him, or would he bottle out again as he had just done? The weather was warm – it must be summer – and the end of the day was drawing in. He chose an area to sleep on the grass, and he collected some dried leaves to make a bed and pillow. The sun had now fallen below the horizon, and darkness prevailed. Robert was no different than any other human: he had a fear of darkness.

He was also frightened about any wild animals, so he had his eyes half-open most of the time. He hadn't seen any animals all day, but perhaps they were nocturnal. He was anxious about snakes, too. He had an aversion to those slimy-looking creatures, though he didn't know why. They were just like any animal: if you left them alone, they'd leave you alone, too. Except, of course, for pythons and the like, but this doesn't look like their habitat. Did he really know that, though?

That night, he did something he hadn't done for many years: he prayed to God for help and protection. To be on the safe side, he mentioned Viviane, too. Then he remembered his prayer in the bank basement. "Thank you, God. I won't let you down this time, I promise."

He only catnapped that night, waking every hour or so – he still had his watch. Every time the leaves rustled or twigs broke with the movement of rats and mice, he woke and froze. No animal bothered him, and eventually, his fear ebbed as he saw the sunrise breaking. It was a beautiful sight, the redness of the sun shining through the light clouds. Birds were chirping in the trees, and a new day was beginning for every creature.

His watch was showing four o'clock, so he left it at that for now. The sun was just rising, and assuming he was still on Earth, then he must have been roughly in the same time zone as London.

He searched around for more berries and had breakfast before setting off again, thinking, *Viviane, what have you got me involved in? Well, I didn't like my life in 2019, so maybe this will be the adventure I so desperately want.* He had no idea of direction, but he kept walking in the same way he had yesterday, using the sun for that purpose. The scenery was changing all the time; he went over moors and then a small forest of trees and lots of pastureland. Some of the pastureland had cattle on it, and he came across a field at one point which had deer grazing.

He noticed that the deer seemed agitated. All heads were scanning the horizon, and ears were erect and twitching with every sound or movement. Robert stopped and watched; he was standing in a small copse of trees next to a tall, old oak tree. He stood behind the tree, peering around the side.

Animals seem to have a sixth sense of danger; the herd was very still now. Robert clung to the tree; he didn't know what was happening, but he could feel the tension from the animals. Maybe it was his own tension, and his nails dug into the tree bark. He then saw a wild boar strolling across the field, but the deer didn't move. They weren't bothered by that.

The tension was still building, and Robert could feel his heart beating fast again, and then, from behind him, came a stalking female lion.

"Shush. Stay still. It's not interested in you. Just stay calm," he heard a voice say.

That's all right for you to say, thought Robert, realizing it was Viviane. The lion's head was low and horizontal, and it walked straight past him without even glancing at him. It did not make a sound as it crept on without breaking a twig. Robert was relieved to see it pass him; it meant she had seen a better meal. Her eyes stared out in front of her, and her ears perked up.

For a moment, Robert was still petrified and couldn't move. He didn't know what to do. Should he run away from the lion? That might make her change her prey to him. Robert tried to back off slowly, but it was as though all his bones were frozen solid. His leg muscles went into spasms as his brain was giving two orders: run, no, stay. He settled on staying, clasping the tree tighter, his nails digging into the bark until his fingers bled. Without a sound, he slid around the tree a little more, out of view. His heart was now pounding so hard he thought it would explode; he could feel the throbbing in his ears.

Just then, the lioness stopped, which made Robert worry even more. Had she seen him? Was he easier meat? Robert did something he never did: he crossed himself even though he was not Catholic. He dared not breathe. Finally, the lioness moved off slowly again, heading for the tasty deer, which she could see in front of her. The herd was motionless. They had sensed the danger; it was now life or death for one of them, and they knew it.

That did allow Robert to breathe again as he realized the lion wanted the deer. As the lioness progressed towards the herd, she had picked out her prey. It was standing at the edge of the main group, and the lion was stalking toward it through the tall grass.

Without warning, she took off like a bat out of hell, racing at forty miles an hour. The deer all knew now that they had to run. One deer realized the lioness was after her, and it raced off, zigzagging and jumping, anything it could do to get out of the lioness's path. The other deer moved in the opposite direction and gathered under a spreading tree. They knew there was nothing they could do for the deer who'd been singled out. Survival is always the essence in these circumstances; animals have that preservation instinct.

Robert watched as the lioness raced, trying to cut off the deer's escape. The deer knew that the lioness was faster than her but that if she could tire the lioness out before getting caught, she might have a chance. The lioness knew that, too, and she was closing in. As the lioness got close, the deer would veer off almost at a right angle. The lion was not so versatile and had to do a much wider sweep. That left her further away again from her prey, and time was not on her side now. She couldn't keep this pace up for long.

Robert sensed that both animals were tiring. It seemed to him that the lioness was about to make one last effort. She got to within six feet of the deer, and then she leaped five feet into the air. Robert had never seen anything like it in his life. He had never been on a safari until now, and here, he had no protection. The lioness landed on the deer's back with such a force and weight that the deer collapsed. That was it. Within seconds, the lioness opened its enormous mouth and bit hard into the throat of the deer. For that one moment, the deer flinched, and then it was gone; it didn't move again.

The lioness got up, standing on all fours, and looked around in triumph, making sure that no other adversary was after her prey. She was panting heavily. She then lay down next to the deer and started to tear it up. After all that running, the lioness needed energy from the food. Robert watched for five minutes, and then out of the woods near him came two lion cubs. They were hardly any bigger than the large cats that he knew from back home. They raced over to their mother, and all three had a good feed.

Robert knew that there was no further danger to him. The lions had had their fill and wouldn't be hungry again for a few days. Robert let out a big sigh as he wound down from the tension and continued his walk. He thought, *I must be in Africa, but that was not what Viviane said. Can I believe her anyway?*

"I told you that you were not in any danger. You must believe in me. You need my help in this strange world. You must trust me," Viviane said, but he couldn't see her.

Robert came to a quick decision: he had to go along with Viviane. he had no other option; she was his only chance of success and life. Trust was a different matter, though.

After an hour, he thought he was getting nearer civilization when, in the distance, he could see a person walking towards him. He was relieved; at least there were humans here! They walked toward each other. *That's hopeful,* thought Robert.

At last, they reached each other; the other youth was a white male about Robert's age. He was smaller in stature, about five foot six, with ruffled brown hair that didn't look clean. Come to think of it, neither did the rest of this youth. He was much thinner than Robert. His clothes were very rustic, which, in honesty, Robert could only describe as rags. They stood looking at each other for a moment. The youth was apparently surprised to see Robert, which struck Robert as strange. Robert still had blue jeans on and a white cotton shirt. Then he realized that he was dressed completely differently than this lad, so he probably appeared strange to him.

Robert held out his hand to shake, but the youth did not move except to raise his hand up vertically, the palm forward as in a high-five position. Robert responded by touching palms, and they both smiled. *So, that is the greeting here,* thought Robert. *I wonder if he speaks English. Well, here goes.*

"Hello, my name's Robert," he said slowly.

The youth reacted equally slowly, saying, "I am Celt."

Robert realized that this lad did speak a type of English, but he must remember to speak slowly. That was lucky, as he didn't know any other language, but it was certainly an old type of English.

"Is there a town near here?" said Robert

"I come from Camelot, over the hill." Celt pointed. "You can come with me if you like. There is no other town near here."

"Thank you," said Robert, and they set off together toward this Camelot. Robert thought, *Where the hell am I? He said Camelot, but perhaps I misheard him? The only Camelot I know of is the legend of King Arthur, and that's what the ghost said.* He kept on looking around him, expecting to see Viviane appear again, but she didn't.

He realized he had to use simple language with Celt as he did not seem very educated. They did manage to converse slowly on their walk. Robert didn't know where he was, only that it was somewhere, at least, where the people spoke a sort of English. Where was Camelot anyway?

He wondered whether this was even England, was there were lions. He asked Celt what country they were in just to see if he would say England, but the youth just looked at him in amazement. "There is only one country," he said. "Here." Robert was now feeling confused and frightened; he did not know what to expect.

Celt told Robert that Camelot was a castle town ruled by King Arthur. His lands reached in all directions as far as you could ride a horse in two days. Robert thought carefully about what he had learned at school. In the period after the Romans left Britain in the fifth century AD, he knew civilization had plunged into anarchy, with warlords setting up small kingdoms all over the country. They were continually fighting one another for more and more land.

King Arthur came to power following the death of his father, Uther Pendragon, and ruled his country with the aid of knights. Robert had learned that if such a person existed, he would have been a warlord and ruled a small area, perhaps as big as one county in 2019. It was thought to have been in the west of England, in the Bristol area, or maybe Wales. The legend placed much emphasis on magic in the area and the adviser to Arthur, Merlin. Such a story was always hard for Robert to believe.

Robert thought, *Not only have I been transported in distance, but also in time. Viviane must be right.* After a two-hour walk, they could see the town in front of them; it was a just like a Disney castle, and around the outside was a stone wall. It sat on a hillock about twenty feet above the surrounding area.

Around the wall was a dry moat about ten feet deep, which meant a distance of thirty feet from bottom to top. In the front entrance was a wooden drawbridge. There were houses of rustic stone, simply one stone laid on another and left to settle down naturally. Some houses were timber cabins of the type Robert expected to see in Switzerland, but not of that quality; he had never been to Switzerland anyway. The homes were spread out all around the town; it looked as though there were some inside the wall as well.

Roofs were mixed, the better ones thatched with river reeds, but others were just square pieces of wood to make tiles. Then there were those that were of metal. Robert thought it looked like tin. As they got nearer, he saw farmers tending their flocks of sheep, cows, and geese. Birds flew all over, pecking at the animal feed. What surprised Robert was that every house except one was a single-story building. The one building that had two floors was the castle, which was made of cut stone and could, therefore, hold the weight of an extra floor.

Robert noted that animals and birds looked much the same as he knew. It looked a beautiful place to live, very peaceful and pleasing to the eye, but he wasn't too sure in some respects. Robert had never liked the Boy Scouts he'd belonged to as a youth. He didn't like camping, and things looked a bit like that here.

Celt had explained that he worked in the kitchen of the castle. He'd been out picking berries for dinner that night and had a full basket. Robert asked him if he might be allowed to stay in the town and if he could get a job in the kitchen as well. Celt promised to speak with his boss, the chef, and eventually, they arrived at the town. Robert stood in front of the main entrance, taking this all in. He couldn't help but think that maybe he was really in a Disney theme park and it was all someone's idea of a joke.

In front of him was the main wall, which he could see clearly now. Again, it was comprised of stones piled on top of one another, not cut into blocks. He hadn't expected that, but it was about six feet thick and seemed to perform its task. The drawbridge was down, so they could walk across. The gate was made of thick planks of wood in a crisscross fashion. The guards behind could see through it to check who was coming.

They knew Celt, so the gate opened with a loud creak. Inside, Robert stood still, flabbergasted, taking a moment to look around. In front of him was the castle. It was also made of cut stone blocks, but it was much more impressive. It had window openings, but no glass, just shutters. The houses outside of the town had no windows or shutters at all.

There were also some smaller buildings scattered around the inside of the outer wall; they were like the houses seen outside. Robert observed that there were no chimneys, and he assumed that any fires inside just smoked out the building. Not good for the inhabitants' health, but it would keep out bugs.

Standing just inside the castle was King Arthur. It was late afternoon, and he was looking out of the window opening.

He felt good about himself. The sun was still shining, and the breeze was refreshing. He picked up his golden crown, which was lying on the table beside him, as it always was. He walked out of the door and stood on the front doorstep of the castle.

He put the crown on his head and stood to survey his kingdom, and a lot further than that as well. He felt resplendent and proud in his gold brocade vest and dark-green pants. He placed his hands on his hips; his right leg was just in front of the left. His head was lifted high and slightly back on his shoulders. He was in his prime, looking across his land, thinking his father would have been proud of him. He was twenty-three years old, and his hair was dark and his eyes blue from the Celtic influence in his genealogy. All in all, he was very handsome.

It's all mine, he thought as he noticed the kitchen boy Celt enter the front gate, his front gate. *Who's that with him? That's a face I don't know.* Arthur prided himself on knowing all his staff and residents personally by sight and name.

Robert had entered the grounds with Celt; he suddenly stopped at the vision in front of him. This must be King Arthur, he thought, and he was in awe. The sight of the king inspired him, but more than that, he experienced a meeting of souls. *What was that about?* thought Robert. Just then, the king raised his head slightly, and a beam of the sun's light reflected from the king's crown and straight into Robert's eye. It was like a beam from God, as though God was telling him something, or was it Viviane?

A voice came to Robert that only he could hear: "This is your new home. Make your mark in this town, and that's the king on the front steps. You need to befriend him."

Celt took Robert to the kitchen, which was outside of the castle building, no doubt because of the risk of fire. The kitchen was as Robert expected: a bland room with five fires down one side and metal utensils everywhere. Robert was concerned about hygiene. Celt introduced him to the head chef, a man called Ulf. Robert told him that he was from out of the area and was unhappy where he lived, which was a five-day walk away, and he asked if he could stay here and work in the castle.

The chef, a rather grumpy man, looked up and down at Robert, surprised at his dress. Robert still had on his jeans and his white shirt, which was now filthy.

The chef said to Robert, "Where did you get those clothes?" as he felt the soft cotton.

Robert, at a loss for words for a moment, finally said, "Um, well, I met a tailor on my travels, and he made the pants for me and gave me an old shirt."

"More likely you stole it, sonny," said the chef.

"No, sir, really."

"Well, let's say I accept that, but remember, there is no stealing here. You can start tomorrow. There are some work clothes over there. Help yourself."

The chef worked from morn till night and expected his staff to do the same; it seemed quite common in those times for peasants to be disgruntled with their lords. The chef was happy to give Robert a menial job in the kitchen, mainly washing up, helping to prepare the next meal, and being a general dogsbody. *Those words haven't changed over the years*, thought Robert. He learned that meals were prepared for about one hundred people at a time. The day started at four thirty, and he had to be up by four. The day ended when the last job finished, but they had no light in the evening other than fires. The chef thought, *We are lucky here to have such a good king as Arthur.*

Celt took Robert to the sleeping quarters, which were in a communal hall that slept about thirty boys. It was very basic: the beds were rustic wooden cots with some form of hard mattress, probably horse hair. There were no other facilities. The only bed available was the one at the farthest end, underneath the opening in the wall, which would eventually be called a window! Robert thought, *This is going to be drafty.* He didn't like camping in 2019, so this made his stomach turn over. But he knew there was no alternative.

There was a communal washroom, which consisted of a wooden bowl with water poured into it from a jug. The water was brown, straight out of the well. The toilet facilities were a hole in the ground that was filled in at the end of each day, and then another one was dug further on. Robert learned that if you drank water, you had to boil it first, but most people drank beer for safety; the alcoholic quantity was small.

He was given that evening off to familiarize himself with the town. It was impressed on him that at his level, he was not allowed into the main castle building. He strolled around town, taking it all in, speaking to anyone interested. He was getting used to the language now, which he later found to be an early form of English. The locals called it Englisc; it was a mix of Germanic languages and Latin.

He walked around the castle grounds and saw the sporting fields, which were outside the main wall. They were very keen on jousting and the like. Horses were the only form of transportation, and many were grazing in the area around the jousting fields, attended to by the grooms. These people were keen to look after their animals. He went over to speak to some of the squires; he found out that a squire was the direct assistant to a knight, such as a valet in generations to come. He got on well with all he met except for one squire named

Scatchen, who reminded Robert of Edward Brice. Scatchen had that same bullyboy trait about him. He had evil in his eyes, so Robert just ignored him and walked on.

He could see several knights in the distance, but he thought he would keep away on the first day. He was learning that there was a definite hierarchy here, and he didn't want to overstep the mark at this stage. He had not been in the castle proper, as he knew that he was not allowed there yet, but he was determined to get in there. For now, he went back to his room as it was getting dark. He settled down for the night with the other kitchen lads. Once it was dark, there was nothing else to do other than go to bed, and he had to get up early.

This was his first night in bed; he lay there at what he thought was about nine o'clock, in the darkness, looking at the ceiling, which he could only imagine, as there was no light coming through the opening in the wall. The trouble was, he imagined all thoughts of scary things, monsters. He had always been afraid of the dark as a child, and this was a darkness that he had never seen before. His mind reeled; he was scared, no, petrified. *I must calm down*, he thought, taking deep breaths. *What am I going to do here? I come from about fifteen hundred years in the future, not that I have any idea what year it is.* He thought that if he had been younger, he would have cried, but he had been brought up with "Big boys don't cry." He wanted to, though, at least within himself. *I am a man now, and they certainly don't cry!* The only saving grace was that the dormitory was next to the kitchen, and the heat from the day's activity percolated through the solid walls. *Almost central heating*, Robert thought.

He even started to think maybe he should have stayed in 2019 and taken the consequences; at least life would have been straightforward.

How can I do the things that Viviane expects of me? What are they? I am only an ordinary person, thought Robert, *not a hero.* Eventually, he drifted off to sleep and dreamed of Viviane. She said to him, "You can do it. Heroes are not born; they develop. You are more than capable of being a hero as your character develops. I have been watching you, and you will become a hero. I will put you in the circumstances to make that happen. Remember, these people are primitive; you have knowledge far beyond their learning, so use it. I'll have further tasks for you in due course, and I know you will live up to my expectations. Just use your brain; it's an incredible piece of equipment. If you don't use it, you'll lose it."

CHAPTER FOUR

Reveille was at four in the morning, and as he woke, Robert was still thinking about his dream. *What did she mean by use it or lose it? Okay, that's it. I'm going to use it come what may. What have I got to lose anyway?*

All the lads got up and washed in the washroom; it was mainly a splash with water. These people did not clean themselves and certainly did not bathe. *Disease must be rife,* he thought. It was not how he had been brought up, and suddenly, he wished he was back home as a child again. Maybe he could do better next time. Then he realized he had to stay; there was no going back.

Most of the men were growing beards, so Robert thought he would do the same. He had always wanted one. He later found out that if you wanted a proper bath, you did that in the river, down the path.

At four thirty, all hands were in the kitchen, awaiting orders from the chef. They learned that today's menu was beef steak and corn mash for breakfast, mutton, peas, and carrots baked in the oven for lunch, and roast pig meat with vegetables cooked in animal fat, which they called lard, for dinner.

Robert's job was to fry the beef steak in large copper pans. *The lard is not very healthy,* thought Robert, *but perhaps they do not have vegetable oil.* He performed his task well; he had always had a flair for cooking. His mother had taught him well at an early age, and he had kept it up with his grandmother in remembrance of her. He was then given an hour off before preparing lunch.

At the end of breakfast, the king said to his knights, "Today, we must tour the western side of the kingdom. We need to show our presence at the various hamlets. Be ready to leave in an hour; it will mean a late lunch. We do not need to wear full armor; official tunics will suffice."

They left to get attired. Their horses were all brushed down by the grooms, and the knights were in their saddles by the steps of the castle in plenty of time. All the knights were in full-length tunics of red and gold with a rampant lion embroidered on the right breast.

The king's chestnut stallion stood beside them. The horse had a luxurious livery of gold lamé blanket and matching hood. The king walked down the front steps like a prima donna, dressed in a magnificent tunic of blues, greens, and reds that depicted the strength of the nation.

He was helped onto his horse by the groom at the head of the procession, which was about to leave. The whole town stopped what they were doing to watch its splendor. For their benefit, the procession rode around the inside of the town wall, acknowledging the cheers of the crowd. The king gave the royal wave back, a slight circular gesture of the hand. Robert was in the crowd and was awestruck; he had never seen anything so glamorous. He looked at the king with a sense of pride and belonging. He hadn't experienced that before either. *I'll have to ingratiate myself into his presence,* he thought.

At the top of the front steps stood Queen Genevieve. This was the first occasion he had seen the queen. She certainly was beautiful in a full gown of gold lamé to match Arthur's majesty.

They headed out through the main gate, and the procession spent the rest of the morning touring through the villages. The king met the head person in each hamlet, usually the farmer, for quick discussions en route. The communities were set up by the king, who had granted a farmer a section of land on which he'd built a manor house. He would then employ staff to work the fields; they needed homes for their families. Before long, there were six or eight houses in a community. Then a shop would come, and a village emerged. A small one was called a hamlet. The farmer produced food for the castle by way of rent. There was no coined money; a barter system had evolved.

The villagers were always pleased to see the king's procession; he would repeat it two or three times a year in each sector. After a long morning, the procession arrived back at the castle. The knights were tired, and all were ready for a sumptuous meal.

Earlier, in the kitchen, Robert had said to the chef, "Do you serve a sauce with the meat?"

"No," the chef replied. "Do you have a suggestion?"

"Yes. In my village, we served mutton with what we called mint sauce."

"That's interesting. And how do you make that?"

"It's straightforward. First, you collect some mint; it's a herb from the garden. Cut it up into minuscule pieces and then add vinegar and sweetener."

"Vinegar, what's that?" said the chef.

Robert had guessed they didn't have sugar yet, but honey would do. He hadn't realized they would not know the word vinegar, though. He explained, "Vinegar is acetic acid used for pickling."

"Why didn't you say so? Oh yes, we pickle things, but it is called pickling juice. Why don't you make this mint sauce for me to try? There is mint in the garden outside."

Robert was pleased that on day one, he could demonstrate his talents. He went outside, collected a significant amount of mint, came back into the kitchen, took a large cutting knife, and chopped it up. He then went to the shelf, took off the jar marked pickling juice, and placed the mint in a wooden bowl. He added a quantity of the juice, and he then experimented, adding honey until the flavor was sweet but still had the sour tang of the vinegar. He took it over to the chef, who tasted it, saying, "It has a bitter taste."

Robert said, "You need to place it over the meat to get the proper effect."

The chef said, "Let's do that." He cut a slice of the mutton, put the sauce on, and ate it. "That's better. I'm impressed. I think the king will like that. Well done, Robert. You've earned your keep today."

At the late lunch, the waiters served the mutton to the whole household, first to the king and queen, followed by the remainder of the court. The king questioned what the sauce was, and he was told it was a mint sauce and that it was to be put on the mutton. The king was indeed impressed when he tasted it. He said, "I like this sauce very much. Give my compliments to the chef."

At that, the chef came out, always appreciative of praise, but he was a fair man. "On this occasion, I must pass the praise over to one of my new assistants, Robert. It was entirely his recipe."

"In that case, you must bring this Robert to meet me. Besides, I always want to meet new members of my town."

"Yes, sire"

Robert came into the dining room. This was his first visit to the castle proper. *Not bad for my second day,* he thought. The room was very bland, but it was impressive. There were several tapestries on the walls, but no paintings like he'd expected. Very long banners hung from the ceiling, depicting the prowess of the nation. There were a few statues around that had been left by the Romans. He was taken over to the king and bowed low before him. He guessed that was the correct thing to do, and he wanted to impress the king.

King Arthur was a handsome man. Although seated, Robert guessed that he was about five foot ten inches. He, too, had a beard and was well dressed in his brocade jacket.

The king looked up, thinking, *Ah, this is the man I saw enter the town yesterday.* He said, "I wanted to thank you for this new sauce you have introduced to us and to welcome you to Camelot. We always welcome travelers to our town. Let's hope you like it and stay. Well done. The sauce enhances the taste of the meat. What do you call it, and do you have any more concoctions like this?"

"It's called mint sauce, sire, and I have many different sauces to prepare for you if you would like."

"Then I would like you to introduce them; please make that happen, master chef."

"I most certainly will, sire," said the chef. Viviane was standing behind him, out of sight, smiling.

The king thought, *I am glad to see this man has changed his clothes.* He looked Robert straight in the eye. It didn't happen very often, but he thought, I *feel a strange affinity for this man. He is, of course, much too humble in status to become a friend, but the feeling is there. I'll keep a close watch on this Robert.*

Robert was delighted and went back to the kitchen. "Well then, you'd better come up with these new recipes for the king," said the chef.

"I certainly will, sir. In fact, I have a sauce for the pig meat," said Robert, aware that in Old England, before the Normans came in 1066, pork was called pig meat. "It's called applesauce; it's made by boiling apples to a pulp and adding honey."

He asked the chef, "Do you have any other form of sweetener?"

"That's a strange question. Of course we don't. Why, do you know of another?"

He wanted to say yes, but he thought better of it. Sugar would not be available for another thousand years. "No, sir."

"Okay, then you prepare this applesauce. There are apples in the store over there," the chef said, pointing.

Robert set about getting twenty apples. He peeled them and cut them up into small pieces, putting them in a large pot. He added a small amount of water and put the pot on the cooker, which was a large iron range. Underneath was a wood and charcoal fire. In five minutes, the water was boiling, and the apples started to break down. After another fifteen minutes, he took the pot off the range, as it was getting too hot. There was no way of controlling the heat.

He let it cool down – the apples were still cooking during that time – and then he put it back on the range, adding an amount of honey. He tasted it, but there was not enough honey, so he added more until the taste was what he wanted. He put the pot aside to allow it to cool down. He said to the chef, "Try this when it cools down." The chef loved it.

Robert asked him, "Do we have any spices?"

"I don't think so, but then, I don't know what they are."

"Do we have any wine?"

"We have wine or mead."

"Can I have a little of each, please?" Robert proceeded to put a small amount of the applesauce into two small cups. The chef returned with two bottles, and Robert poured a small amount of each one in each pot and stirred.

"Now try each," he said to the chef, who did, savoring the taste of each.

"Wow," he said. "I like both, but I prefer the one with mead." Robert knew that mead was a honey wine often drunk in Old England, and he thought it would be a good substitute for cinnamon. The chef said, "We'll serve the mead applesauce with the pig meat tonight. Well done."

Robert was feeling pleased with himself: two new sauces in one day, and he had other ideas.

That evening at dinner, Robert's sauce accompanied the pig meat, and everyone loved it and came back for more. The king again requested the presence of the chef. This time, he brought Robert with him. The king once more congratulated the chef, who again said it was Robert's creation. The king was now very surprised, the second time in one day. He said to the chef, "We cannot waste this young man's talent. I suggest we promote him to take more responsibility in the kitchen." Again, Viviane was in the background, smiling.

"Thank you, sire. I will certainly do that," said the chef. The king watched as Robert left the room, in thought.

Robert got his first step up the ladder; he was now put in charge of five kitchen hands. Over the next few weeks, he came up with lots of ideas for new recipes. He introduced more fowl when it was available. The king liked that and called for his farmers to respond and cultivate more chicken, geese, pheasants, and swans. Robert got on well with the other boys in the kitchen. He felt like one of them, and they responded to that. He thought about his previous job at the bar in Bromley; if only the chef there could have seen him now.

The weeks were passing by, and now he was keen to help in the garden in his limited spare time. He was particularly anxious to grow herbs: rosemary, thyme, and parsley. They had all these plants, but they were not cultivated very well. Robert tried to improve the soil with fertilizer so that he could use more sauces for the cooking. He was now feeling a part of this community. Every time he passed the king while walking, the king would always say hello. Once, the king stopped to talk to Robert; there was a connection forming.

He saw that they ate sheep when it was mutton, which meant it was at least a year old, by which time the flavor had started to deteriorate. Robert went to the chef and said, "When cooking sheep, it is better to use those that are less than nine months old. The flavor is significantly improved."

The chef replied, "It would be costly to do that. The sheep at that age are small and would cost the same as a large one."

Robert said, "That is true, but the flavor is so much better."

The chef killed a young sheep and served it to the king the next day.

The king enjoyed it so much that he ordered a decree that the farmers should kill the sheep at less than nine months old. They would be paid more for per pound, as the sheep would be lighter. They would then call that meat by a different name.

The king went down to the kitchen personally. The chef whispered to Robert, "This is unheard of, the king coming here."

The king said to the chef, "I needed to come down to where the work is done to see what happens. It's only too easy to forget the things that go on down here just to make a meal for all the court. You must let my household staff know if there is anything you should need."

"Thank you, sire. All of us much appreciate that," said the chef, thinking he would not let this opportunity pass by.

"By the way, Robert, what would you like to call this new meat of mutton less than nine months old?" said the king.

"I'd call it lamb, sire." Robert was truly delighted that the king had asked him a question.

"That's a strange name, but so be it. In the future, sheep that are less than nine months old will be called lamb," the king said, and so the birth of a new word happened. As the king left the kitchen, even he thought he did not visit the kitchen enough. He was also thinking, *There is something special about this Robert person. I must find out what.*

CHAPTER FIVE

Robert was rising in prestige in Camelot now that the king had taken notice of him. All the court responded by recognizing this newcomer, following the king's example. Everyone enjoyed Robert's company and his food, except, that is, for Squire Scatchen, who was jealous of Robert's increased status.

Robert spent a lot of his free time, of which there was more since his promotion, around the sports fields. There were many knights in this area, and Robert thought he would like to be one. He wondered how that happened. He was now allowed to talk to them, and they were happy to speak to him because they enjoyed his food.

Scatchen was now getting paranoid with jealousy. He had a very mean, bumptious demeanor and was annoyed at the attention Robert was getting, and he made it clear to him. He had been heard to say to other squires, "Who on earth does this new upstart think he is? I'll give him what for if he doesn't change his ways." Scatchen had already been chastised by his knight, Sir Galahad, who admired Robert. However, for the moment, Robert kept out of Scatchen's way.

Robert had his personal bedroom now. It was small, but at least it was his. It was a cleared room with a bed and a chest of drawers, not that he had much to put in there. At least there was no smell from the other boys' dirty bodies. He had a few sets of clothes now, purchased with his rising earnings. He needed to get rid of his twenty-first-century clothes, which revealed him as an outsider. Local clothes were very basic woolen jumpers and trousers and some animal skins. The skins were expensive and reserved for best wear, and they did smell somewhat.

He still had his little extras, like the watch. He was concerned that the watch battery would run out soon. He needed to work something out for that. He knew that the Romans were thought to have made batteries from a zinc and a copper plate in sulfuric acid. He would try and see what he could do.

He also had his bar of gold – he was sure that bar had jumped into his hand – but he would keep that quiet for now; it might come in handy later. He hid both items in his drawer, which had a lock. He was pleased with his new room; it gave him freedom and privacy. He had not altered the time shown on his watch. There was no point, and he didn't know the correct time anyway. He couldn't even show it to anyone, but it made him feel happy to have it in his drawer. It had been given to him by his grandmother, so it reminded him of his past life. He did miss some aspects of his old life, but he still had no idea of what he had to do here.

He went to see the alchemist to have a chat with him about his thoughts on electricity, although he could not be specific. He said, "I need some sulfuric acid, a bar of zinc and one of copper, oh, and two clay pots. Do we have that?"

"That's interesting," said the alchemist, who was of the old school, a real scientist of the future, with fuzzy hair and a Father Christmas beard. "As it happens, I do have a bottle of what I think you are seeking. The Romans left it when they left the country, and it has been sitting on the shelf for all those years. I don't know what to do with it, so you may as well have it. The zinc, copper, and the jars, I have." He went from drawer to cupboard to collect the items. "You seem to have knowledge of alchemy. I would be pleased to hear your theories someday."

"I'll be glad to share them with you," said Robert. "I'm going to try and make electricity as the Romans did." Robert knew that some historians thought that the Romans had a form of battery for electricity on a small scale. Those types of advances were forgotten when they returned to Rome.

"Electricity? What will that do?"

"It is a form of energy, like the heat and light of the sun. If it works, we can make light for the evening time. Only in small quantities, but we would still need a lot of sulfuric acid."

The alchemist was impressed. *There is a lot to this man that not many realize. He will go a long way here if he can do what he says*, he thought. But the alchemist was skeptical, although he desperately wanted new inventions. *He'll suggest turning the sun's energy into light at night soon*, the alchemist sniggered to himself.

Robert spent the next few days putting together his domestic battery: two pots, each containing sulfuric acid, with a metal bar connected by a piece of wire. He found they had an abundance of copper. He then got hold of a glass jar, inside of which he put a thin piece of wire connected to his battery. He had to figure out a way of extracting the air from the jar. He did that with the aid of a bung and a small syringe used on the animals.

He then went back to the alchemist and showed him his invention. After half an hour, there was a small amount of light emitted from his lightbulb.

The alchemist was very impressed. "How did you know that?"

"One of those things," Robert said, touching his nose.

"I'll set about seeing where we can get more of that sulfuric acid. Can you leave it with me? I'll show the king. I'm sure he will allow a search in the district and beyond," said the alchemist

Robert went back to his room while the alchemist went to see the king and showed him the invention that Robert had made.

"What is that?" said the king, in deep amazement at the sight of light coming from the makeshift bulb.

"It makes light; it's called a battery. We need more sulfuric acid to produce more electricity on a bigger scale. Can I arrange for knights to go into the districts to collect what is available, please, sire?"

"You certainly can. This is a promising idea. You're a man of knowledge. What do you make of this person called Robert? He comes here with new delicious recipes, and he makes this electricity. What else can he do? Is he a magician or wizard? Who knows? But I'll leave it you to organize the excursions to our neighbors."

"Thank you, sire," said the alchemist not knowing how to reply to the rest of the questions.

The king made a mental note that he must very soon speak with Robert to find out more about him. *He seems the type of man we need. I wonder what else he knows.*

Viviane was pleased with Roberts's progress. She came to him in the next night and sat at the end of his bed. Robert was awake, thinking, and she said to him, "You are doing well. Show the inhabitants what you can do. They will love and trust you. That's very important, particularly with King Arthur."

"I understand, but what am I supposed to do?" said Robert

"It will all become clear to you as time goes by. It is better from your point of view that you discover it. That will make you strong and become the hero you want." She left him, and he fell asleep.

Time was moving on now, and it was three months since Robert had arrived in Camelot, although time didn't mean so much to Robert; one day was just like the next. He was beginning to feel settled now. There would be no point fighting fate anyway. He knew there was nothing he could do about it. He did miss his local pub in Bromley, but here, he felt he would be able to influence things, whereas, in Bromley, he was a nobody. He still wished he had a family; perhaps that would come, too, one day.

Robert was amazed how small Camelot was compared to cities in the twenty-first century. Camelot only had a population of about two hundred people, but it would be easier for him to become established, and he liked that.

As Robert had free time, he went to his favorite place: the sports field. As usual, there were lots of horses around. Growing up on the outskirts of London, he had never ridden before. Horse riding was expensive in 2019. But he wanted to try now, so he went to a groom that he was particularly friendly with and said, "I'd like to try riding. Do you think your master would allow me to ride his horse?"

The groom said, "I'm sure my knight won't mind. He's spoken very well of you. He particularly likes your food sauces."

"I haven't ridden before, so I may need some help."

The groom said that he would help him and took Robert to the horse's face, saying, "Talk to the animals in a friendly manner; they like to know who's riding them. If you are cruel to them, they will throw you."

Robert whispered sweet words to the horse; amazingly, the horse did seem to react and understand.

After the introduction, the groom handed Robert the reins, saying, "See what I mean?" He helped Robert onto the horse's back. As he climbed, the horse turned his head to watch Robert get on. The groom said, "There, he's watching who got on his back. You'd look if someone got on your back, wouldn't you?" The king was watching out of an upstairs window in the castle.

The groom showed Robert how to hold the reins. He said, "Just talk to the horse, encourage him forward with a gentle kick on his hindquarters. When you want him to go faster, kick harder, always making your kicks confidently. Do not tap, or the horse might think your leg is just flapping. They like a positive command. When you want him to stop, pull in the reins slowly at first to get him to slow down. Then with more strength to get him to stop."

Robert took all that in; he was a little nervous. "It's so high up here; it seems much higher looking down than it did from the ground." He kicked, commanding the horse to move forward, and the horse started walking. Robert just led the horse around the arena, loving it. Once he had settled in, he felt a real contact with the horse, patting its neck and talking to it. The horse's head was bouncing up and down in response.

Sitting behind Robert, bouncing up and down, was Viviane. She loved riding when she was alive. "Ride him, cowboy," she whispered.

Robert relaxed and waved his arm around, saying, "John Wayne, eat your heart out."

After ten minutes, he was feeling much more confident and asked the horse to go faster with a sharp kick in its rear. The horse went into a trot, and Robert was jogging up and down. Feeling a little bouncy, he slowed down and walked the horse back to the groom and slid off.

"How did I do? It felt good," said Robert as Viviane flew off.

"You did great," said the groom, and Robert went around to the front of the horse and breathed into its nostril. The horse seemed pleased and neighed its pleasure.

As he watched out of the window, the king thought, *Robert maybe not of royal status, but I feel a real commitment.*

As it happened, Queen Guinevere was also out riding around the paddock. She looked very regal in her elegant riding gear. She thought, *I've been out here for a while now. That's enough exercise for today*, and she headed back to where the grooms waited.

Just then, Scatchen turned the corner and came over to Robert and said aggressively, "What were you doing riding my master's horse?"

"Oh, sorry, I didn't realize," said Robert.

"That's a shame. You should've asked me first, and I would have told you no."

"It's my fault," said the groom. "I thought it would be all right. Your knight likes Robert."

"That's not the point; you don't have that right," said Scatchen, who was much bigger than the groom, and he went for him, punching the groom in the stomach. Robert reacted immediately; he knew a bully could not be left unattended. He pulled Scatchen back and set upon him, punching him in the face. A fight ensued. Robert was now a stout man and able to deliver heavy punches. Soon, the squire had a black eye and a bloody nose and was lying on the ground with blood pouring out of his nose.

"Attaboy!" could be heard as the wind suddenly whooshed through the trees.

"What was that?" said the groom. Robert said nothing, knowing exactly who it was.

Scatchen was now fuming, his face turning a bright shade of red. Knowing he could not fight Robert fairly, he pulled out his knife from its sheath and sprang up from the ground. He walked stealthily around Robert, waiting for the moment to pounce. He saw his moment and raised his hand, but then his arm froze; he was unable to move it. Robert instinctively raised his right arm to deflect Scatchen's wrist. Their wrists met in a spasm of pain to them both, but it was enough for Scatchen to drop the knife. At the same time, Robert raised his knee into Scatchen's groin. Scatchen reeled on the ground in agony.

A gleeful smile appeared on Viviane's face, but only Robert could see it, and she said to him alone, "I told you I would be here for you. We make a good team."

All this was seen by Scatchen's knight, Sir Galahad, as well as by the king at his window. Galahad was watching from the other side of the field and was pleased with Robert's response. The queen had just arrived to get off her horse, and both Robert and Scatchen got up and bowed to her.

"That isn't how we behave in Camelot, but I will leave it to Sir Galahad to deal with you both," said the queen as she had seen Galahad walking over.

The king, from his window, had heard and seen all this happening. He, too, thought, *I'll leave this to Galahad.*

Galahad reached the scene and acknowledged the queen, who was now leaving. Standing behind the queen was Viviane, looking more beautiful than any of the ladies of Camelot, but only Robert could see her, which gave him more confidence.

"Come now, lads, no fighting. Leave that to us knights," said Galahad, but he was pleased to see that Robert had handled himself well and justly. Robert immediately went on the defensive, fearing that he was being chastised, and he opened his mouth to say something. Sir Galahad interrupted, saying, "Don't worry, I saw everything from over there. You were defending the groom, and Scatchen had no right to attack either of you. Leave this to me. You are welcome to ride my horse anytime. In fact, we need to get you one of your own." Sir Galahad grabbed Scatchen and led him into the castle by the scruff of the neck.

The queen met Galahad at the castle afterward and said, "We cannot have that behavior in our kingdom."

"I agree, ma'am. I do apologize," said Galahad. "I have given Scatchen the sack, but I think the king must banish him from the kingdom."

Robert felt at ease and left the area. Two hours later, after Robert's lunch duties, he was called to see Sir Galahad in the castle. He was now getting apprehensive again, but he went over to the castle and met with the knight.

"Come in, son, and have a seat," said Sir Galahad in a fatherly way.

Robert felt more relaxed; the approach seemed friendly. He sat down; the chairs were serviceable, not comfortable, but he didn't care. Sir Galahad was about forty years old, with slightly graying hair. Robert noticed earlier that Galahad was tall at six feet; most people were shorter in this town. Galahad looked as though he had many battle scars, but that also seemed to be common in this land. He did appear to have a pleasing nature; you felt comfortable in this man's presence.

"Well now, you seemed to handle yourself well today and jumped in to protect my groom, who was being abused by my squire. I will not stand for that treatment from him. We knights are here to protect all the population, not to attack them. That applies to our squires also, so I have given Scatchen the sack. The king will hold court tomorrow with the intention of exiling him from the kingdom."

"Oh, is that necessary?" said Robert, not wanting to cause unnecessary hostility.

"Yes, it is. This is not the first incident, and he is no good for me on that basis. I have been watching you for the last few weeks, and you are handling yourself well in Camelot. I would like to offer you the job of being my squire."

"Thank you very much, sir. I am very honored, but I don't know what I would have to do. May I ask what it would entail?" Sitting on the empty chair next to Robert was Viviane.

"Of course. A squire looks after a knight in all respects. He would, for example, help him to dress for jousting tournaments. He deals with the knight's household matters and, of course, would be with him in battle. The pay is considerably more than you currently receive. Your prestige would rise within the community; it would also mean free access to the castle."

"Sounds good to me. Go for it," Viviane whispered to Robert in her girlish manner.

"Then I would be honored to take up that appointment, sir," Robert said rather formally. "There is one thing I would like to ask you, sir." He was still surprised about seeing a lion in what was now clearly ancient Britain. "When I arrived here, on the way, I saw a lioness attacking a deer. Are there wild lions in this country? I had understood there were none."

Smiling, Galahad said, "Well, not really; they are not indigenous. When the Romans were here, they brought lions and many other animals over for their gladiators to fight in the arenas. They set up many arenas in the country. The Romans were here for over four hundred years, you know. These animals and others were caged, but when they left, they released any animals that were alive. The lions and other creatures such as zebras fled into the woodlands to live and breed. You may see the odd lion around the countryside. Do not be too concerned, though; the farmers have been killing off any they find. I'm surprised you saw one. I thought they were now extinct."

"Well, I did see one, and she had two cubs," said Robert

They got up and shook hands. "I will arrange the transfer with the chef," said Sir Galahad. "Tomorrow, I will spend the morning with you, explaining how things run in Camelot."

"Thank you, sir. I look forward to that."

Robert was over the moon. He was rising through the ranks with such speed; he had only been here about nine months and was now earning real money. He would never have done so well in 2019, and his prospects were good; he knew that now. *Come to think of it, I wonder what year this is. There is no way of knowing. The locals do not use that reference.*

The only item they had to tell time was the sundial, by which Robert had set his watch. He gathered that they had the same seasons. It was summer now, and the weather was warm and sunny. Not too hot, though; it rained about once a week. He heard that in winter, it rained more and sometimes, they even had snow. The only real reference to the passage of time for the locals was the moon; they talked about the lunar month. The knights and above knew of the year from the season changes, but there was no basis for a starting point.

Everyone tended to go to bed as it got dark. They couldn't see otherwise except by the light of some small oil lamps, but they were not very effective. The oil was expensive. They had some light from fires, though. Because of the stone walls, it was always cold in buildings, particularly in the castle. Even in summer, fires were lit. Wood was free, and it helped to keep the buildings dry. That evening, the chef told Robert that he needn't report for work in the morning as he had spoken with Sir Galahad. He thanked Robert for all his help and said that if he remembered any other recipes, to please let him know. Robert readily agreed.

That night, Scatchen left Camelot of his own accord. He knew he had gone too far, and he thought he would end up in the town jail or even be stoned in the stocks. That pleased Arthur; it saved him the task of exiling him.

The next day, Robert reported to Sir Galahad at sunrise. Once again, Viviane was in the chair next to him. Sir Galahad said, "Welcome to my household, Robert. This morning, I'm going to fill you in on what happens at Camelot. Together with a little history of the realm and further afield."

"When the Romans left our shores, there was a state of chaos. There were no traditional leaders. Anarchy set in, and for many years, the country was broken up into small communities. Each community had its ruler; there were many wars between the kingdoms to get consolidation. Now there are a dozen domains, and the overall country is called Avalon, although no one knows exactly where it begins and ends. The Scots from Caledonia are, of course, a separate country divided into clans or tribes of their own.

"King Arthur Pendragon inherited the crown of Camelot from his father at the age of eighteen. That was five years ago, so he is about your age now. Arthur's father was very strict. There have always been suggestions of magic in the lands. Those of us who are educated know that there is no such thing. There are many so-called witches who know much about the countryside. Herbs and things of that nature, they understand, and they will give prophecies for the future and potions for ill health. It has been shown that they are wrong as many times as they are right. Arthur's father outlawed all witches and wizards. Many were killed, and that caused discontent in the land. That is currently forgotten, and we have moved on now.

"Our land extends about twenty leagues in all directions. The land is tilled by farmers, who are given their land in return for them supplying food to the castle. They also get protection from the castle troops, but in the case of war, they must fight with the forces.

"Arthur is the king, but the nation is run by the knights, with Arthur as our chief. We meet weekly in the main hall, which I will show you soon. The knights all sit around and discuss whatever problem exists. The squires sit behind their knights at these meetings. You will experience that for yourself; the next meeting is tomorrow.

"The ethics of the nation are to provide a safe harbor for the population and justice for all. The king becomes a judge and resolves disputes. One day, no doubt, an independent judge will sit and hear complaints and resolve them, but that is all in the future.

"There, that is enough for now. I will show you to your new quarters inside the castle proper."

"Nothing about me in that little speech, was there," Viviane said to Robert, somewhat put out that her life had been forgotten. Robert knew when to keep his mouth shut; his mother had told him all those years ago, "Never argue with a lady."

Robert had not realized he would be moving again. He was impressed with his new room, which was inside the castle. It had an oil light and was larger than the previous room. The bed was more comfortable than his previous one, and he had another chest of drawers, so he moved his belongings over. The room also had its own window opening with shutters. After the move, he took the opportunity to explore the castle. It was much as he had imagined. It was very bland, with bare walls other than the tapestries and other colorful hangings. There were several oil lamps around the building in corridors. A few statues remained from the Roman occupation.

Many of the rooms opened out onto one another; furniture was simple, all wood and practical rather than beautiful. There was a large fireplace in every room. He had noticed earlier that they didn't have chimney pots on the roofs, just long chimney flues to the top of the building. All tables and chairs were well made by craftsmen, but there were no extra luxuries.

Later in the day, he was walking around the town and was amazed at how his prestige had risen following his skirmish with Scatchen. News got around quickly in Camelot. No one liked Scatchen, and people were glad to see the back of him. Men were doffing their hats to Robert out of respect; the ladies gave him that extra smile, and he liked that. For the first time in his life, he was somebody.

That evening, he took his seat at the dining table. Now he was on the other side of the fence. He always made a point of being kind to the servers as he remembered being one of the kitchen staff himself.

At the top of the table was King Arthur, sitting next to his wife, Queen Guinevere. The knights and their wives spread out from there, and the squires were last of all. Guinevere was a beautiful woman of about twenty. She had long, dark hair in a braid down to her shoulders and blue eyes with a hint of green.

There was one knight, a Sir Baldwin who had ideas; he found the queen very intriguing. He was a young man of twenty-five, and he had not been in the court long, coming from a neighboring town further up the country. He made the point on this evening of going to the head of the table, acknowledging the king but bowing graciously to the queen, telling her how enchanting she looked this evening.

Now, the king was not a jealous man as such, but this knight was overstepping his situation, the king thought, but he let it go without comment. The queen was flattered, however, but seeing her husband's slight annoyance, she just said thank you. Sir Baldwin retook his seat at the table next to Sir Galahad.

The king was a very sturdy-looking fellow with short, dark hair. All the other men had rugged complexions, probably from living much of the time outdoors. The king and queen were well dressed in beautiful robes; they wanted to look the best at the table. Robert thought that the other occupants probably acted accordingly and dressed down so as not to outshine their majesties. They had a delicious meal of roasted lamb cooked with rosemary and mint sauce, served with green beans. Robert felt proud of himself. They were his recipes, and everyone loved them.

The next day, Robert started his duties early by getting Sir Galahad ready for his meeting. At mid-morning, they both took their seats, Sir Galahad and all the knights in a large circle and the squires sitting behind. The king dealt with the questions raised; most were quite straightforward and quickly put aside. The last item was more contentious.

The king said, "It has come to my attention that the adjacent warlord is raiding some of the outland farmers to the east. My suggestion is that our defense knight, Sir Galahad, take a party of twenty soldiers over there to assess the situation and then give whatever assistance is necessary."

There was a difference of opinion expressed. One knight thought the king should go with the full army. Another thought that only one knight should go to liaise with the warlord. Finally, the king's original suggestion was accepted. Robert concluded that although the knights ruled the kingdom in total, in reality, it was the king who had the final word, and most knights went along with what he said without question. It was a dictatorship in reality.

Robert thought after the meeting that the king and the knights would be served better with a table in front of them at these meetings. *It will be much more impressive*, he thought, and he had heard of the famous round table in the legend.

I'll see if I can speak to the carpenters to see how practical it is to build one.

"Now you are thinking clearly. Don't forget to have the king painted at the table's head. The table must be good enough for its memory to last for thousands of years, although the table itself will be gone by that time," Viviane whispered in Robert's ear.

"Thank you. I'll remember, Viviane. May I call you that?" he said

"What else would you call me? I may be a spirit and have powers beyond your comprehension, but I am still a girl at heart."

Later in the day, Robert went to see the carpenters, with Viviane flying behind. There were two in the castle's employ. One was an elderly gentleman who had been doing this work all his life and loved it. Anyone could tell that from the quality of the things he had around his workshop. The other carpenter was his young apprentice. Robert said to the older gentleman, "Is it possible for you to make a table for the king that is ten feet in diameter and divided into sixteen segments? Each section will be painted with a knight except for one, which will have a portrait of the king and will be at the top of the table."

"You are not asking for much, are you?" the carpenter said sarcastically but with humor. "Seriously, yes, it can be done. It will take a long while, though, probably about a year. I will have to make it in sections, four- to five-foot squares of wood, and then join them together and cut it circular. It will have to be at least three inches thick, but yes, it can be done. If we cut down the trees now, it should be ready this time next year. The quality, I assure you, will be out of this world."

"Excellent. Please go ahead. I will pay for it out of my earnings," said Robert, thinking that "out of this world" was probably right. The carpenter was excited with this project; it was much more interesting than the mundane jobs he was typically asked to do. He immediately set about the task have the best oak trees cut down.

Sir Galahad started preparations for the excursion into the outlands. It would take three days on horseback, and each rider would have two horses to allow one to rest. They needed a wagon for provisions. The expedition would last at least two weeks depending on what they found. When touring, you had to expect anything. As promised, Sir Galahad gave Robert his own horse, a beautiful white stallion. He loved and befriended it, spending many hours of his free time grooming it. He was becoming quite experienced at his riding; he didn't want to delay the expedition.

CHAPTER SIX

On the fourth day, they were ready to set out, Sir Galahad, Robert, and twenty soldiers. There were two provision wagons with spare horses. Weapons were restricted to swords; they had very little else. Robert had noticed the castle had lances, spears, knives, pikes, and various forms of axes, mainly of stone, which were used more like a club. They were all stored in the main castle, but they were not considered appropriate for this trip.

They assembled in front of the castle steps, as was a tradition on these occasions, Galahad and Robert at the front and the other soldiers behind. At that moment, the king came down the steps to say goodbye to Galahad and impress upon him that this matter needed to be resolved at all costs.

"Use whatever force you need," said the king.

Galahad said he would do his duty, and the king then moved sideways to Robert and said, "Look after Galahad for me. He's a good man. I rely on him immensely and take care of yourself as well."

"I will, sire, and thank you," said Robert, acknowledging the king's concern, and they shook hands.

They mounted their horses and set out at a slow walk so as not to tire the horses. Galahad turned to Robert, smiled in a fatherly way, and said, "The king has taken a particular interest in you. He has never come to see us off before on these expeditions, nor does he shake hands with anyone. I can see I will need to keep a watch over you."

The pace was slow, which was good for Robert; he could then see the different countryside, which became hillier the further east they went. It also gave him more time to get used to the riding. Riding a horse in an arena was one thing, but in the wild, it was entirely another. They passed many farms on the way, and the procession stopped to freshen up and get more supplies. It was necessary to rest the horses and to be seen by the tenants en route to let them know that the king was there to look after them.

On the back of Robert's horse was Viviane. He knew she was there, but no one else did. He was sure once that he could feel her body. It was as though she was a young girl again; he could feel the softness of her body. But then he pulled himself out of his dream, or was it a dream?

By the fourth day, they were nearing their goal. They saw that some areas of ground had been destroyed by fire. They got near to the farmhouse and could see there were six horses in front of the building, which was little more than a large wooden shack.

Galahad said, "That's strange. Something is not right here. There shouldn't be that many horses in the front yard. You stay back with the wagons, Robert. You other men, come with me."

They rode off at a gallop to the farmhouse. Outside it, they jumped off their horses. Galahad knew this was trouble. He pushed open the door without knocking. Inside were six men intimidating the farmer, who was known to Galahad. "What's going on here?" the knight said.

The farmer, visibly relieved at Galahad's arrival, said, "These are men from the local warlord that I reported."

The warlord's men immediately, and without warning, went on the attack. The leader flew at Galahad with his knife in his hand. Galahad was quick; he raised his arm and clouted the arm of his assailant with his club, and the man's knife slid across the floor. Viviane, who was always in the background, focused her eyes on the knife, causing it to slide out of the way. Galahad brought his other hand up in a fist that went straight into the man's face. "You'll have a black eye from that," he muttered as the man fell to the ground, unconscious.

Behind him, Galahad's soldiers had come into the fray, and the warlord's men were heavily outnumbered. Punches flew, and the warlord's men were soon brought under control: six bodies lying on the floor.

The farmer said, "I'm so grateful to see you, Galahad. This situation has been going on for a long while now. Men from this warlord regularly attack us. We refused to swear allegiance to him. I am loyal to King Arthur. I have known the King Arthur, and his father before him, for many years."

Galahad said, "We are here to look after you. The king commands it. Does the warlord come with them, or do they always come on their own?"

"No, the warlord hasn't been here."

Galahad sent one of his men back to bring Robert over with the wagons. When they both returned, they loaded the six unconscious men in one wagon and tied them up. Galahad arranged for half of his men to be housed at the farm; they were given quarters in a barn. The other half camped outside and guarded the prisoners.

Galahad said to Robert, "You and I and the remainder of the troops will ride out to the warlord's castle tomorrow. It is about a day's journey to the east."

In the morning, Sir Galahad, Robert, and the troops set out. In the wagon, the captives were now awake but had sore heads. By the end of the day, they were still not at the warlord's castle. Galahad said to Robert, "We need to camp here tonight; I don't want to arrive at the castle at this time of the day, with nightfall coming."

They camped overnight, and the captives, who were still tied up in the cart, were left there. Galahad remarked, "I'm not making them too comfortable."

Robert inquired whether Camelot had many fights of this nature. "If so, what weapons do you use?"

"There are usually two or more incidents during the year, but most are resolved without a fight," said Galahad. "That is the hope here. As for weapons, we have the usual swords, axes, and pikes. Our foot soldiers are mainly equipped with these. The knights are on horseback. We have lances in case we come across other knights from a different realm."

Robert thought, *If only I could introduce them to guns.* Gunpowder might be difficult, but he would consider that. "Do we ever get in the situation where we fight a large army?"

"It's interesting you would say that. We are always thinking that one day, that will be a possibility. Why?"

"Well if you do, then you need longbows and arrows."

"You must acquaint me with those," said Galahad. "I have heard that the Romans had such weapons, but I think they called them crossbows."

"Crossbows fire a dart and are much smaller. A longbow shoots an arrow, which is much longer; the arrows cover a further distance. When fired from a longbow, the archers can effectively start shooting arrows when the opposition is further away. That way, you either kill them or frighten them off before they can retaliate."

"I want to hear more about this bow and arrow. Did you say the men who fire the arrows are called archers?"

"That's it," said Robert.

That night, camping under the full moon, Robert had another dream about Viviane. She told him, "Now you're getting there. See how easy it is when you use your brain? You have all the knowledge, so use it. Gunpowder is not beyond your capabilities."

In the morning, they rode on to the warlord's castle. They arrived at the gates under a white flag and were shown in under escort. At the main entrance, they were met by the warlord. The ruler's castle was a smaller version of Camelot. It also had a defensive wall around it with a gate and drawbridge, but only six other houses for the servants and what appeared to be a dormitory building for soldiers.

Galahad went to the cart and let the captives off, throwing them on the ground to make a point to the warlord. He said to the ruler, "I think these are yours. We need to talk about this." The warlord glared at his men as they were unceremoniously dumped on the ground.

Galahad said to Robert, "You go and sit with the staff in the kitchen and see what you can find out from them, and I'll speak with the lord."

The six men were released by their compatriots and sulked off with their bruises. The leader looked daggers at Galahad and muttered, "I'll get you for this. You'd better watch your back."

"In your dreams," said Galahad as he walked inside the castle with the lord; the atmosphere was electric. The warlord was a brute of a man, grossly overweight and round. Like everyone, he had a beard. Galahad was emphatic that these attacks on King Arthur's farmers had to stop. Arthur would protect them by force if necessary. "We will bring the full force of our army to attack you if necessary. Don't take this as a boneless threat; we will not allow your intimidation to continue."

"These farmsteads are in my domain. They always have been and always will," said the warlord.

"That is not so. There was the war ten years ago between you and King Uther, Arthur's father, which Uther won, and the new boundaries were drawn up in the peace settlement."

"That may have been the case then, but not now. I want my lands back and will fight for them if necessary," said the warlord.

Robert got down from his horse, with Viviane following him, and he went into the kitchen area to speak with the servants. He sat down at the long table and found out from the servants the warlord would not be backing down. Not in the long term, anyway. Viviane was flitting around the room, checking on the dirt in the kitchen; she had been a kitchen hand when she was alive and would not tolerate a dirty kitchen. She scraped off a finger of dirt, held it up for Robert to see, and screwed up her nose. Robert laughed, and a kitchen hand said, "What's funny?"

"Oh, sorry, it was just a thought," said Robert. Viviane was moving around, having fun, making faces at the servants.

Discussions in the main hall went on for another hour, getting nowhere. The warlord could see he was not going to get an agreement, and he realized this would have to be settled by a battle. He was not ready for that now, so he agreed to leave things as they were, thinking, *I'll take this up again when I can get reinforcements.*

On that note, Galahad came out of the castle keep and went to Robert, who was already waiting outside. Galahad said, "It's all arranged, for now at least. He has agreed not to interfere with our tenants. I'm not sure that I trust him, though"

Robert, on the other hand, had learned that the lord wanted more territory. He was prepared to fight for it in any way possible. He expressed these views to Sir Galahad, who responded that it did not surprise him.

They headed out of the castle and on back to the farm, which they arrived at the next day. They assured the farmer that all would be well from now on. If there was further trouble, then he must send word to King Arthur immediately. That would result in the full army coming to war.

On that basis, they headed back to Camelot. On the way, Galahad said to Robert, "When we get back, you must produce for me the longbow you described and demonstrate your theory."

"Gladly." Robert was pleased that his ideas were being listened to. It made him feel important. He'd known that one day, it would happen, but he hadn't realized he might be the person to introduce the longbow to ancient Britain. Robert was keen to learn which year he was in; he inquired casually of Galahad, "What religion does Camelot support?"

"Camelot is an ancient kingdom, so we believe in the power of nature, trees, the sky, sun, and stars, the wind that blows through our lives. We do not have a particular god. When the Romans were here, there were a few people around the country who revered a good Jewish man by the name of Jesus Christ. He came from a country occupied by Rome a long way away. That poor soul was crucified to save all the world's people, they say, but that has all gone quiet in recent times. I did hear that there is a monk named Augustine whose followers are touring the country, spreading the teachings of this Jesus Christ, but they have not been to our area yet."

Robert thought carefully. From his memory, he recalled that Augustine landed in Britain in the late 590s AD. The date now must be somewhere around 600 AD. *Wow*, he thought, *this is unbelievable.* No one in Camelot would believe his story, so Robert knew he must keep quiet about it. Maybe, one day, he could get back to the twenty-first century, but then he thought, *Why would I want to do that? Perhaps life will be better here.*

It was a long journey, but eventually, they arrived at Camelot. They retired as it was the end of the day, and all slept well after such a trip. The following morning, Robert set about producing his bow. He went to see the assistant carpenter again and said, "Do you have willow tree strips of wood?"

"Not willow, but I do have oak."

"Sorry, but it has to be willow, which is more pliable. I need a strip of willow about two inches wide and six feet long. It needs to be rubbed down smooth and end up about one and a half inches wide at the center, tapering down at each end to one inch. Can you do that?"

"Yes. Come with me and choose the tree. There are many around the lake; willow trees like the water. What with the table and the bow, you should see if you can get us extra helpers," said the carpenter.

"I will speak to the king about that," said Robert, thinking, *I doubt he will take any notice of me.*

They went down by the lake; it was about three acres in size.

"I don't like this lake," said Viviane in the background, and Robert wondered whether this was where Viviane had died.

At the far end could be seen the spring that fed it. The water just bubbled out of the ground; it crossed Robert's mind as to whether this was the source of the River Thames. The water moved down the lake and then formed a river at the other end, heading to the east. The water was shimmering in the sunlight; fish were leaping. Robert thought, *They are beautiful trout*, as he looked at their markings.

There were many willow trees around the lake.

"This is an excellent trunk, just right for the purpose you need. I can make what you asked for from this. In fact, I can make quite a few. Did you call them bows?" said the carpenter

"Try the one next to it," Viviane whispered to Robert.

"Um, can we look at the next tree," Robert said to the carpenter.

"Yes, let's have a look. Actually, you're right. This would be a better tree. How on earth did you know that?"

Robert smiled, and so did Viviane.

The tree was cut down, and they cleaned off the branches. They took the trunk back to the workshop. "That should do the trick," said the carpenter.

"Yes, that's good. The more you can make, the better, but the bows need to be accurately made. Straight, not bent. When shall I come back? I also need arrows; they should be round, about half an inch in diameter. Two feet long. They should be of oak, and again, they must be perfectly straight. If they are bent, they will not fly straight."

"Give me a day. Come back tomorrow."

They parted, and Robert went about the rest of his duties. Later, he went to the blacksmith, saying that he needed twenty-five arrowheads. The blacksmith looked at him blankly. "What's an arrowhead?" he asked.

"Oh!" said Robert, and he proceeded to draw one using charcoal on a piece of wood.

"That looks dangerous."

"Only if it's coming toward you," joked Robert

"Okay, I can do that; do you want them in iron or copper?"

Robert thought steel, but maybe it was too early to go down that road! "Iron. The point must be sharp. It has to penetrate flesh," he said, and he agreed to come back tomorrow. He now had to go and collect many bird feathers for the flights. He wasn't sure which ones would be best, so he got a variety.

Next, he went back to the alchemist to see how he was getting on with the sulfuric acid. The alchemist said, "You're in luck. I managed to get hold of three bottles of the acid from various local castles. No one wanted them there, so I managed to make some trades."

"That's wonderful. Thanks," said Robert, and he took the bottles back to his room. He made his batteries the same way as before, but larger now, and this time, he had prearranged with the glass blower to blow several bulbs. Robert inserted the wire for the filament and then extracted the air as before. Viviane said, "You be careful. That stuff can kill you, and I have more tasks for you in the future. Pour the acid very slowly."

He now connected everything up, following Viviane's advice, and he took his contraption into the castle as it was getting dark. He asked Sir Galahad if he could give another demonstration. Galahad readily agreed and said he would get the king. When all were gathered, Robert lit his lamp.

The king said, "Robert, you are a wonder. You must show someone from the castle how you do that. We will call him the lamplighter. He can do that each night to help with the evening light in the castle." The king gave Robert a big smile, the sort of smile that came with emotion. Robert returned it; he felt a real bond forming.

"I'll be glad to, sire," said Robert.

He went back to his room. He suddenly felt elated. *I can bring something to this community. I'm going to be a success here. I don't need to go back to the twenty-first century. My expectations of life are simple: I want a wife and children in a town where I am respected. Thank you, Viviane. I am going to make this work.*

Chapter Seven

Today, Sir Mordred was doing his duties. He was instructed to go to the three farms on the west side of Camelot, all of which lay about five miles from town. Mordred was a young man, as were most of the knights, but he felt he must work hard to establish himself with the king. The knights had their own hierarchy, with the king on the top rung. Today, Mordred needed to go to each farm and see that the farmers were happy and producing good crops and if they needed any special help.

There had not been any interference with farmers from outsiders on this side of Camelot in the past, so Mordred was expecting to have a quiet day. By midafternoon, he arrived at the third farm; the first two farmers had had no problems. This farmer, Giles Mandrake, was having difficulties with a wild boar. Giles was a burly man of about fifty; his wife was younger. Most men married younger ladies. They were good for housework and having babies.

"I am having difficulties with a boar," said Giles. "I think there is only one, although it's difficult to say. You know a boar is just a pig, and they stick their snouts into the ground, looking for truffles and other food. The problem is that they destroy the ground cover and the crops that are growing."

"Oh, I see," said Mordred, not having come across that problem before. He didn't know much about the details of farming. He was a fighter through and through.

"Is this a new experience, or has it been around for a long time? I don't remember you mentioning it when I was here three months ago," said Mordred.

"It is new. I thought we had gotten rid of all the wild boars in this area of Avalon, but this one turned up out of the blue."

"I'll go back and report the situation to the King Arthur. I am sure we can deal with this. It is only one, though?"

"Yes, I'm sure of it."

"All right, I'll be in touch."

Sir Mordred returned to Camelot and arrived late afternoon, just as the sun was setting. It was getting dark, so he didn't report the situation to the king at that time. There was to be a meeting tomorrow of all the knights.

At ten o'clock the next morning, the knights took their places in the circle. King Arthur was at the head as usual for their monthly meeting in the main hall of the castle. Various minor items were discussed. At the end of the meeting, Arthur said, "Are there any other matters arising?"

"Well, sire, I do have something..." Mordred said hesitantly.

"So, what is it Mordred?"

"Well, sire, I did my rounds of the three farms to the west of us as usual yesterday. I have to report that the last farm I called at, the one run by Giles Mandrake, is having problems with a wild boar."

"Wild boar? I thought they were extinct years ago," said the king.

"So did I, sire, but apparently not, and this boar is causing damage to the ground and, therefore, to his crops. If it is left unabated, then we must expect a smaller crop this year."

"What do boars do? I am not that familiar with them."

"Well, you realize they are pigs, sire. So, they look for truffles under the ground," said Mordred a little sarcastically.

"Yes, I do know what a boar is," said the king, feeling like Mordred was talking down to him. "Hmmm, we will have to do something about this. They are large, heavy animals. So, I want you, Mordred, to go with Sir Galahad. Take two of the strong workmen from town and capture the boar. It will make an excellent meal. You will need to take the hoist to lift it."

Sensing that Arthur was getting a little frustrated today, Galahad intervened, saying, "We will certainly do that, sire," and with that, the meeting ended. Galahad, who was the more senior knight, said to Mordred, "Let's arrange that for tomorrow. I will get two strong lads and the wagon with the hoist, and we'll leave to go to the farm at nine o'clock. We'll need to take shovels and any other digging implements as we will need to make a trap. I'll bring my squire Robert with me. It will be interesting for him to see the wild boar."

Arrangements were made; the town had a special wagon that had a winch on the back in the form of a wind-up drum. "That should take the weight of a boar," said Galahad. At nine the next morning, the five of them set off in the wagon and with four extra horses for Giles Mandrake's farm.

When they arrived, they said to the farmer, "Can you show us where the boar normally operates?" The farmer took them to the area where he had seen the animal last, which was at the end of a wooded section. The fields alongside were plowed and had been planted with corn. They could see where the boar was causing the damage. The corn was trodden down, and the ground was dug up. Robert was surprised at how much damage to the crops these animals made.

Galahad planned to dig a pit at least six feet deep. He ordered the two workmen to dig it at the edge of the field, near the woods. That took them two hours, during which time Galahad and Mordred cut down twelve thick stakes and shaved the ends into sharp points. Robert said, "I'll help with the digging. It will be good exercise for me."

The stakes were securely fixed at the bottom of the pit so that their points were sticking upward. The top of the pit was then covered with light branches and leaves. On top of that were placed several apples. Boars like apples.

"All we can do now is wait," said Galahad

"I think it would be better now to wait at the farmhouse. You must, of course, spend the night with me. The boar will come out at night," said the farmer, and they left to go back to the farm.

In the morning, they all rode out to their trap and found that the boar had fallen into the pit and been impaled on the spikes. "That was a success," said Galahad. "Now we need to get it out. That will take a great deal of effort. Just look at its size. It must be at least three hundred pounds."

Robert and Galahad pulled around the hoist on the wagon and fed a thick rope under the creature. They tied the rope to the winch, and the five of them then set about raising the boar. It was challenging work even with all the helpers, but eventually, the animal was in the wagon. Galahad told the two workers to ride back to Camelot with the boar to get it butchered while it was still fresh. The rest of them would fill in the pit, which seemed the simple part.

The workers set off with the wagon, which was now heavily laden. They could only travel at a walking pace; it took an hour to get to Camelot. They deposited the boar at the butcher's shop. The butcher was very pleased and immediately commenced cutting the meat up into steaks. They were then hung up on hooks to cure in the special hut alongside the butcher's shop.

Back at the pit, Mordred had just started to fill in the pit with Robert. Now, the farmer had told them that there was only one boar, but unbeknownst to them, lurking in the bushes to the side of the pit was the boar's mate. Boars are intelligent animals, and this one was still, staring out at what had happened. It knew what had occurred and was mad.

This animal was at least two hundred and fifty pounds and had large tusks on either side of its snout. It charged straight out of the bushes, without a moment's warning, at Mordred, who was standing at the edge of the pit in front of it. Perhaps it was just as well that Mordred didn't know what hit him, as he went straight into the trap, landing on an upturned spike. It was over in seconds; Mordred died instantly. The boar wasn't as smart as it thought, though, because it went straight in on top, and the spikes went into the boar as well.

It squealed dreadfully as the spikes were not long enough to go through both Mordred and the boar. Galahad could see the animal was dying, so he picked up a spare stake and thrust it through the animal's head. Robert felt nauseous at this point, and he quickly turned away, breathing hard and vomiting up his breakfast.

Galahad stood back in shock at what had happened. He said, "I'll have to go to Camelot and report that we need some serious help here." He and Robert took their horses and sped back to Camelot, where they found the king at the front of the castle.

"Sire, I have some shocking news. There has been a terrible accident. Another boar killed Mordred, and we need help to get him and the boar out of the pit," said Galahad.

The king was shocked and saddened. "This is awful," he said, feeling somewhat guilty as he had been rather abrupt with Mordred yesterday. "You must take whatever you need and bring the body back."

Galahad arranged for six men to go to the pit with another wagon and hoist the body out. They eventually got both out, poor Mordred and the boar, and they took them back to Camelot. Mordred received a decent funeral two days later.

They erected a large pyre on the edge of town, and Mordred was placed on top. The king lit the pyre; he always thought it was his job to do for a knight. The spiritual leader said words of comfort for his friends, although Mordred had no family in Camelot. The pyre burned for two hours before turning to ashes, which were spread over the ground once cold.

The boar had been handed over to the butcher once again. He was extremely pleased as he now had enough meat for several months, although he expressed his regrets for Mordred.

CHAPTER EIGHT

King Arthur and Sir Galahad were so pleased with Robert following his invention of the electric light that they gave him three days off to rest; he took the opportunity to develop his bow and arrows. He selected one of the bows and polished it up. The carpenter had taken him at his word; the bow was straight. He carved a grip for his hand and added a string made of catgut, and he twanged it; it had real force and sound.

The blacksmith had made the arrowheads. Robert selected three, which he fixed on the arrows. He then needed to set the feathers to give the arrow stability in flight. It was tricky, but he managed it, and he now had three complete arrows. He made a small finger clasp of leather to protect the fingers when drawing the bowstring back, and the job was complete.

So, he took the rest of the day walking outside the castle complex. There was a twenty-foot-high wall surrounding the castle for protection in case of a siege. The instructions to the tenant farmers were that they must come inside the wall in the event of an attack.

That morning, Viviane had been sitting on the edge of Robert's bed. She'd said to him, "It's time you looked around for a wife to give you the family you desperately need. I can't help you in that department."

"I have been looking, but no one is as beautiful as you."

"Flattery will get you nowhere." Even so, she'd perked up.

Today, he decided he would just walk and talk to everyone he met. The townsfolk had all heard of the strange lad who was thought to be a wizard as he knew so much. That pleased him; now he had become so accepted. He even doffed his cap to people as he passed them.

He went past one farm, and in the barn, he saw a lovely young lady milking a cow. She also had long blonde hair, which she kept shoulder length, and blue eyes that sparkled in the sunlight. She was about five foot six and of a slim build. She reminded Robert of Viviane a lot. She saw Robert coming and smiled. It was a beautiful smile, a beam that went from side to side on her face. There were a lot of girls working inside the castle and in the surrounding fields, but this girl really had something that attracted Robert.

He went over to her, but before he could speak, she said to him, "It's good to meet you. I've heard a lot about you in town."

He felt flattered and said, "I have been away for a while, but it's good to be back. It's nice to meet you, too. My name's Robert."

"I'm Gwen, named after Guinevere, but she is much more beautiful than I am."

"Not at all," said Robert, feeling a little shy and self-conscious.

Gwen blushed. "I'm almost done here. You look as though you're out for a walk. Would you like some company?"

"I'd love that."

After five minutes, she said, "That's it. I'm ready. Let's go for that walk."

"Why don't we go down by the river fed by the lake. I like it there, and it's very peaceful." They set off, chatting all the way. Robert had always found it difficult to talk to girls because he lacked confidence and didn't want to be put down. But here, it was different; he was far more knowledgeable than anyone in this realm. He was now getting used to the strange dialects these people had. *I feel one of them now*, he thought. When they got down to the river, they sat on the side of the bank, listening to the water quietly flowing.

"It's like the sound of silence," Robert said to Gwen. The water was bubbling along over the stones. It was shallow at this spot, and the fish, which Robert knew were trout, could be seen swimming around each other playfully.

"I like that. Pure silence does have a sound, and it comes from within," said Gwen.

Robert liked her. *This lady is a thinker.* They looked hard and long at each other. Not a word passed; it was as though they were talking through telepathy. They started to get closer, leaning toward each other until their lips touched lightly. The excitement rushed through both their bodies.

They pulled apart, feeling a little guilty, and Gwen said, "We should be heading back, but let's go past the lake. I have a story to tell you there." They walked along the river until they reached the lake. Gwen said, "Let's sit here a minute."

They sat down, and she said, "There is an old legend that a young girl drowned in this lake. No one can remember when. There were these two young lovers who always challenged each other to do various feats of endurance. On one occasion, they challenged each other who could swim across the lake the fastest.

"The weather was not good on that day. It had been a very cloudy morning. By the time they got to the lake, the rain was coming down in buckets, but that did not put off the two heroes. They stood about where we are today, took their clothes off, and dove naked into the water. As you can see, it's about five hundred feet across, which should have taken them about ten minutes.

"That day, the bad weather was closing in fast, thunder and lightning raged, and the lake was looking like a sea. The wind was blowing the water into waves. The girl was struggling, unbeknownst to the boy, who was pushing ahead, thinking that he was winning. His goal was now in sight.

"He then realized that his girlfriend was in trouble, but by the time he got back to her, she had gone. He dove down to try to get to her, but he could not find her in the rough, dirty waters. After ten minutes, he realized that there was no hope."

"She died on that day, and ever since then, she is said to reappear to help anyone if they call to her. She is known as the Lady of the Lake; her real name was Viviane. No one knows what happened to the boy."

Robert was almost in tears listening to the story. *So that is your story, Viviane, how sad*, Robert thought, and a tear finally did down his face. He was really saddened. He knew that girl now, or at least her spirit, and he said, "That is an amazing story. You did say her name was Viviane?"

"Yes, that it was," said Gwen. "Why?" She could see Robert was visibly upset, as though he had lost a friend.

He couldn't tell Gwen his story yet. Perhaps one day. Besides, he didn't want to admit that he had been a bank robber. Come to think of it, she wouldn't know what a bank was. Instead, he said, "Oh, no reason. Do you think her ghost comes back? If she has one, that is. Do you believe in ghosts?"

"Well," said Gwen, "one day, when I was much younger, I was a naughty child. I wandered off to here and got lost. I was sitting on the bank just over there, crying. I saw a vision come out of the water, a ghost-like girl figure. It said, 'Don't be afraid. Your house is over there,' and she pointed in that direction. The apparition sank back into the lake like a sheet falling into the water. I went home the way she had pointed."

Robert thought about it all. The Lady in the Lake? That last story did sound like the ghost he knew. They got up at that point, brushed off the grass, and started to walk up the bank. Gwen was in front of Robert, and he suddenly had one of those déjà vu moments. The hairs on his neck stood up on end, and he thought he heard a chuckle behind him. He turned around in a flash, and there she was, Viviane, smiling.

"Fear not. Gwen can't see or hear me yet. You are doing an excellent job. Gwen is a sweet girl. Take care of her. Your tasks will become more complicated soon, so have strength," said Viviane as she sank back into the water, thinking of her betrothed that she had lost.

Gwen suddenly turned and said, "What's wrong? Are you all right?"

"Oh, I'm fine. It's just that…" Feeling a little silly, he stopped and turned back. "It's nothing, just my imagination."

They set off for Gwen's home. When they got back to the farm, her father was outside. Robert said to Gwen, "Thank you so much for the afternoon. I enjoyed being with you. Can we do it again?"

"Yes," she said. "I liked it, too. I would like to see you again."

Robert kissed her lightly on the cheek and left, glancing back after fifty feet to see her still watching him. She gave a small wave, which he returned.

Gwen's father said, "He seems a nice young man."

Robert and Gwen would soon be spending1 many an afternoon on those special walks that only young lovers know.

That night, when Robert went to bed, his mind was active, thinking, *I am here to help Arthur in some way, not just to bring him electricity.* One of the situations of that period in England was settlers coming in from Europe. The Vikings were particularly aggressive, but they were not until later in time. Now it must have been the Angles, Saxons, or Jutes. Whichever it was, he knew there would be battles soon. Robert knew now that he had to improve the town's defenses. That night, lying in bed, he was aware that the town wall needed ramparts. *The army needs bows and arrows and steel, and I am the man for this task. I will make Camelot invincible.* He eventually got to sleep.

The next day, Robert reported for work again and said to Sir Galahad, "I have made the bow and arrow for your consideration."

"Good," said Galahad. "I'll get the king. He must see this as well."

In one hour, they were all standing in the unobstructed sports field for the demonstration. Robert said, "Sire, please remember the arrows may go astray; it is a skill that needs to be learned by your future bowmen."

"That's understood, Robert. This is not a test of you, just the bow and arrow," said the king. "Please, carry on."

Robert had placed a log about a hundred feet away. The king inspected the bow and gently pulled on the string. "Hem, that's tight," he said and handed the bow back to Robert.

Robert held the bow vertically in front of him. He placed an arrow to the string and pulled it back as far as he could with the finger pad. He aimed it as best he could at the log – he had never done this before – and he let the arrow go. It flew from the bow at an enormous speed, and he watched it for what seemed like seconds. It went past the log by at least another fifty feet.

"I'm sorry, sire. I missed the log."

"What a useless shot," Robert heard Viviane say, laughing. She seemed to be with him all the time now.

The king was speechless before collecting himself; he could see the value of this weapon.

"That is incredible, Robert. Well done. It went way past the log and traveled at least one hundred and fifty feet. With practice, it could be even further, and accuracy will follow. This is marvelous. We will be eternally grateful; it will make our army invincible."

The king gave immediate orders to his carpenters to reproduce the bow and arrow in significant numbers; he could immediately see the advantage an army would have with this weapon.

"Sire, may I speak with you, or should I talk to Sir Galahad first?" Robert said.

"That's all right, Robert. You and every citizen can speak to me."

"In that case, sire, the bow and arrow will give you a great advantage if the castle is attacked. The arrows fly a great distance, but what is needed is a platform for the archers to stand upon behind the town wall. It must be four feet below the top of the wall; it is called a rampart. Men can then be placed along that rampart and fire arrows into the enemy outside as they advance. The arrows will not go through armor, but soldiers on foot will not have armor. Also, the extra height of the wall will make the arrows fly further."

"You have a good man here, Galahad. Look after him," said the king.

"Yes, sire, I intend to."

The king then turned to Robert. "You seem sure we will receive an attack. Why do you think that?"

"Ah, that's a difficult one to answer, sire." Thinking quickly, he went on to say, "It came to me in a dream, sire. Raiders will arrive from the east."

"Now, that is interesting," said the king. He had heard that settlers were in the east of the country, near the town of Winchester. *This young man must be a wizard, but we will make the most of him.*

That evening, when Robert went to bed, he was lying awake, deep in thought as usual. Now he realized why he had been sent back in time. If this was the King Arthur, the legend known from books and films, where were Sir Launcelot and Merlin? They played an important part, or maybe it was just a legend.

The next day, all the trades of the castle were organized to build the rampart platform suggested by Robert. The carpenters were making bows and arrows in their hundreds. Robert said to the master carpenter, "I realize this is going to delay the table manufacture, but safety comes first."

The carpenter said, "We'll manage both, Robert, but some help would be handy."

Robert went to see the blacksmith, who was standing in his shop, wearing his leather apron, to find out how he obtained his iron. He learned it came in as pig iron; the pig was the name of the container the iron was cast in.

Robert said to him, "Can we melt down the metal and add carbon by way of crushed charcoal? Charcoal is high in carbon. It will make a much stronger metal called steel; the carbon gives it strength."

"Well, I could give that a try. We would need to create immense heat to melt it, though. Leave it to me, and I'll see what I can do." The blacksmith then had to make an exceptionally large furnace with special clay sides to do the job, but after three days, he had gotten the heat in the furnace to what was needed.

Robert's plans were coming along well; the platform took shape and was up in a week. The bows and arrows were constructed. The archers were practicing shooting the arrows, and they were getting better at it every day. They collected the arrows each time, as they were still scarce. The distances were getting longer; they were reaching at least two hundred feet now and building up to three hundred. The king had offered a reward for the first archer to reach three hundred feet. That was a real spur, and the accuracy was getting better.

As the rampart was now erected behind the town wall, the queen wanted to walk all the way around. She dressed that morning in pants rather than a dress, saying it would be more appropriate. She walked the wall with her lady in waiting. Coming the other way was Sir Baldwin, dressed in his fancy clothes and with a feather hat. Approaching the queen, he removed his hat and bowed, saying, "Good morning, ma'am. It's a lovely day for a walk, and you are looking very becoming in your pants."

"Thank you, kind sir," said the queen. She knew she should not feel this, but she was attracted to Sir Baldwin. They talked for a few minutes while the lady in waiting moved a discrete distance back. The queen then carried on walking, thinking, *I really must not get involved in a liaison.*

Robert, in the meantime, was advising the archers who were practicing. "Accuracy is not the most important thing; it is all about the speed at reloading." When they fired, the arrows left dozens at a time. Hopefully, some of them would find their targets, if not all; the important thing was to reload.

The king was pleased; he realized that this weapon would one day make the nation great. He knew that Robert was crucial to the kingdom, and he had spoken with Sir Galahad to say it was time for Robert to become his personal adviser. Galahad was upset at losing his squire, but he realized this was in the interest of the realm. King Arthur always had it in his mind that one day, the country would be known as Greater Avalon! That had been his father's hope, and Arthur loved his father's memory and wanted to do right by him.

So, Robert was now in direct contact with the king and accompanied him on all important matters; a real bond was forming between the two. In the meantime, the blacksmith came to Robert in a very excited manner, saying, "I've been trying to find you. I did as you said, and a new metal formed. It is shinier than the old iron and sounds different when you hit it, more of a ping than a clonk. I have also made some bars from it, and they are so much stronger than the iron."

"Good," said Robert as he inspected the shiny new metal. "Can you please make the arrowheads from that new metal in future. This metal is to be known as steel; it is much harder than iron and copper. You should use it in all the swords in the future. Copper is too soft, and iron is brittle. The steel is much stronger." The blacksmith immediately set about making more of this steel.

Robert was again feeling pleased with himself. He thought the castle would be safer now. He was imparting knowledge to the people centuries in advance. He was careful not to alter the course of history, just giving it a little help along the way. Robert was also spending more time with Gwen. She was impressed that he was now the king's adviser, and she was becoming hopeful that he might ask her to marry him. Robert enjoyed being with Gwen very much.

The blacksmith was very busy now making swords of steel. When he had several made and polished, there was to be a contest to test which of the swords were stronger. Ten men, five on each side, set about a contest, not to the death, but merely to test the swords. One team had iron, and the other steel.

Everyone was dumbfounded to find that all the iron swords broke when hit by the steel swords, everyone except Viviane, of course. She was just watching, smiling in admiration for her protégé. The steel swords were hardly marked after the contest. The king was once again amazed at Robert's ingenuity. He said, "Is there no end to your genius? We must keep this steel a secret; otherwise, our enemies will have it as well, and then there is no advantage."

The king realized that he was becoming close to Robert. In a way, he sensed it was because they had similar backgrounds. They were both only children, and neither had living parents; there was a bond forming.

That afternoon, Robert was not working, and he went to see Gwen. She was in the barn on the outskirts of her father's farm. The barn was full of fresh hay, and she was standing on the top of it, looking down at him. She realized how much she was in love with him; her face was turning red with the thought of him standing below her.

She was a young woman now, and passion was building up inside her, Robert was feeling aroused, it had been so long since he had a girlfriend, and he slowly climbed up the haystack. Neither of them said anything that afternoon; there was no need, they just made love.

They both realized that this was what they wanted for the future. Gwen wanted to have a husband and a family, just like her parents and their parents. After their lovemaking, she said, "You had better leave the barn before me. I'll stay here and wait a while."

Robert left quietly. Gwen stayed, a beautiful smile on her face. *He's mine now*, she thought.

That evening, the king had arranged a feast in the castle for the villagers. Feast days were the only break from the tedium of work, and tonight, the king had a special announcement to make. The castle was always decorated, but tonight, the singers and bank had arranged a special performance of songs and dances to delight their audience. A feast was laid out on the front table of suckling pig, chickens, geese, venison, and duck, with all the trimmings. The villagers came up in turns to help themselves to food on wooden plates. The more wealthy brought their own pewter plates and made sure they took them home with them.

After the show, Arthur stood up and said, "I have an announcement to make. Robert has been a blessing, for me personally and for Camelot in particular. He is enhancing our defenses against any foe that might exist, and he assures me he will be done shortly. He has given us bows and arrows, a rampart for our wall, and the new metal called steel. He has shown us electricity. In recognition of that and other things I am sure will evolve, I am going to knight him, so I would ask him to kneel before me." The king gestured for Robert to come forward.

Robert was amazed, and walked over to the king in awe; he was truly grateful for the recognition, something he never thought he would have, and he knelt before the king.

King Arthur said, "Robert is not a name that is in keeping with the position or the character of the man, so I am going to change it to Merlin."

The king tapped his shoulders with his sword, saying, "Arise, Sir Merlin."

A great cheer went up in the room, and then the crowd chanted, "Merlin! Merlin! Merlin!"

Robert, now Merlin, was completely overcome. His throat was closing up, but he knew he has to speak. If only his parents could have seen him now, but perhaps they could. He waited patiently for the cheers to die down; it gave him a moment to get his breath back. He lifted himself off his knees, and with tears welling in his eyes, he stood and faced his audience, who were now quiet. That is, except for one lady ghost, who was flying around the room in jubilation, but no one in the gathering could see her except Merlin.

"Your majesties, friends, and fellow citizens of this great land, may I thank you for this great honor. You have welcomed me into your town and made me feel part of it. I hope I will be able to live up to the honor you have given me, and I welcome the name change. Merlin is an exceptional name. Thank you."

He sat down after the applause, thinking, *So, I am Merlin in the legend. That explains a lot. Now I do have to live up to that. I didn't alter history. I am part of it.*

CHAPTER NINE

The king was becoming concerned about the warlord to the east. He had received word from a messenger that the warlord was getting very aggressive once more and threatening Arthur's farmers.

The messenger stated, "The warlord has been killing the farmers' cattle as they would not swear allegiance to him." This time, the committee of knights had no hesitation in confirming that it was necessary to send the full army into decisive battle. The king turned to his adviser, Merlin, and said, "Do you have any other thoughts? You have done wonders for defense. Do you have any thoughts on the attack that we are not aware of?"

"Well, yes, sire, as a matter of fact, I do. The Romans had what is effectively a giant bow and arrow, called a ballista. It is a large wooden bow that is transported on wheels and fires rocks at a castle wall, gradually making a breach wide enough for ground troops to enter."

The king thought for a moment and said, "Hem, I think I have seen one of those contraptions. Now, where was it…? I remember! When I was at that spa town built by the Romans called Bath. There was one there, I am sure of it. The baths have gone into ruin now, although the spring is still there. Bath is not that far from here, perhaps a five-day ride, and it is then only three days from there to the warlord's castle.

Here's what we will do. Galahad, I want you to organize four men to ride to Bath and get hold of this ballista. Bring it to the warlord's castle, which will take you about eight days. We will leave here with the army in three days' time, and we should arrive at the warlord's castle at about the same time."

The plan was put into action, and the four men, with Galahad leading them, took off for Bath the next day. Merlin took the opportunity to spend some quality time with Gwen before they headed off to war. He was excited by the prospect. He had never seen a war, even though he knew his job would not be to fight actively.

In this period of rest before they left for the attack, Merlin saw Gwen every day. They spent all day together, walking in the countryside. They stopped at quiet spots and made love.

Merlin said to Gwen on one occasion, "It's beautiful making love to you under the sky."

Gwen replied, "You do realize I might have a baby."

"I know." There was no birth control – he knew that – and he added, "That would be nice. I would love to have a baby with you, and a family. I miss being part of a family so much."

Gwen was finding it difficult to remember Robert's change of name to Merlin, and she had to admit making the odd mistake, but she liked the name Merlin. Gwen's father was happy his daughter had seemed to find love, not that he knew all the details.

On the fourth day, it was time to leave. The party of a hundred men set off, leaving a small garrison to guard Camelot. Travel was slower this time as the soldiers had to walk. The king, twelve knights, and Merlin rode horses. Merlin took turns walking to give a boost to the morale of the soldiers, although he was now a knight, and the soldiers appreciated his actions. By the sixth day, they had arrived a mile outside the castle, and they made an encampment there. Natural water was at hand from the local stream. Tents were erected as they expected to be here for several days.

The party from Bath was seen in the distance on the second day, hauling on an object, which turned out to be the ballista. Arthur had been right on his timing. *The castle is located on a hillock. This must be standard practice in the country, easier to defend from the high ground,* thought Merlin.

The ballista would be ideal for hurling rocks at the gate. Out of sight of the castle, Arthur's men practiced firing it. It was straightforward: the bow was wound back, and a rock was placed in the hurling basket; then it was fired. Everyone had to keep away from the basket, though, and when fired, the whole thing shook and jumped. After three attempts, they seemed to have it mastered, but only time would tell.

The next morning, King Arthur, Merlin, and four other knights rode to the castle under a white flag. A party rode out to meet them from the castle, also carrying a white flag. They discussed the situation; the warlord had decided that he wanted to take over Arthur's land this side of Camelot.

Arthur responded, "That this is not an option, and if you don't concede, I will attack and destroy your castle. You will lose your whole territory."

The warlord laughed and said, "We'll see about that. Your father was lucky last time our countries were at war, but this time, it will be different."

"So be it," said Arthur

They had reached an impasse, and each party withdrew under their white flags to prepare for battle. Arthur pulled up his new ballista; it was placed outside the front gate to the castle, about two hundred feet away. The defenders could do nothing about it other than watch in amazement. They had never seen anything like it. They could have come out of the enclosure but chose not to do that. If they had, they would have been picked off by Arthur's archers. They were not sure what the contraption was, though.

Arthur's men then collected large rocks to be hurled at the gate and piled them up. There was still little the opposition could do; they had not seen a ballista before. Since the Romans had left all those years ago, no one had used a ballista. The soldiers had sealed themselves inside the castle walls.

Arthur had lined up fifty men across the back of the ballista, all archers, and the opposition was wondering what that was about, too. The enemy had not even seen a bow either. That left Arthur with another fifty men. They were better at hand-to-hand fighting with their new steel swords; they lined up behind the bowmen.

At the signal from the king, the ballista fired at the front gate. It missed by yards, falling well short; the guards inside the castle could be heard laughing and jeering. By the third shot, the men had found their range. The rock thumped against the gate. By the twentieth shot, the gate was beginning to break up. Merlin, who was standing behind the ballista, guiding the men with their aim, was pleased with the results. "Well done, lads. We'll soon have the gate down," he said to the launchers. Viviane, who was standing behind Merlin, nodded in agreement.

Another ten shots and the gate started to fall apart; two more shots and the gate had fallen. "Now we have them," said Viviane to Merlin. Behind the gate were about twenty soldiers waiting to come out. Before they could move, Arthur's bowmen had raised their bows. They fired a volley of arrows straight at where the gate had been, and ten men fell. There was no laughter then.

There was a pause as the warlord got more men to come forward. Those men left were not so keen about having to clamber over the dead bodies of their comrades, arrows stuck out of the fallen soldiers. Another volley, and more men fell on top of the fallen. At that stage, Arthur calculated that the warlord had twenty-five men dead or out of action. Most bodies were in a pile by the front gate. Arthur moved his infantry forward under the command of Sir Galahad. With swords drawn, they entered through the gatehouse.

There were only a few men around now who came at them with swords. Sir Galahad saw immediately the man he'd fought with last time at the farmhouse. He had seen Sir Galahad also, and if looks could kill… Both had swords and shields, and they were going to battle it out, come what may.

They eyed each other. Galahad had a steel sword, while his opponent's was of iron. Both shields were iron. Galahad tripped around his foe with light feet. Suddenly, he brought down his sword, which was fended off by the opponent's shield. Galahad thought, *I'm getting too old for this hand-to-hand fighting,* as he felt the shockwave go back up his arm. Needless to say, so did his opponent, although neither would admit it even to themselves. They spent the next five minutes shuffling around, getting the best position. Galahad wanted the high ground to jump down on his foe.

It was a cat-and-mouse game with the occasional clash of swords and shields. Galahad did manage to get a slash in across his opponent's chest, but it was not deep. His foe did not surrender as Galahad had hoped.

At that moment, the other soldiers of the warlord seemed to be giving in. Several threw their weapons on the ground, the accepted way to surrender, responding to the superior power of Arthur's army. Merlin had taken a back seat in the battle; he knew he was not a hand-to-hand fighter, but he was determined to change that for the future. It was too late for Galahad's foe, though. He was distracted by the events, and Galahad ran him through the midriff with his blade, and he fell back and died in agony. Viviane, at that point, acted. She did not like to see unnecessary death. She raised her hand, and a white light was emitted. All the opposition fighters froze in time.

Arthur called a ceasefire. The warlord was at an upstairs window of the castle, looking out. Arthur said, "You've lost. Don't waste any more life. Surrender."

"I'd rather die fighting, and my men will follow me."

His soldiers didn't agree and were now able to move their arms. They dropped their weapons immediately, throwing their arms in the air in surrender, and were taken prisoner.

Arthur was left with no alternative now; he turned to look at Merlin, who said, "You have no option now, sire." The king had to burn down the central keep. Although it was stone, most of the interior was wood. Arthur laid fires at the doors and threw burning torches through windows on the ground floor. He also poured in oil, which took flame quickly, and soon, the castle was a mass of flame. Flames could be seen shooting up through the floors as each one fell in with a crackle of burning wood, and the heat was enormous. Arthur's soldiers had to move back from the walls. At that stage, Arthur had expected all the inhabitants to come out as prisoners. That did not happen, and Arthur wondered if he had missed a secret passageway escape. No, he hadn't. After three hours, the fire dropped, and the castle was burned out inside.

Once the building had cooled down and they could get in safely, Arthur's men went from room to room, carrying out the dead bodies. There were ten in total, all thought to be members of the warlord's family. Arthur arranged decent burials for them. He rounded up all the prisoners and walking wounded. He told them they would be free to live in Camelot providing they gave allegiance to himself and Camelot. Peasants and soldiers changed sides with rapidity in the fighting between warlords. Some of the wounded died within the day. They, too, were given decent burials. Any surviving at that point were taken back to Camelot for recuperation.

Arthur took an inventory of each man and his profession. There were three each of carpenters, blacksmiths, and masons and then twenty general helpers. The castle and all surrounding buildings were demolished.

King Arthur declared that all the warlord's land was now part of Camelot, and a contingent of men under one knight went around to all the local farms with that news. Most farmers were pleased, saying that the warlord had been a tyrant, demanding high taxes and offering nothing in return. They, too, were happy to give Arthur allegiance. Merlin was especially happy to learn there were three more carpenters, just what he needed for his tasks.

Arthur was pleased with his soldiers and gave them a bonus. He had managed to extract some treasure from the warlord's castle, which Arthur shared amongst his people. It took five days to return to Camelot, except for the ballista, which needed eight. Everyone was glad to be back home, especially Merlin, who was missing Gwen.

While Arthur had been away, Sir Baldwin, who had not gone with the war party because of a stomach problem, had been making advances toward Queen Guinevere. He was discrete at first, but the queen was flattered by his pleasurable voice, so soft and becoming. Arthur had a gruff voice, and she had missed a man's advances. She got on well with Arthur, but the grass was always greener on the other side, as her mother had said to her when she was young.

The castle was empty for most of the day as everyone of note was at war, and the evenings were particularly quiet. Dinner was still being served, although there were only four people at the table that night. The queen was at the head of the table alone, and Sir Baldwin went up to her and said, "It might be inappropriate, but could I sit next to you, on the other side of where the king would normally sit. I thought you might like some company."

"That's kind you. Please do. My husband won't mind," said the queen.

They spent the whole evening chatting, and the other two diners departed when they had finished their meals. The queen was feeling amorous with all the flattery, and they both forgot themselves. Their hands touched accidentally, or was it? An electric shock went up both their arms. "What was that?" said the queen

"That was a spirit telling us to kiss," Said Baldwin, and they did, a tender kiss. Fortunately, no one else was in the room by now. The queen enjoyed it, wanting more, but she came to her senses, saying, "I'm sorry, Sir Baldwin, but we cannot do this. If Arthur found out, we would both be in serious trouble, and nothing is private in Camelot."

Sir Baldwin was sad. He knew he had nothing to lose; he could be off in a second and leave the town, but he realized the queen couldn't. He became formal, paid his respects to the queen, kissing her hand, and left the room. The queen was sad, but she knew she had done the right thing. She decided that evening that she and Arthur must have a child.

When the king rode into town, cheers welcomed the whole party; the residents left behind had worried that some catastrophe might strike while the king was away, but now he was back. *Very satisfactory*, thought Arthur. He had increased the size of his domain by a quarter. That meant more rent to keep the dominion going. He also thought he could increase the number of his soldiers.

His land now stretched from Bath right down to the end of Cornwall and up to lower Wales. He thought his father would be proud of him, which was important to him. He recognized the large input that Merlin had made; he was now more than an adviser to the king. Arthur was developing a genuine affection for Merlin as a friend. They had so much in common. They were both only children. Arthur's mother couldn't have had any more children. She knew she'd only had Arthur through witchcraft. Both Arthur and Merlin wanted to have family and a brother.

Arthur was hearing rumors of settlers who were raiding the east coast of the country. They were ruthless killers, taking whatever land they could find. Fortunately, his kingdom was on the opposite side of the country and, for the time being, safe. He was conscious of keeping defenses up as much as possible, as one day, they would want to come here. He so much relied on Merlin to give him innovative ideas. Arthur was coming to the conclusion that Merlin was a sorcerer seeing into the future. That was, of course, against the law in Camelot, but he didn't want to go down that road.

Merlin still had one more card up his sleeve, gunpowder. Merlin knew gunpowder was known and used by the Chinese as far back as 1000 BC. Where would he get saltpeter? It did not occur naturally in Britain. Merlin knew the other ingredients, and sulfur and carbon were not a problem. He remembered from his school days that saltpeter was potassium nitrate. Merlin went to see the alchemist again and asked, "Where would I get potassium nitrate?"

"That's a tough question," said the alchemist. "That would be a compound of potassium and nitrogen, which, to my knowledge, does not occur naturally in this country, but I believe it may be possible to make it, although I've never seen it done."

"How would I go about it?"

"Well, let me think. We would need enormous quantities of cow dung, urine, and rotting straw. It would all need to be collected up in a large heap and covered for about a year. Hopefully, some of the crystals formed would be potassium nitrate. I think common salt might help as an activator. It's worth a try."

"Good," said Merlin. "Let's do that."

Viviane, who was watching, thought, *Maybe he doesn't need my help with everything.*

Merlin set about collecting all the ingredients mentioned and put them in a pile in a sunny place to get the heat from the sun. He covered the pile with a mixture of skins and cloth.

He resisted the temptation to check the collection each day but did look every month or so.

The carpenter was extremely pleased to get the extra help from the adjoining warlord's carpenters. He told Merlin that the table would now be back on schedule. The carpenter had calculated at first that he needed four quadrants, each with sides five feet long. He could put them together to make the right size, but he then realized that would mean the tree they came from would need to be at least ten feet in diameter. Oak trees are not easy to find that size, if at all, so he had opted for half a quadrant, making eight sections, which would come from a tree eight feet in diameter.

Some of the oldest trees in the forest would fit that bill. He had two such trees cut down of that size, and then he cut three-inch layers off the tree trunks so that he had ten segments, two being spares, that would be shaped to have five-foot sides and curved at the end. Merlin went along to see them and said, "This is coming on very well."

The carpenter said, "Well, this is the very rough wood. We have a long way to go yet. Each segment must be rubbed down, polished, and then painted and polished again. The table then must be assembled in the main hall. Once it's in place, it cannot be moved again; it will be far too heavy." The carpenter confirmed that the king didn't know of the plan. Merlin wanted it to be a surprise.

Things were quieting down at Camelot now; they had destroyed the adjoining warlord. There were rumors of settlers again causing a nuisance on the other side of the country. The settlers favored what the Romans called Britannia because the weather was so much more temperate. Their country, in the center of mainland Europe, was not as fertile. At present, they were not a threat to Arthur, but he felt that would change. The knights took turns going to the surrounding communities to see that all was well. Only good reports were coming back to Camelot, which pleased the king.

Gwen was now becoming a special person to Merlin; he knew he loved her and wanted to spend the rest of his life with her. He had come to terms with the fact that his life was here in this century, not back in Bromley. He knew he could make something of his life here, and he wanted a wife to love and a family. They spent most of their spare time together, walking the countryside, fishing, and relaxing. It was always good to catch some fish to vary the diet of meat. Merlin's new steel hooks were an improvement on the old iron ones, which always rusted.

CHAPTER TEN

Although the settlers had not been a problem yet to Camelot, Arthur knew that they needed a plan for dealing with them. The regular monthly meeting of the knights was tomorrow, and he intended to raise the issue.

The next morning, at about eleven o'clock, the knights met in the main hall of the castle. They were all seated in a circle with their squires behind them. Merlin had not appointed a squire for himself as he did not intend to fight or joust personally. Arthur started off the meeting by saying the only item on the agenda today was the procedure they should adopt in case the settlers move over into their realm.

One of the knights said, "Sire, do we have any information as to whether that is a likelihood?"

"No, not at the minute, but I believe it is inevitable. They started on the east coast and are working westward. It cannot be long before they are here," said Arthur

He went on to say, "We have, thanks to Merlin, improved our weaponry. Following the addition of bows and arrows, we also have the ballista and steel swords. Merlin has developed the ramparts on the city wall, which will make our defense more secure. He tells me that he is working on another project that will improve our chances further in case of an attack. Is there anything else we should be doing? Do you have anything to say, Merlin, as you mentioned this to me recently?"

"Sire," said Merlin, "I know history, which always repeats itself, and one day, these settlers will attack us. It has happened many times in the past to this island on which we live and will happen again in the future, rest assured."

"I agree, and we must accept that and plan accordingly," said Arthur, not realizing that they lived on an island.

No one could add any other options except to keep regular patrols to the east of Camelot. That was the direction from which any danger would come. All agreed to that, and a rota was to be established.

Arthur finished the discussion by saying, "We must keep ourselves on alert at all times. If anyone comes up with any ideas, they must bring them forward to me without waiting for a regular meeting." With that, the meeting closed.

Arthur went over to Galahad and had a private word. "Can you please organize the regular patrols that we just agreed."

"Certainly, sire. I will put that in hand right away."

After a few days, Merlin's love for Gwen had grown to a fever pitch, and he felt it was time to settle down. He saw no opportunity for him to get back to 2019, and why would he go back? It offered nothing for him. He was a hero here. He wanted to marry Gwen, but he was troubled.

Gwen was completely unaware where Merlin came from. He thought long and hard about this subject. How could you start a marriage with such deceit? What would she say when she eventually found out, as people usually do? He was perplexed. How would he tell her? Would she even understand? He knew he had to give it a try. *Keep the story simple*, he said to himself. *It's no good telling her about a city in the future when you live in Camelot.*

He started to pluck up the courage to tell Gwen. *At least the weather is kind today*, he thought. He chose a grassy area in a field and said, "Sit down here, darling. There is something I need to talk to you about." She sat down, and Merlin joined her.

Gwen thought, *Maybe he's going to ask me to marry him.* She wanted that.

"This is very complicated to explain," said Merlin, "and it will be difficult for you to understand, or even believe. I come from a different century far in the future. I was brought back in time by Viviane, the Lady of the Lake, you know, the one in the story you told me about when we first met."

"I always thought there was something strange about you on that day when you heard my story, but tell me more," Gwen said, not understanding what the implications were.

"Yes, but I couldn't admit it then. You would not have believed me, nor would anyone else for that matter. I would simply have been made a fool. Viviane brought me back in time so that I could give Arthur some advantages from my future life to make him into a mighty king. He will become the first king of all England. That is the name that will be given to this land in time. You know I have given him batteries, steel, and longbows, and gunpowder will follow. There will be other things I will introduce soon."

Gwen was, as Merlin suspected, disbelieving. *Does he think I am mad?* she thought. "Why are you telling me all this now? And what is gunpowder?"

"Don't worry about the gunpowder. All will be clear soon. I told you because I love you, and I want us to be married and settle down with a family of children. It wouldn't be fair to do that without telling you my story. Otherwise, if it ever came out in the future, you would be annoyed and think of me as a fraud. I couldn't bear that."

Viviane had kept out of the discussion, but she was nodding her head in agreement.

"I love you, too, but I don't know that I can believe what you are telling me. I do believe in the spirit of Viviane, as you know, but are you simply telling me this because you know that? I don't really care where you came from as long as you are with me. But will you ever want to go back to the other time?"

"No," said Merlin. "I have considered that very carefully over the past months. Definitely not. I did not get on very well in the future time. When I first arrived here, I did, but not now. I have no living parents; they died when I was ten years old. I have no family and got into a bad company of robbers. That is the reason Viviane chose me for this task. She told me that."

"Tell me how it all happened," said Gwen

Merlin related the story, but he kept it simple, using words and situations that Gwen would understand with her limited knowledge. He couldn't mention the bank raid – she wouldn't know what a bank was – so he just said it was a robbery. By the end, in half an hour, she was still not believing, but at least it explained how Merlin knew about so many things.

"Darling, thank you for telling me all this, but you are going to have to let me think this through in detail," said Gwen.

Merlin now wondered if he had done the right thing. Perhaps he shouldn't have told her, but they agreed to leave things over for the time being. Merlin took her home and said goodbye. Then he went back to the castle, feeling depressed. Had he messed up? He loved Gwen so dearly. Merlin went to bed early that night, missing dinner; he had no appetite,

Gwen was in turmoil. She didn't want to tell her parents; they wouldn't understand and would probably tell her to move on to a different boy. *I love Merlin*, she thought as she lay in bed. *What is the worst that can happen?* Tears ran down her face in her turmoil. She was upset; she wanted a simple existence without these headaches. Eventually, she got to sleep. When she dreamed that night, Viviane came to her in her ghostly appearance.

"You are troubled, Gwen," said Viviane. "Do you remember as a child how I directed you to your home? Well, this dilemma is similar. This man loves you, and you love him. Life is never straightforward. No one knows what is around the corner, and that's how it must be. Merlin's intentions, as we must now call him, are good. He will make you a good husband for the rest of your life, however long that will be. Marry him and be happy. You are an intricate part of his tasks."

In her sleep, Gwen rested her subconscious mind deeply. She knew what to do. The next day, she went to the castle to see Merlin. He saw her coming and felt apprehensive. Was she smiling? Did she look happy? He didn't know, but he walked over to her as she came through the front gate.

Gwen stopped and said, "I love you so much. It wouldn't matter to me if you came from one of the stars that we see at night. You don't, do you, by the way?" She laughed and fluttered her eyelashes at him.

"I love you, Gwen, be assured of that, and I don't come from one of those stars," said Merlin.

Merlin got down on his knees in front of Gwen and said, "Will you please marry me, darling?"

Gwen smiled. "Oh yes, you just try and stop me! Is that how you propose marriage in the future?"

"Well, some do, I think we should go and speak with your parents and give them the good news. I don't believe we should tell anyone my story, though, I would be ridiculed, perhaps even thought of as a wizard, and you know what that would mean in this country."

Gwen agreed, and they kissed deeply and headed off to her parents. On the way, they were quiet, both deep in thought about Viviane.

"I wonder what Vivian's full story is. There must be more to it than meets the eye. Why is she getting involved?" said Gwen.

"Hmm, I have always thought the same. Why was she chosen as a spirit instead of the many thousands of other people who have died in the past?" said Merlin

"Probably some kind of witchcraft.".

Merlin put his arm around Gwen and said, "Well, she brought us together, and I will always be grateful for that." They kissed again. Relief was spreading over Merlin from head to toe.

They went in to see Gwen's dad, who was in the outhouse sharpening his tools, and Merlin said that they would like to get married. Gwen's father and mother were very pleased. They knew that Merlin was a good catch and thought that he would take care of Gwen. A date was set for next month, when the spiritual leader would arrange the marriage.

It would be a very strange affair for Merlin, who had always imagined a Christian wedding. That was not an option in this pagan society. The spiritual leader would bless the couple in the name of nature, the sun, the stars, and the woodland.

On the big day, there was a short service followed by much celebrating, eating, and drinking. Camelot loved a party. The drinking got out of hand sometimes, but that was their only vice. The whole town, including the king and queen, were present and offered their blessings, and the king and queen gave the married couple a lovely gift of furniture.

The couple was also gifted their house by the town. It was a small cottage just outside the outer wall of the castle. Merlin had specifically asked for a window opening with a shutter, which was agreed to. When it was furnished, it looked very comfortable, and Gwen was so pleased to have her first home of her own with Merlin.

When Arthur had returned from the battle with the adjoining warlord, Guinevere had decided that she and he had to get closer. The incident with Baldwin must not be repeated, and she decided to have a baby so that they, too, would become a family. Baldwin had left Camelot to seek his fortune elsewhere.

It was now several months since Merlin had laid down his dung heap. He hadn't looked at it for weeks now, so he finally did. It was changing. It smelt vile, but the alchemist said, "That's because it is fermenting," which is what he thought it should be doing. The alchemist added, "Another six months should do it, if it works at all, that is."

The next six months went by very quickly, what with getting the cottage the way they wanted it and Gwen now expecting a child. Merlin was over the moon; he had always wanted to settle down and have a child, and now it was happening. He had never guessed it would be in the seventh century, though. They didn't see much of Viviane during this time; she knew Merlin could handle things for now. She knew she would be needed later on.

In the evenings before sleep, Merlin and Gwen would lie in bed talking. Gwen would often ask Merlin about his other life in the future. He found it quite difficult to explain things; he told her that buildings were much taller and had basements under the ground. He told her that they had a better means of transportation than the horse, called a car, saying that it was like a closed-in wagon but with an engine to power it. "I can't explain to you what an engine is because there is nothing remotely like it in this land. I suppose you could say it's like a mechanical horse. Men will fly in cylindrical vehicles called aircraft.

"As for buildings, you know how Arthur's castle is two floors high? Well, in my time, buildings are twenty floors high, and many are even higher." This amazed Gwen. One of Merlin's difficulties was explaining time. Gwen knew that the sun rose on the east side of town in the morning and traveled across the sky, setting on the west side. She thought it went underneath the earth, which she thought was flat, coming up the other side in the morning. She understood that made a day.

She also knew there were four seasons, winter, spring, summer, autumn, and back to winter, which made a year. There was no calendar as such; Merlin had told Gwen there were three hundred and sixty-five days in a year. So, he made his own calendar. One day, he took a plank of wood and some charcoal, and each day, he added a mark on the wood until he had six. On the seventh, he crossed through the lines, making one week. That way, he could have some idea as to how the year was progressing. He knew that would be an aid when battles were planned in the future. He was aware that there would be battles.

One bright day, Merlin decided it was time to look at the dung heap once more, and he took the alchemist with him.

"What do you think," he said to the alchemist.

"Well, it looks done to me. Let's clear the top away. The saltpeter should be underneath." Sure enough, at the bottom was a pile of dark crystals. "With any luck, that is potassium nitrate."

Merlin collected the crystals and mixed them with a similar quantity of sulfur and charcoal. Both the last items were readily available. He took a small amount, placing it on a clay saucer. They walked to the castle, where, just inside, was an oil lamp that was always burning, as starting a fire was difficult. He overlooked the fact they didn't have matches.

Merlin lit a splint from the lamp and placed it onto the powder they had made; it flared up instantly. Merlin felt pleased with himself, but he didn't let it show.

"There," he said to the alchemist. "Gunpowder." Another demonstration was immediately set up for the king. He looked on in amazement, as he always did with Merlin's demonstrations, saying, "Merlin, you will never stop surprising me. What do you do with it?"

"Well, sire, you can make bombs with it."

"Bombs?" said the king. "What on earth are they?"

"Well, sire, the gunpowder is put into a sealed container with a taper coming out. The taper is lit, and they can be thrown at an enemy to explode on impact or placed on the road to blow up someone or a wagon passing. You can also use it to project missiles out of a cannon or bullets from a gun."

"The last part, I don't understand at all, but talk to me about that later. In the meantime, I want you to organize the production of this material on a massive scale."

"I will," said Merlin, "but it takes about a year to make."

Merlin arranged with every farmer in the district to build up piles of dung and straw. They had to collect urine if possible and add it to the heap, then salt, and cover it for a year. When they had finished building one pile, they needed to start a second and then a third, and so on. That way, there would be a continuous production line in place.

He joked to himself, *It's the start of the Industrial Revolution.* He arranged with the alchemist for copious quantities of sulfur to be purchased from traders. He then went to the charcoal makers; charcoal was the primary source of wood to burn for heat. Also used for cooking, it lasted much longer than burning live wood, and the heat was more controllable. Burning wood in an atmosphere starved of air made charcoal. After several days, the black chunks of partly burnt wood emerged.

Merlin made sure that from now on, the forestry men would produce much more charcoal, which would be crushed down to a powder. That would then produce gunpowder and steel; he had then set matters in hand for the gunpowder production. They would have to wait a year for the first batch. Merlin knew the community would need it.

It was now early in the year, springtime, and the trees were beginning to bud, as were the wildflowers in the countryside. Animals were full of the joys of spring and looking for their mates. It had been a mild winter, one which had needed less charcoal for heating, meaning more for the store.

Merlin was now on excellent terms with the king. They saw each other many times during the day, and Merlin had become the king's chief adviser. He knew what was happening everywhere and planning for the future. Last month Gwen had given birth to their son, a beautiful baby they had named Aelfred. It had been Merlin's idea because he knew that one day, a King Aelfred would unite England properly and burn the cakes.

Queen Guinevere had also given birth to a baby boy; they had named him Cheadda. Arthur told Merlin that it was a common name in his kingdom. *Both Aelfred and Cheadda will grow up and play together*, thought Merlin. That was all he could hope for in his wildest dreams. One day, young Cheadda would become king after Arthur, and so, the list of English kings would start to grow.

Things were quiet now, and Merlin was careful not to alter the course of history. He did feel he would like to leave something behind that wasn't in the legend. He had observed while traveling around the kingdom that there were many Roman villas around the countryside. When the Romans had left, they'd just up and went, not taking anything with them.

Most of the building materials had been removed for recycling and building new houses. The inhabitants weren't interested in the flamboyance of the Romans. Old statues had been abandoned, in many cases to fall over. Some had been broken by the weather and vandalism; when a conquering army left, there was always a bad feeling. Heads of statues were just lying on the ground. Merlin noticed one head on an excursion. It was life-size and the exact image of King Arthur. He carefully strapped the bust to his horse and took it back to Camelot.

The next evening, he went to the king and said, "Look what I found, sire. This is the spitting image of you." He showed Arthur the bust.

The king looked at it very deeply, turning it in all directions. Then he said, "It's nothing like me. I don't look like that." Merlin realized the king didn't know what he looked like. There were no mirrors, and the only reflections were from water. The problem then was that the reflection was reversed so that left was right and so on. The queen agreed with Merlin; it looked just like the king. Merlin put the bust in his room for the time being. He was working on an idea as to what he should do with it. He wanted to pass it down the generations to prove that King Arthur was real.

CHAPTER ELEVEN

$\mathfrak{A}$s fate would have it, the very next day, King Arthur said to Merlin, "I would like you to go down to our tin mines further into the West Country and bring back three bales of tin. These mines have been in production for many years in a region known as Cornwall. Take two knights and four archers for protection. I have been hearing rumors of thieves attacking travelers on the moors between here and Cornwall."

Merlin had, of course, heard of the Cornish tin mines, as well as those for copper, and he knew that copper and tin make bronze. The next day, he set off with his escort for the two-day journey to the mines. They took two wagons, one to carry the archers, and everyone else was on horseback. The other wagon was to bring back the tin. In the back of one cart, hidden, was his bust of Arthur. Merlin had a plan.

As they traveled west over the moors around the River Exe, they saw about a mile in front of them three men attacking a lone traveler. The knights immediately took off, galloping to the rescue. Merlin went with them to add a show of strength. It was not necessary; by the time they reached the traveler, the three attackers had ridden off.

The traveler said he was eternally grateful to the knights for their presence, as they had undoubtedly saved his life. Highwaymen were vicious, and life was not precious to them. The traveler was also heading to the tin mines and gladly accepted Merlin's offer to ride with them. He introduced himself as Martin, saying that he had a house near the mines. They were offered a bed for the night, which all were glad to accept.

Martin was a good-looking man in his early thirties, a traveling salesman by trade. He journeyed the whole country selling household implements. That evening, they had a satisfying meal and a comfortable night's sleep. Martin's house was different that most: it had two floors. Merlin thought, *He must do well with his sales.* His hose was much better than the damp ground they'd been expecting. The moors could be very cold at night, even in summer.

During the night, Merlin came up with another idea. *While I am down in the Cornwall mines, why don't I see about the construction of a cannon now that we have gunpowder?* He convinced himself that Viviane would be pleased with that, which she was. She was purposefully keeping more in the background now that Merlin was finding his own feet.

In the morning, just after the sun rose, he got hold of a small piece of parchment and charcoal. He made a plan of the design for his cannon, including all the dimensions. After a good breakfast, they all said their goodbyes to Martin, and Merlin went to the tin mine, which was a mile away, to purchase his bales of tin. They produced the tin from furnaces, and it was poured into casks to make blocks, which were called bales when cold. They loaded three bales that had been made the week before into the wagon.

Merlin spoke with the metal worker, asking him whether he made bronze. "Oh, yes, it's been made here for centuries. My family has always been here doing this job," the worker said

"Good. I have two tasks for you," said Merlin. "I'd like you to coat this bust in bronze. Is that possible?" He carefully lifted the marble bust out of the wagon.

The metalworker looked at it in detail. "It's certainly a beautiful piece; it should take a coating very well. You can watch if you like. I have a vat of bronze. All we need to do is dip it in there, remove it carefully, and then we'll leave it overnight to dry and set."

Merlin felt very hot from the furnaces in the metalworking shop. The metalworker dipped the bust in the bronze for a minute or so and pulled it out with grips and set it down standing up. "There, that is the start. We need to repeat the process tomorrow, and then, when it has cooled down, we'll just clean it up."

"Thanks, but how do you stand this heat day after day?" said Merlin.

"Oh, you get used to it, you know. I've done this all my life. What is the other task that you mentioned?"

"I would like you to make two cannons to this specification in bronze," said Merlin. He handed the metalworker his drawing.

The metalworker studied it carefully for several minutes. "Is that a seven-foot-long barrel, with a six-inch tube down the middle to the rear? I assume the bulbous end is the rear."

"That's a small hole that goes down to the tube. The back of the cannon, as you say, is bulbous. The completed cannons have to be mounted on a heavy-duty timber trunnion with solid wooden wheels."

"A timber what?" said the metalworker.

Merlin realized he shouldn't have used that word. "Oh, sorry, I meant a very heavy wooden trolley. It must be robust enough to be pulled by six or eight horses. In addition to that, we need fifty balls made of iron, six inches in diameter, that will fit in this barrel. It is essential that the interior of the barrel is smooth so that the balls can slide up and down it quickly."

The metalworker scratched his head. "I can arrange that, but it will take considerable time. The barrel, as you call it, would be cast in two and then welded together. The woodwork, I can get done. You call this a cannon. What's it used for?"

Merlin, not wanting to give the man the full explanation, said, "It's a decorative item for the entrance to our town. Even so, it must be in perfect condition, particularly the inside of the tube."

"That goes without saying. Everything I make is perfect. I'll put that in hand and have it delivered to you. It will take about six months; I assume the costs are chargeable to King Arthur, which we will deduct from our taxes due."

"Agreed," said Merlin, overstepping his authority, but he knew that when he explained all this to the king, he would be pleased.

Merlin left the bust with the metalworker and returned the next day. The metalworker said, "It all went well today. The bronze had cooled and solidified by this morning, so I put the second coat on, and here it is. You will need to leave it overnight again to cool down. Well, what do you think? It stands up on its own now."

Merlin was impressed and said, "It looks just like King Arthur. I'll leave it to dry a little longer, though, because it has a long journey home."

They left the bust to dry for another two days. The metalworker told Merlin that he had started the cannon project and was making the first cast. "The cannons, I will have delivered to Camelot in about one hundred and eighty days."

Merlin set off for Camelot with his escorts, very pleased with himself. Maybe he had altered the course of history a little. He now had a statue of the head of King Arthur; no one could then deny that he lived.

When back in Camelot, he went to the king again and said, "This is what I have done to your bust." The king was still not impressed but said with a little sarcasm, "If it pleases you, then I am delighted as well." Arthur didn't realize the significance of this bust, and Merlin wasn't going to say anything more.

"Oh, there is one other thing, sire. While I was at the mines, I exceeded my authority. I ordered production of two cannons."

Arthur said, "Cannons?"

"Yes, sire. These are the guns that will one day be the primary weapons used in battle, but you will have them now. It came to me in a dream while I was away. When they arrive, I will explain all to you, but they will take half a year to make."

Arthur said, "Well, you know I trust you implicitly, Merlin. I await their arrival with anticipation."

Merlin needed to make sure the bust he had made was named, so he went to the blacksmith and said, "I have another task for you. Can you make a plate for this bust that states: 'King Arthur, King of all England'?"

"I certainly can, but to what does King of all England refer?"

Merlin wanted to be careful with what he said. "One day in the future, this country will be called England."

The blacksmith thought it was a joke, so he just nodded. "It will be ready for you tomorrow."

The next day, Merlin went to collect his bust, which was now sitting on a plinth with the plaque on it that Merlin had asked for. He took the bust to the castle and placed it in a prominent position in one of the recesses in the wall.

The castle had been adorned internally in the last three months. The ladies had been making banners, tapestries, and other needlework. This was because, in three months' time, the whole court would be traveling to Sarum with all its refineries. Sarum was an old town near the ancient stone temple called Stonehenge. The temple went back two thousand years; it was comprised of large, vertical stones in a circle, with stone lintels on top. On to that had been placed a wooden roof.

The roof had crumbled away only last year, so it had lasted very well. Sadly, it was gone now, and the building was open, a temple to the sun god. On the summer solstice, the sun shone through the main entrance and caused a beautiful shadow at the other end, onto an altar. It only happened once a year when the sun was rising over the horizon. On that day, which was in mid-June, people came from all over the country to worship. Afterward, a one-week sporting event was held to test the prowess of the various kingdoms. All of this was explained to Merlin by Sir Galahad. Merlin knew of Stonehenge from the twenty-first century, but he was surprised to learn it had originally had a roof.

"It is more of a festive occasion than a religious one," said Sir Galahad.

Merlin had heard that everyone went along with the ceremonies. Arthur had told Merlin, "We will be attending with twenty knights and an entourage. It is a week of pageantry, so we will take tents for everyone to live in and have fun. The purpose is for the kings to get together and for each court to enjoy the games. It will be interesting to see how many kings attend this year."

Merlin was very pleased. *It will be a good outing*, he thought. Each of the kingdoms that attended always wanted to show off their prowess and strength. Each realm wanted to prevent other warlords from claiming more land, so they wanted to see which of the other kings was the weakest.

Merlin went back to Gwen and told her what was planned. She thought it best if she didn't travel all that way with young Aelfred. Merlin agreed; he would have plenty of company on the route. The queen said she would not journey either, having to look after young Cheadda.

As the weeks went on, more preparations were made each day until the final day before they were to set off. Merlin went back to the carpenter to see how his table was progressing. All eight segments had been constructed. They had each been sanded down smooth and polished with a varnish type of lacquer. Four of the divisions were painted on top with a knight in full armor. A nameplate had been left on the upper part so that the name of the knight could be inserted. When a knight died in battle or from natural causes, then a new knight's name could be added, saving the need to repaint the whole table. Merlin was very impressed with the artistry and congratulated the carpenter and his assistants.

The travel time to Sarum was about eight days; they had to move slower than usual because of the wagons. Two wagons were carrying the tents; one was to set off a day early so that it would be at the first night's stop and the tent erected before the king's arrival. At that time, the other tent wagon would set off so that when the king arrived at each campsite, the tents would be erect.

Merlin said goodbye to Gwen and Aelfred. He would miss them both, and it would be at least a month until he saw them again. They left Camelot early morning on the big day, a party of sixty people. They headed out in an easterly direction. It was a slow pace, but the riding passed the time. Merlin enjoyed horseback riding. He'd always thought himself as a bit of a cowboy in his earlier life, and his riding skills had now advanced. At the end of the day, they arrived at the large marquee. It was not furnished inside; everyone is expected to sleep on the ground. It was a question of all sharing, but it worked out fine. They enjoyed an excellent meal, and the wine flowed.

The next seven days were the same, but Merlin was getting a little saddle-sore by the end. He was glad when they arrived at Sarum.

Merlin could see how Camelot had gotten its plan when they arrived at Sarum. It was a much older town than Camelot, probably dating back a thousand years or more. Camelot was a replica of Sarum but on a much larger scale. Sarum was on a hillock with a massive circular wall around it. Merlin observed that walls at that time were plain, with no projections for would-be archers to hide behind and then come out to shoot. He must remember that for future designs.

Inside the outer wall were houses and shops; it was the major town in the area. Sadly, it was starting to go into ruin now, as it was too small for what was required, and the townsfolk were talking about moving to a new position nearby. Merlin thought, *That's progress, I suppose, but it is a shame. The locals must preserve old towns.*

They stopped there for provisions before heading off to the plains, which were a little to the north. Merlin took the opportunity to look deeply into Sarum; he was keen to see how these ancients lived.

Chapter Twelve

I t took about an hour to get to the temple at Stonehenge. It was bustling with people; banners were draped from every stone, and flags were hung on stands of catgut. A kaleidoscope of colors blazed everywhere, reds, mustard yellows, blues, and greens, as the whole area was covered with tents. Merlin thought, *It's a pity these folks have not yet discovered the actual yellow color.* He couldn't remember the pigment that made it, so he let that one pass and just said to everyone how lovely the colors were!

When Arthur arrived, he took the opportunity to lead his procession around the perimeter of the site. Arthur waved to the other kings, but the message was clear: I'm here in strength, so be careful. He knew that Camelot was the strongest kingdom in the vicinity even before Merlin's inventions.

Arthur's advance party had chosen a site for them. The first tent had been erected, and three more were now speedily put up, and within two hours, they were all settled. Sleeping was still camping, just a spot on the floor, but the weather was fine now. It was midsummer, and the ground was dry. By that time, the day was coming to an end, so the cooks prepared a meal of beef stew and rice, which all enjoyed. Merlin realized that they wouldn't have potatoes for another thousand years.

The next morning was the eve of the summer solstice. Merlin took the opportunity to wander around the site to see what other communities were doing. Most were much the same as Arthur's, though a different race of people occupied one section. He could tell that just by looking at them. He was sure they were the settlers about whom Arthur had spoken. They were fearsome looking and dressed for war. They carried their helmets because of the heat, but they looked very aggressive and ferocious. Their helmets had horns that shone, and they carried shields and swords even though this was a festive occasion. Merlin wasn't sure why; did they think they were going to war? Perhaps they were. Standing next to Merlin was Viviane, but only he could see her.

"These are the people you have to careful of; they will cause trouble to Camelot and King Arthur. You need to make sure he is well prepared," said Viviane.

Merlin went back to the camp to report to Arthur. He was also a little surprised that the settlers were here at all. He had heard that they had made a settlement south of a town called Winchester, which was not far from here. Merlin knew the settlers would cause trouble at some stage because Viviane had told him. Now that the settlers were moving west across the country, Merlin was anxious to get the gunpowder prepared as soon as possible. Although Arthur had brought bows and arrows, he wanted to keep them hidden. Only he had those, and he did not want the settlers forewarned. He knew that one day, they would be needed in the battle that was sure to come.

The next morning was the summer solstice. It was an early start because, at sunrise, the whole encampment was in the temple. They were not particularly sun worshipers, but it was more of a symbolic gesture. After that, the sports began. There were horse races, jousts, sword-fighting contests, and crossbow competitions.

Merlin didn't enter any of them; he was not competitive in that way. Neither was he trained for them. He enjoyed watching the games, and he noticed that the settlers won many of the contests. They were clearly a competitive people, and he could see trouble brewing for the future. There were times during the week that several of the kings had meetings to discuss matters affecting them all, and the settlers were excluded. They had expressed some threatening views to several of the kings. They were interested in widening their realm and wanted to take over the whole country; there were two small kingdoms between Arthur and the settlers.

Arthur hosted a meeting between those two kings and a third one who was slightly higher up the country. They would be at the mercy of the settlers if they got as far as Camelot. Arthur asked Merlin to come with him. They all expressed their concern at the settlers' aggression, but it was evident that they did not want to form an alliance. Everyone wanted to hold onto their bit of Avalon. "One day, things will be different," Arthur said to Merlin.

"Oh, they will, sire, they will, of that you can be assured, but not in our lifetime," said Merlin.

The four kings agreed that if the settlers moved in their direction, they would inform the others. If necessary, they would then form a joint army. Arthur criticized the other kings for trying to stand alone. "United we stand, divided we fall," he told them. He was not prepared to divulge his secret weapons, though.

That evening, there was an altercation between a bunch of the settlers and a group of knights. It was all over a trifle, one of the settlers came too close to one of the knight's wives, and a brawl broke out. *Nothing unusual in that*, thought Arthur, but the ferocity of the fighting was intense. The settlers were enjoying the fight and broke various bones of the opposition. *These men need to be taken in hand*, thought Arthur. He just hoped he could get defenses improved before they turned on his kingdom. He vowed never to underestimate these people.

It was now approaching the last day of the festival, when the jousting finals would take place. Sir Galahad had already gotten through to the final and was standing on the edge of the sports field. He watched the last two knights joust in the other semifinal. Merlin went up to him and said, "Good morning, sir. How are you?"

"I'm fine, thank you, and how are you? I want to see what the opposition is like," said Galahad.

The two knights were standing at opposite ends of the field, both in shining armor and holding their lances beside them. The lances towered over each of them by at least six feet. At each end of the field were tents decorated with the insignia of each contestant, and banners were flowing in the breeze. The sun was bright, and it was a beautiful day. The grass was a brilliant green, as though it had been painted with the reflection of the sun. Each jouster had his squire, who made sure his knight was ready and suited up in armor. It took a long time to put on the armor because of all the layers. Each layer had to have bandages under it to stop any chafing of the skin.

It was a grand occasion. The horses were in regalia; one was as white as snow, and the other was a piebald. Each knight got up on his horse, aided by his squire, who had to push with all his might. The knight was now hefty in full armor. Once on his horse, he was handed the lance, which he raised to the level. Each knight rode over to his lady. If he didn't have one present, then it was any lady who was in the royal tent. He lowered his lance to her, upon which she tied her kerchief. The knight raised and lowered his visor in salute and then rode back to the start position.

They faced each other. Between them was a rustic fence made of tree branches. It was nearly time for the contest. Sir Galahad said to Merlin, "Watch for the stance of each rider when they leave."

The starter in the middle of the fence raised his arm. He brought it down hard, at the same time running backward, away from the jousting area. The two horses started to move, slowly at first, but then spurred on by the riders, they galloped toward each other.

Galahad said, "You see how the left rider is hunched over, while the other is bolt upright. Bending over makes you a smaller target, but the disadvantage is that your head is lower to the horse. The one thing you don't want is a hit to the head; it would break your neck. The idea is to aim at the center of the chest so as the knock your man off the horse. But if your head is too flat, the lance might rise from the chest to the head. Of course, in battle, you just want to kill him any way you can, but this is a friendly contest."

They raced toward each other at great speed, and Galahad said, "You need to get into a gallop as soon as possible. A horse's gait changes from trotting to galloping. In a trot, the horse uses all four legs independently, giving a bumpy ride, whereas, in a gallop, the front and rear legs go together. That makes the ride smoother. The one thing you don't want in jousting is for the lance to be bouncing up and down." Merlin hadn't galloped on a horse yet, but he liked the idea of that. The speed appealed to him.

In under a minute, the two riders reached each other. There was a loud crash as the lances hit the metal armor of the other knight at the same time. Both only glanced off to the near side, which meant they slipped past the opponent. Both riders were still on their horses. "Nil, nil," said Galahad.

Each rider carried on to the end of the field and got ready to change ends. After first resting, removing their visors and taking some deep breaths, the exercise was repeated.

Merlin said, "How do you hold the lance so still?"

"Well, it's all about balance. If you look, you will see that the lance is divided into three sections. The handhold is in the first third, and the lance itself is tapered. When you put your hand in the hold, the lance is made so that it is equally balanced at that point. Lances come in many sizes, from ten to fourteen feet long. The longer, the better in a battle as your lance will get to the opponent sooner. Conversely, it is much heavier and therefore not so stable, so it is a matter of choice. For a jousting contest, which is only to knock the rider off the horse, not to kill him, then lances are standard at twelve feet long for fairness. You ought to try it sometime."

"I'm not so sure about that. It looks a bit dangerous to me," said Merlin.

The jousters were ready now. They turned to face each other, and the starter set them off.

"See how they are both in the same upright stance this time? The one knight learned from his mistake," said Galahad.

They came at each other fast, and one got his lance into the perfect position. He caught the opponent right in the center of the chest. Crash! The noise was deafening as the man fell off the horse with a great clatter. He did not move. Several people rushed over to him and took off what armor they could. He was unconscious but still breathing. The referee declared that this was a knockout, and the joust was awarded to the knight still on his horse. After five minutes, the injured man came to, and after removing the rest of his armor, he was declared alive!

"These days, if you are breathing, you are deemed to be okay," said Galahad. "Well, that's the man I will be contesting later this afternoon."

Everyone stopped for lunch. Galahad and the other knight, whose name was Lancelot, did not eat much to make sure they were fit for the final round. Lancelot was from another kingdom some distance from Camelot. He was a young man in his late teens. He still had a lot to learn, but he was a good jouster. Galahad talked to him over lunch and thought that he seemed very amiable. Galahad was much older, of course, in his forties, which gave him the advantage of experience in the joust. Launcelot had the benefit of younger age and less fear. Merlin was also at the lunch table next to Galahad and thought, *I wonder if this is the Lancelot from the legend?*

"If you want to change kingdoms at any time, I'm sure there would be room for you at Camelot," Galahad said to Lancelot.

Maybe it is, then, thought Merlin.

"Thanks for that. Actually, there has been some discontent in my kingdom, and may the best man win this afternoon. Let's enjoy a beer afterward. It's very thirsty work; this jousting," said Launcelot.

Galahad had asked Merlin to act as his squire this afternoon as his new squire was feeling ill, probably from too much wine. Merlin was pleased to help and spent the next hour getting all the equipment ready for the joust.

It took a further hour just to get Galahad into his armor. It was a very complicated operation, with under-bandaging to stop the rubbing of the metal on his body. But he was finally ready, and they shook hands.

"Good luck, sir," said Merlin, and they saddled up the horse, Galahad's favorite, a piebald named Spotty. Galahad got on the horse, aided by Merlin, and felt comfortable in the saddle. Merlin handed him his lance.

At the other end of the field was Lancelot, who was already on his horse. They acknowledged each other by saluting with their lances and moved into position to start the joust. Their lances were in the horizontal position, ready to go. The starter lifted his arm and brought it down sharply. Both riders rode toward the other and were in a gallop within a few seconds. They were speeding down each side of the fence at a tremendous pace, and their lances crashed into one another. Both lances broke, but both riders remained on their horses.

Galahad was not happy with himself. He knew he'd had an excellent aim and hit, so he decided to use his stronger lance made of oak. Lancelot had the same idea; he too was unhappy with his performance. They went back to base, changed lances, and prepared themselves for the second run. Again, they set off at a furious pace. This time, Galahad got his lance at Lancelot just a second in front. That meant that his lance pushed Lancelot off his line before Lancelot's lance contacted Galahad. Round two to Galahad, and he was feeling much better with himself now. Round three went the other way, and Lancelot knocked Galahad off his horse. They were even again at one fall each. The next round went to Galahad, so he had the advantage going into the last round: one ahead.

Galahad knew he had to win this tournament for his prestige. They lined up for the final run. Lancelot was somewhat despondent at being one down, which meant he had to win this round to stay in for a final joust. If they ended in a draw, then it would go on until the first jouster fell.

That was not necessary, though, as Galahad knocked Lancelot off his horse in that round also. He had won the tournament and did a parade around the field for all the spectators, who were cheering madly. He rode over to King Arthur, who was in a place of honor, a specially erected tent for all the kings present. They saluted each other.

Several of the other knights in Arthur's camp had fared well in various other events during the week. It had been a good week for Arthur's prestige, and there was a lot of drinking and partying that night. Galahad and Lancelot had that special drink after their event. It was noticeable how the settlers were outsiders and kept to themselves.

Merlin was happy to be leaving tomorrow and getting back to Gwen and Aelfred. That evening, Arthur, Galahad, and Robert had a discussion in a separate tent about the settlers. Arthur said, "We need to know what their intentions are." Merlin stated that he had overheard earlier in the day that a meeting was to be held tonight at the settler's camp. Galahad and Arthur exchanged opinions as to when the settlers would act.

Merlin excused himself by saying he needed a natural break and left. Viviane, who had been flying around the tent, was becoming concerned, and she waved her finger at Merlin, shaking her head from side to side. Merlin thought that although he had introduced many weapons, he was not involved in the actual fighting, and he felt he needed to take some positive action.

Viviane became visible to Arthur and Galahad and said to them, "You two had better go after Merlin. He will need looking after. He is not up to dealing with the settlers yet, but you will not remember speaking to me about this." Arthur and Galahad looked at each other, thinking, *What was that?* They left the tent.

Merlin walked towards the settler's tent. It was dark outside, but shadows of several people could be seen on the inside through the canvas. Merlin discretely sat down against the tent wall and listened; he checked around: all clear.

He could hear them talking. It was broken English, but he could decipher it. They were saying that they needed to take over all the land between them and Camelot gradually, one kingdom at a time. At that moment, two hands grabbed Merlin by the shoulders and lifted him up.

There were two of them. One said, "Well, what have we got here, then? A spy in our midst."

Suddenly, behind them appeared Arthur and Galahad with knives in their hands. They knew they had to act quickly and silence these two before reinforcements arrived. Arthur grabbed one from the behind and sliced his throat, and Galahad did the same to the other. Both men fell to the ground without a sound. Viviane was there, watching with a large smile on her face, thinking, *I do need to keep a close watch on Merlin after all.*

Arthur looked around. There was only silence; no one was coming. "Back to our camp, quick," said Arthur. On the way back, he said to Merlin, "That was foolish. You could have gotten yourself killed. The town needs you alive, and I do personally. Please don't do anything like that again; you're not trained for it."

Later that night, Viviane came to Merlin in his sleep. "Listen to what Arthur says. You are not trained for hand fighting. I need you alive; there is much work for you to do. Devote your time to improving the defenses at Camelot. Oh, and don't forget that bar of gold I placed in your hand at the robbery."

In his dream, Merlin said, "It was you, then. I was sure I didn't pick up the gold."

In the morning, there was much gossip about the events of the night before and the two dead bodies outside the settlers' tent, but no one knew the truth. The settlers knew it had to have been one of the other kings, but they had no idea which. One of their leaders said, "These locals will regret this action. I personally will kill at least ten for each one of those good people killed last night."

Later in the day, they disassembled the campsite and loaded the wagons for the trip back to Camelot. Merlin had informed Arthur of what he had learned from his exploit last night, which just reinforced the need for Camelot's defenses to be upgraded.

The journey home was uneventful. They had some rain on the way, which made traveling unpleasant, but they all arrived at Camelot safely. They had seen a pack of wild boar, but the animals had kept away from the procession. Merlin had to remind himself that there were still wild animals in this country, but he had not seen another lion since the first day.

When they got home, Merlin was keen to see how his saltpeter works were getting on. He felt sure he was going to need gunpowder before too long; he knew that the settlers would rule a large part of this island before their demise. He had to smile, though, knowing that Britain would get rid of one set of invaders only to be replaced by another. *That's life*, he thought, but for now, he had to defeat them and serve King Arthur, who had now become like a brother to him.

The dung piles were doing fine, stinking to high heaven. Another six months should see the first collection. Merlin's mind turned to another direction: he had been reminded by Viviane of the bar of gold he had brought with him. Although gold was valuable then, there was little he could do with it. There were no markets as such, so he thought that he would like to have it made into an individual sword for the king. *That must have been what Viviane meant for me, of course, Excalibur*, thought Merlin. The sword would be a ceremonial one, as it couldn't be used in battle. The metal was far too soft, especially now with his steel.

Merlin went to see the blacksmith and told him of his thoughts. He did not say where he'd gotten the gold, but after a while, he realized he had to come up with an explanation. He came up with the story that when he was on the far side of the country, he went to see an alchemist with an iron bar and he turned it into gold. Merlin said he didn't know how he did it, but as he couldn't use it, he wanted to give the sword as a gift to the king. That explanation seemed to go down well; they always liked a bit of magic in those days. The blacksmith thought, *If you believe that, you'll believe anything*, but he liked Merlin.

Viviane, who was watching, shook her head in disbelief. *How could he say that?* she thought.

The blacksmith mentioned that he had acquired some red jewels over the years. He left the smithy and went into his house, which was adjoining, and came back with six large rubies. "They are magnificent," said Merlin.

They shone bright red in the sunlight; they were so perfectly cut that bright white stars could be seen gleaming in them. The blacksmith said, "Can I put them into the hilt of the sword?"

Merlin said he was very grateful as it would set the sword off well. He wanted this sword to go down in history, which he knew it would.

Merlin said, "I'll think up a way of giving it to the king in a spectacular way."

He went to the carpenter. All the segments of the table were now complete; It was just a matter of assembling them now in the main hall. That meant that the king would have to be told. Merlin said, "Leave that to me. I will work something out."

CHAPTER THIRTEEN

𝕬rthur was concerned about leaving the settlers to themselves to go against the local kings whenever they felt like it, as he knew they would. He had thought about leading an army to take the fight to them but had decided against it. The other local kings were still not interested in joining him, which he had discovered from envoys that had been sent out every week.

For the time being, Arthur had strengthened the castle wall, making sure that the rampart platform was stable for the bowmen to use when necessary. He tested the archers' abilities weekly to ensure they were getting more accurate. He was pleased with the progress; the steel blades of the swords were also a vast improvement. He knew the settlers would only have iron, or maybe even copper. Merlin had been thinking of ways to detonate the gunpowder, but other than using a fuse, which was not available, he was stumped.

He did come up with the idea of large bags or boxes of gunpowder which could be ignited by a flaming arrow. He was aware that for best effect, the explosion should be in a confined area. *I'll have to work on that*, he thought.

Arthur constantly thought of his new companion Merlin. He was now more than a friend, and Arthur knew he completely relied on him. Merlin was transforming the military strength of the nation, and Arthur realized he now thought of Merlin as a brother.

Several months had now passed since they'd returned from Stonehenge. Autumn had set in, and Camelot was getting ready for winter. Every day for the last three weeks, Merlin had been up on the ramparts, scouring the horizon in the direction of Cornwall, looking for his cannons to arrive. He was becoming impatient; the agreed time had long passed now, and the cannons should have been here by now.

Merlin went to see the king. "Sire, the cannons have not arrived yet, and I am becoming concerned. Can I have your leave to go and see what is happening to them?"

"Of course you can, but you must take two knights to protect you."

"Thank you, sire; I will set out in the morning."

The next morning, the three set off on horseback for Cornwall. It was quicker this time as they did not take the wagons. Merlin had thought they would meet the cannons coming the other way. That was not to be, and they arrived at the mines on the third day. Merlin went straight to the metalworker's yard. As he entered, in front of him were two gleaming bronze cannons, each mounted on a huge wooden trunnion. He jumped off his horse and rubbed his hands along the barrels. They were just as perfect as the maker had promised. He felt the inside of the barrel: smooth, just as needed.

He went over to the metalworker, saying. "Sorry, but I couldn't wait any longer. I was concerned in case they were waylaid en route. I've looked at them. Thank you so much. They are perfect."

"You are welcome; I do apologize for the delay. The problem was that the cannons developed so much interest locally as to what they were. I was always answering questions," the metalworker said, smiling. "The trunnions, that was what you called them, wasn't it? They caused a lot of commenting and laughter. Several residents wanted one to carry their babies. They are ready to go, though, and I have arranged for them to go to Camelot tomorrow."

"Thank you. We'll ride back with them as well for added protection," said Merlin.

All arranged, they left the next morning early, two cannons each pulled by six horses. There were four outriders, Merlin and his two knights. It was a slow journey with the guns, but eventually, they arrived at Camelot. They had been seen way off from the ramparts, and a guard had gone to advise the king of their safe return.

Arthur was at the front gate when they arrived. He looked at the weapons, not knowing what they were for. He said to Merlin, "They are magnificent quality."

Merlin said, "Sire, I suggest for the moment that we place one on each side of the front gate. It will be for appearance, but any adversary will not know what it can do and be scared."

"I don't know what it can do either," said Arthur, laughing.

"Let me explain, sire. The first thing to do is put gunpowder into a small linen bag. That is pushed down the barrel and rammed to the end, tight," he said, holding the barrel. "Then an iron ball is placed in the barrel, and that, too, is pushed to the end. A small amount of loose gunpowder is put in the hole at the rear of the barrel" he said, touching the hole. "That gunpowder is then lit, which will set off an explosion in the powder bag. That forces out the ball, which is hurled three hundred feet or more at the enemy."

"I had fifty shots made. They are iron, and our blacksmith can make more. These wheels are wood and will not last more than ten years being moved around, if that. In due course, we can replace those with ones made of steel, which will be much stronger and last longer. Let me demonstrate, sire."

Merlin loaded the barrel with the gunpowder sack, followed by a cannonball. Then he filled the tube at the back with loose gunpowder. "The cannon must have plenty of room behind it as, when fired, there will be a big kickback," he explained to Arthur.

Merlin shouted, "Stand back!" and he lit the gunpowder. Within seconds, the cannonball was hurled out of the barrel with an enormous bang. It traveled about two hundred feet, thumping into the ground. The cannon jumped back about two feet as well. Merlin emphasized, "When you fire it, you must make sure no one is standing behind."

"Yes, I can see that. The explosion would frighten off an adversary without the ball flying. Thank you for the demonstration. It's just one more astonishing weapon you have invented. I can't hear anything," said Arthur as he waited for normal hearing to return to his ears.

Arthur then arranged for one of his men to collect the cannonball. Merlin said, "I think we should provide the soldiers who fire the cannons with earmuffs to deaden the noise a little."

Arthur was very impressed. "I think they will be ideal where you said. I agree the gunners need hearing muffs; I will arrange that." Each cannon was placed on either side of the approach to the drawbridge, a pile of twenty-five balls in a pyramid by each.

Merlin was so pleased with himself. He was convinced now that this was the task that Viviane had set for him. What Merlin hadn't expected was that he was becoming very close to Arthur. He had never had a close friend like this. *Can you be friends with a king?* he asked himself. *Perhaps it is possible in these days.* Merlin was determined to try.

The next few days were quiet. Merlin took every opportunity to go on the ramparts to look down on his new cannons. He was very impressed, and one day, he was with the lookouts on the wall and spotted six riders approaching Camelot. There was always apprehension when a group of this size approached the town, especially now with the concerns of the settlers, and these men looked like soldiers. Did they have an unseen army behind them? The guards rushed to find the king inside the castle.

Arthur speedily went to the wall and climbed his new rampart. He looked over the battlements. He was glad of this device; it gave real protection for the guards and the town. He could see the men approaching, and if they were enemies, they couldn't see him. The riders were conscious of the anxiety they might be creating. The leader erected a white flag, and the men proceeded up to the main drawbridge. It was then lowered, and on Arthur's instructions, the gate was raised for them to enter the town.

On the other side of the gate was Sir Galahad, who greeted the six men. He recognized the leader immediately. It was Sir Lancelot, the knight he had fought in the jousting contest final at Stonehenge.

"Greetings, Lancelot," said Galahad. "It's good to see you again. What brings you to our neck of the woods?"

"It's good to see you as well," said Lancelot. "I still need to challenge you to a return for that last joust! But that's not why we are here."

The men got off their horses, and Galahad and Lancelot shook hands. Galahad said, "Anytime, friend." They took their jousting seriously.

Lancelot said, "Can we talk in private?"

"Certainly. Tell your men to water their horses and come with me. He led Lancelot into an anteroom inside the castle.

Lancelot said, "When we met last time, you implied that there might be room in Camelot for me. The situation in my kingdom has deteriorated to such an extent that our king has almost capitulated to the settlers we saw earlier in the year. Five other knights and I decided that we had had enough. We wish to change our allegiance to King Arthur, but we would like to keep our knighthoods if that's acceptable."

Galahad said he would have to speak with the king. He was sure that the king would be glad to have more experienced fighting men in his court. He was distressed to hear the situation in the neighboring kingdom. He asked for more details but said, "Let's bring King Arthur in on this conversation."

In an hour's time, a meeting was arranged for the six new knights, Galahad, and King Arthur to discuss the problems. As always, Merlin was in on the discussions.

Arthur said, "You are very welcome here. We need more knights, and Galahad has spoken for you. However, what is the situation in your kingdom? I met with your king in the summer, and we agreed that we would keep in touch if there were problems with the new settlers. I have heard nothing from him."

Lancelot responded, "Sire, after we returned home from the jousting, all was quiet for a month. Then there were incursions into our land, a few unrelated incidents, but the king did nothing. As expected, the settlers took more liberties, and they have now virtually taken over the realm. We are in the situation now where we six knights have left the court and seek to join forces with you. We know that once they take over our previous realm, they will start on you, and you must be prepared. They have also commenced actions on the kingdom next to yours."

"I feared as much," said Arthur. "I implored your king to join with me and fight the foe. He declined. You are very welcome to join our kingdom, and you can keep your knighthood status. We are preparing our defenses; we have a new rampart on the wall and unique weapons that we have developed. We can discuss those later. I was very impressed with your efforts against Galahad in the joust. We certainly need as many soldiers as we can raise." Arthur was still somewhat anxious about giving details of his weapons to strangers, even if they were well referenced.

"I endorse that," said Galahad. "It will be a pleasure to serve alongside you."

Launcelot said, "I saw that you had a rampart on the top of your wall. That is something I saw in the past in Londinium. They have one there and found it very effective in a battle for pouring hot oil on the attackers."

The king added, "Yes, it can be used for that, but ours is primarily for archers to fire arrows from longbows."

"I'd certainly like to see that. I've not heard of longbows," said Launcelot

"You will; I will be testing the ability of the archers daily from now on."

The meeting was completed, and the six knights were led to their new quarters. Merlin took the opportunity to speak to Lancelot. He wanted to find out how long they had before an attack. Lancelot said, "I do not know, but at a guess, I would say about three months, but it will undoubtedly depend on the weather. With winter coming, they may delay until the spring."

Merlin thought, *So, here's Sir Lancelot. The picture is now complete.*

Now it was back to work. He might have three months to perfect his gunpowder bombs. He knew he must work to do it in a month and set about it right away. Checking with the dung heaps for saltpeter, he collected what he could at that stage and set up more heaps. He mixed up the gunpowder as before and was now getting concerned as to storage. The last thing he wanted was for a stray light to set off an explosion in the town, which would destroy his supplies and the town itself.

He went to speak to Arthur. "Sire, we have a problem as to where we are going to store the gunpowder. We are clearly going to need its help in the coming months, but we don't want it going off prematurely; otherwise, we may blow up the town itself. We need a storage facility that we can get to easily, but our enemies can't. It should be out of the main town in case of an accident, but not far, possibly in two stores to split the risk."

"I see," said Arthur. "Let me see what we can come up with." He relied so much on Merlin now.

"Thank you, sire. There is one other thing. This last year, the carpenters under my instruction have been making a roundtable for you and the knights to sit around. The table is for your parliament meetings. It seats sixteen knights including yourself, and I would like permission to install it for you in the main hall."

The king was pleased as always by Merlin's ideas and said, "Thank you, Merlin. I was thinking that sitting around in a circle is not ideal when you have so many knights, especially with Lancelot and his colleagues joining us. Please get the table set up at once, and again, many thanks. We'll have a celebration when it's up and running."

Merlin went to see the carpenters and told them the good news: they could get on with the table construction. They said that they had already made the sturdy legs. They needed to carry all that weight, so there were ten of them. The carpenters spent the next two weeks installing the table. All the sections needed to be joined, glued, and securely fixed with dowels. After two weeks, it was completed. Another three coats of varnish were applied to give the table a gleam.

The unveiling of the table was at a large ceremony attended by all the townsfolk. Everyone was impressed by the size of it and the quality of the artistry. Merlin said, "This table will go down in history." A feast was held that evening to celebrate; Merlin noted that a feast took place on every occasion possible.

That night before going to bed, he did as he had always done, going to his calendar and putting another notch in it for the day that had passed. The plank of wood was getting full quickly now, and it only counted the number of days passed. He realized this was not enough; he needed to record the number of years. He took five minutes to work out that he would keep the days as they were while recording the number of years on the back. That way, he would be able to work out his age.

Chapter Fourteen

After two weeks, no definite plan had emerged regarding the storage of the gunpowder. Merlin took the bull by the horns and went to Arthur and said, "Sire, we need to build two stone stores outside the wall of the town. They must have only one entrance, from tunnels starting on the inside of the town wall. That way, if there is an unexpected explosion, it will be out of the town itself. The damage will be kept to a minimum. No adversary will be able to get into the stores from the outside; we need to be careful our enemies cannot gain access. Needless to say, we will have them well-guarded by the guards above on the wall."

Arthur responded, "I like the idea, I am sure these settlers will be here sometime over the winter. They are land-hungry; I will arrange for the builders to start straight away. Will you oversee it, Merlin?"

"Glad to, sire."

The next morning, the town masons were at the main gate to meet Merlin. He organized for them to go to the local quarry and bring back as many stones as they could. "You must build two rooms, one on each side of the town wall, inside the dry moat. Each room must be at least twelve feet square and high enough to cover the base of the outer wall."

It took the three days to collect suitable stones and bring them back to town. On the fourth day, they started to build each arsenal. Inside the dry moat, they built the first arsenal with the rock going four feet above the base of the town wall. He told them urgency was required; they must work at a fierce pace because all feared an early attack by the settlers.

They put their backs into the work, and in six days, one room was ready. There were no windows or entrance into the room. From the outside, it just looked like a part of the wall itself. Merlin was pleased with the result. The exterior would be guarded from the ramparts above by soldiers. The builders wondered how they would get into the chamber.

The answer came forth immediately as Merlin set about building the staircase down to the room from inside the wall. They excavated the earth from inside the town, inserting a lintel under the wall and creating a new opening. They installed stone steps down. There was a considerable amount of soil removed and distributed over the ground outside of town.

The king was keeping a watch on the progress. He came to Merlin and said that he was very pleased with his work and that it would serve their purpose well. The king took Merlin's hand in his and shook it hard, saying, "You are an incredible friend. I don't know what I would do without you." He had never done that before with that amount of feeling. Merlin was pleased as he squeezed the king's hand.

It had taken a month to complete the first arsenal; now they set about building the other one on the opposite side of the town wall. In the meantime, Merlin transferred the gunpowder into wooden casks. They were sealed and stored in the arsenal already built. He lifted them off the ground on slabs of stone to prevent any ground moisture from getting into the barrels

Merlin was concerned as to dampness in the arsenal generally, though, which would be inevitable during the winter. That would render the gunpowder useless. He set about installing salt trays all around the room to absorb the water from the atmosphere. Salt was available in town, but it was very expensive. Merlin decided to go into production, setting up a process to extract sea salt from the ocean. Camelot was quite near the sea on the northern shores of Wessex, which would be Devon in 2019.

The beaches in this region were traditionally long and sandy. Merlin partitioned off areas so that he could collect sea water to make a lake. The lake was then left to dry off in the sun. By increasing the flow of water into his lake, he was gradually able to build up salt on the ground. The townspeople hadn't realized that the sea contained salt. They even said it tasted better than what they'd had before.

He also set up kilns at the back of the beach, which were continuously heated by charcoal. In these kilns, he placed sea water. As it dried off with the heat, salt deposited at the base. Charcoal was now readily available, and this turned out to be the quickest way to produce salt, but he needed such copious quantities that he could not possibly obtain enough in the short term.

He knew, though, that in time, the production would increase. Any extra made would be eventually traded with adjoining kingdoms. He felt proud at the end of the day, standing at the back of the beach, looking at his work and taking great satisfaction in what he had done. How he had changed since his misguided youth. His mother and grandmother would have been proud of him now if they'd known, but perhaps they did.

By the time the other arsenal was finished, another month had gone. Merlin now had produced enough gunpowder to fill both arsenals. He had plenty of salt to fill the trays to keep the arsenals dry. The advantage was that the salt would absorb the water and it could then be recycled by drying it off, extracting the water. Merlin now had a good supply of salt, much more than he'd initially predicted. They were indeed trading it with their neighbors who did not have access to the sea. *Camelot is becoming an industrial nation*, thought Merlin, pleased with himself. The extra income to the town helped finance its defenses.

Both the king and Merlin felt the workmen had done a good job; everyone felt a little safer now. The workmen were given a bonus for their excellent work, which was how things worked around Camelot. Arthur said to Merlin that they now had their salt and gunpowder production. He was anxious not to let anyone outside know about the gunpowder, although he knew that at some stage soon, they would find out.

Merlin and Gwen were so much in love that neither could believe how much, and they loved their small son, Aelfred. They talked about maybe having another child. Merlin knew the importance of having a brother or sister as he had none. That night, they both decided to try very hard.

There had been little news of the settlers in the past months. Arthur had taken the precaution of sending daily scouting parties. Launcelot led the scouts around the section of the kingdom that was nearest the settlers. He was settling in well into Camelot. The farmers were pleased to see Lancelot and the knights on their rounds; it made them feel safer. On that day, Lancelot was at the furthest point from Camelot. In the distance, he saw a group of about thirty people coming their way.

It was a mixed bunch of men, women, and children. He didn't think there was any immediate danger, but he knew that caution is always the better part of valor. He waited until they were near, and then he went out to meet them with a white flag. They told him that they came from another kingdom, where the distant settlers had ransacked the town. The king had been slain, and the settlers had taken over all the property, evicting the tenant farmers from their homes, which consisted of five families. Many people had died in the fighting, and the farms had been set alight. "We were lucky to get away," said the leader.

"We're heading for Camelot as we've heard there is a charitable King Arthur there. Hopefully, he will take pity on us." Lancelot was distressed at the plight of these good people, especially since King Arthur had taken pity on him and his companions not so long ago, but he knew that Camelot was filling up. How many more refugees could it take? That was not his problem, and he said, "We are knights of Camelot and will escort you to town."

They all arrived in Camelot that evening, and Lancelot went to see the king, explaining what had happened. Arthur was concerned, too. While they would always help stranded people, there was a physical limit to what they could do, and he was aware that his land was getting used up. Agriculture was the main trade in Avalon. Arthur was charitable, though, and he told the refugees they could settle outside of town and build their houses where they could.

Again, there were different tradesmen with them: another carpenter, a blacksmith, and an alchemist. Of course, all men were expected to fight if required. They were advised that in the event of trouble from the settlers, they must come quickly within the walls of the town. Merlin said, "The town has grown so much we should call it a city now."

The king replied, "For the town to expand, we will need to build a new wall farther out."

Arthur felt more confident now that he had the gunpowder and new soldiers. The new men learned how to use bows and arrows. Some took to it like a duck to water; others did not. He now had a strong army, and Merlin had also been learning to improve his shooting. Furthermore, refugees were arriving almost daily now. They were all told the same: set up homes outside the walls of the town.

Plans were drawn up to expand Camelot and build a second wall two hundred feet out from the existing one. Work was started straight away by digging the ditch on the outside of where the wall would be. If the settlers attacked soon, the new wall would be another line of defense. That ditch took a month to dig. Once done, the outer wall was commenced, but it did not affect the inner wall. That was still the primary defense of the town for the time being.

Slowly, it was rising, stone by stone, which came from surrounding quarries. Anywhere they could find it, the stone was recycled from old demolished buildings. Merlin had used his knowledge once again and told the king that the top of the new wall should have higher sections so that the archers placed on top of the new rampart could move and take cover while reloading and then come out into the open to shoot. Merlin knew that would be more important in the future when guns were invented.

The king, as always, went along with Merlin's advice, and the wall was built in that fashion. The rampart this time was part of the stone structure, which meant the wall must be thicker, but they were able to obtain more stone from the quarry.

The months were passing by now. Still, there were no more problems with the settlers. Merlin went to the blacksmith to see how the sword was progressing.

The blacksmith said, "It's all done," and he produced what Merlin could only describe as the most beautiful thing he had ever seen. The jewels had been added to the hilt, and the blacksmith had managed to find a few more, blue sapphires this time. The blade had been shaped and etched into a pattern. In Merlin's eye, it was fit for the best of kings, and Arthur was certainly that.

In three days' time, it was a feast day. In the evening, under the dim light that Merlin had invented, together with the firelight, King Arthur was sitting next to Queen Guinevere at the head of the dining table. After the main meal, Merlin left the room and returned with the sword in its scabbard. The blacksmith had also made that. He walked up to the king, and the room became silent.

Merlin said, "Sire, the blacksmith, and I would like to present you with this ceremonial sword. It is a sword fit for the first king of Greater Avalon."

Arthur took it, grabbed held the hilt, and slid the sword out of the scabbard, holding it high in the air. There was a gasp that went up throughout the room. Arthur said with a tear running from his eye, "Well, we are not yet Great Avalon, but one day, maybe. This is a very emotional moment for me, and words fail me. Thank you so much, for this is a wonderful gift that I will treasure all my life. It is a tradition in the realm, Merlin, that you must name it for me."

"Then we will call it Excalibur, sire."

"Excalibur, that is an excellent choice for such a magnificent sword. You know that Excalibur means it is magic," said Arthur.

"I do, sire," said Merlin. "It is the sword that belongs to the real king of Britain, as the country will eventually be known."

"Well, that was quite a speech," said the king with a smile. "You seem to have knowledge beyond all recognition."

Viviane was circling the room, smiling. She was pleased with her protégé. Arthur was still holding up his sword, and Viviane, still invisible at the other end of the room, lifted her arm and pointed at it. A white lightning flash of energy went from her finger to the tip of the sword. The whole audience was dumbfounded.

Arthur did not know what had happened, but the sword felt different now. It was as though it had a mind of its own and was imparting energy and thoughts to the holder. At the moment of the flash, he could also see Viviane, but he said nothing.

The festivities continued for the rest of the night. Arthur ran his sword through his fingers. It felt exquisite; the energy was still there. *This is an incredible gift. This man Merlin is now truly becoming my brother. I must soon make an announcement,* Arthur thought.

The next day, it was back to work for all the workmen who were building the new city wall. Merlin and Gwen's house was farther out than the new wall, so that spared their home.

Chapter Fifteen

arious knights were doing the daily patrols still to the outskirts of the territory, checking on any movement of the settlers. It was now months later than when Arthur had anticipated trouble would come. He was becoming a little more complacent. Today was Lancelot's turn to lead the scouting party, which consisted of six men. They always had a plan to visit as many farms on the route as they could to show a presence to the tenants and assure them of their safety.

On this day, they had included a house that was more like a small castle on their route. When they were near, they could see a little flag waving out of an upper floor window. They rode towards the house. As they approached, they saw there was a young damsel at the window, and she was clearly in distress.

Lancelot acknowledged her waves and went to the front door and knocked. After five minutes and two more knocks, the door was opened.

"What do you want?" the occupant said gruffly.

He was not known to Lancelot, but he looked scruffy and smelled. Seeing that he was aggressive, Lancelot said,

"Good morning, sir. I am here on behalf of King Arthur. You have a young lady in the upper window who is clearly in some distress."

"So? That's my business, not yours," was the reply.

"On the contrary, sir, every citizen of this country is the concern of my lord, the king. On his behalf, I demand to know what the problem is." The door was immediately slammed in Lancelot's face.

Lancelot walked around the side of the building, ignoring the owner, if that was who he was. He stood below the window and called out to the girl, "What is the problem, young lady? Can we help you?"

She said, crying, "I'm being held prisoner, locked in this room."

"Who is the man I just spoke to?"

"He is my protector; I come from a village over there." She pointed to the east. "The settlers came to our village and burned it down; my husband was killed trying to defend the village. I managed to escape, and this man took me in, but he is brutal and very demanding. He only lets me out to do his cooking and to have his way with me. I can't take it any longer. I would rather die."

"Fear not," said Lancelot. "We will sort this out."

Launcelot went back to the front door and banged on it hard, so hard, in fact, that the door nearly broke. He thought, *If the owner doesn't open the door, it will be easy to break it down.* The owner did not come to the door this time, and Lancelot drew out his sword and said, "If you don't open the door, I will break it down and enter."

"You'd better be prepared to fight, then," could be heard in muffled response. The door remained closed.

"My pleasure, sir," said Lancelot. He raised his leg and kicked in the door. *This villain must be taught a lesson*, he thought, and he made sure the door was smashed to splinters before he entered. The room was now empty; it was a very basic room, no comforts here. There were only a solid wood table and two chairs. There was a cooker of sorts, which was a pot hanging on a chain over what would be a fire when it was lit. No internal water or other conveniences.

Lancelot crept upstairs. He did not want to be surprised by the villain jumping down on him from the higher ground. He knew he would then be at a disadvantage. He could see that the upper-floor landing was clear, so he proceeded up. That landing had one room off it. He kicked in the door, and again, the room was almost empty. It just contained one small bed, and it had that musty smell that everyone hates. He could see the bugs hopping on it. He left the room as quickly as he could.

There was one more staircase up to the top, which was the floor where the girl was being held. He guessed that the assailant had gone in with her. These stairs led straight up to the one room. He crept up and put his ear to the door. He could hear talking inside and knew he had been right. He could smash in the door, but that would mean the man could be behind it and would be above him. There was no alternative; it was not practical to gain access from the exterior of the house. The door was flimsy. He could see that it was only an attic room and the door was not intended to resist being kicked in.

He decided the best approach would be to get a log that he could use as a ram. If he used a foot, he would be off balance for a few seconds, during which time he would be vulnerable. He quietly went downstairs to find something to use.

In the meantime, his assailant in the room had not heard anything for several minutes. He wondered whether the knights had ridden off in the other direction.

Lancelot went outside and found a small log that would be suitable. He carried it upstairs as quietly as he could. He laid his sword on the top stair, and with one huge push, he slammed the log into the door lock. The door gave way. At the same time, he dropped the log, picked up the sword, and rolled head over heels into the room.

His adversary was taken by surprise, which was Lancelot's intention and gave him a moment to get to his feet. The man grabbed the girl, holding a knife to her neck.

"Get back, or I will slit her throat. She's no good to me anyway, and she couldn't satisfy a pig," he said

Lancelot said, "Well, you should know about being a pig," but he backed off, not wanting the man to harm to the girl. Lancelot knew that all cowards are bullies. He guessed that the converse was true. He thought he would rather face this man downstairs once he had gotten the girl away.

"Okay," said Lancelot. "Let's sort this out downstairs." He stood aside so that the man could move downstairs with the girl. While he had the girl, the man thought he had the upper hand. If he killed her, he knew he was dead, and there would be no trial here. He thought maybe he could negotiate his way out once he was downstairs. He led the way down, backward so that he could keep the knife against the girl's throat.

They were soon on the ground floor. Lancelot would rather be out in the open, where he knew what he had to do. The other five knights had gone outside, anticipating what was happening, and they thought it was best if they kept out of the way for the moment. They did not want the man to feel too overwhelmed, or he might just kill her. Life was cheap.

The man just wanted to get away now. He didn't want the girl anymore. He took her outside, playing into Lancelot's hands, although he didn't realize it. Outside, he kept a horse, and he dragged the girl toward it. He said to Lancelot, "Let me on the horse, and I'll ride off with the girl and release her up the road."

"You treat me like a fool, sir. No, you release her now. Then you can ride off."

The man didn't fall for that one either, telling Lancelot to stand back, which he did as the man jumped up on the horse, still holding the girl. Now he could not hold the knife at her neck as she was still on the ground. Lancelot saw his opportunity and acted in a flash. He ran forward, raising his sword and bringing it down as hard as he could on the man's arm. The blade slashed into his flesh, and Lancelot could feel it hitting the bone.

The man let out a yell as Lancelot had never heard before; his arm was just hanging, and his hold on the girl was gone. The blade had sliced through the tendons, and his arm was useless. Blood was pouring out, and Lancelot knew he would die from loss of blood soon. He was in such agony that he fell off the horse and to the ground.

Lancelot went over to him and put the blade of his sword through the man's ribs and into his heart. He was dead within seconds. "That was a merciful release," said one of the other knights. "He would have died anyway."

They all agreed, and they carried the man's body back into the house and laid it on the table. Then they set a fire beneath it, left the room, and watched as the house burned down.

Lancelot turned to the girl and asked, "What is your name?"

"Ainsley."

"Well, Ainsley, my name's Lancelot. I'm a knight in King Arthur's Camelot. You had better come back with us."

She readily agreed. Lancelot looked at her for the first time. She was lovely, about twenty years old with long, dark hair and such a sweet nose. They all set off back to Camelot. When they arrived, Lancelot had to report the events to the king, which was the custom. Arthur agreed with Lancelot's actions. "We must always help the people in any way we can. We must fight bullies and protect our subjects. Give her a job in the castle household."

Over the next few months, Lancelot saw much more of Ainsley. After two weeks, they were officially courting. Ainsley was so grateful to Lancelot for rescuing her from that tyrant. She knew that wasn't any reason to get married to Lancelot, but they got on so well together, and that was good. Did Lancelot want to settle down, though? He wasn't so sure he enjoyed his independence.

Launcelot spoke one day to Merlin, man to man. "Does married life work for you? I have to say you look very happy, but I have doubts about marrying Ainsley."

"It works well for me, but I understand it may not work for everyone. It is, I believe, up to each individual, but whatever you decide, I will support you," said Merlin.

Launcelot thought long and hard about it over the next few weeks before coming to the decision to marry Ainsley. He went to see her one day and said, "It is a big decision. I believe marriage is for life, but I would like to make that commitment to you."

Ainsley was so happy that she jumped up, threw her arms around Launcelot's neck, and kissed him hard on the lips.

"I take it that's a yes, then!" said Lancelot.

"You bet," she said.

Arrangements were made, and on the big day, there was a feast held at the castle, during which the king carried out the ceremony of marriage. The whole town got on with the drinking, which was customary. The king had given them a house to live in near to Merlin's. After the ceremony, they went back to their new home together.

Things had quietened down in Camelot when, one day, Merlin was on the rampart with Arthur. There were still no signs of the settlers. They were chatting and enjoying the atmosphere. It was a beautiful morning. The sun was high, and the scenery was spectacular: rolling countryside with hills in the distance and the green of summer grass with its distinctive smell. Some people were allergic to the grasses, but not Arthur or Merlin.

Merlin enjoyed these quiet moments of speaking with Arthur alone; he felt that Arthur enjoyed them as well. They could converse without being overheard. Over the past year, they had become very close friends. Merlin, being an only child, had never had a brother, which he would have loved, and he felt that Arthur was taking on that role. This was the nearest he had ever felt to anyone other than Gwen.

They were watching the countryside when they both caught sight of a trailer being pulled by four horses and carrying four men. A second trailer was being drawn behind by a fifth person; it appeared to contain supplies. Arthur and Merlin did not comment but just kept watching. They were talking about other things as the travelers got nearer. Finally,

Arthur said, "I wonder what they want. They are clearly heading this way."

"I am always apprehensive of strangers coming. We don't get many as we are off the beaten track." As they came closer, Merlin knew who they were likely to be by their clothes, but he didn't say anything more.

Arthur joked, "They are wearing dresses, which must be some new fashion."

"No, sire, they are monks."

"Monkeys, Merlin?" said Arthur, mishearing.

"No, sire, monks. They are religious men. They follow the teachings of Jesus Christ, who was crucified some six hundred years ago."

"How do you know all these things, Merlin?"

Merlin just smiled. "Shall we go down to meet them?"

Arthur and Merlin went downstairs to the main gate, where the party was just arriving. The leader came up to the guard, saying, "I am Augustine. I come from Rome on behalf of Pope Gregory the Great. I bring news of the religion of Christianity to the people of Britain. Please allow us entry."

The king, who was standing back, looked at Merlin, who smiled, and he took that as a sign that he should let them in and said, "Gentlemen, you are welcome to enter Camelot." The guards opened the gates. The entourage came in, and they drove the wagons to the front of the castle. "Let's go and see what they have to say," said Arthur. They went to meet them as they got out of the wagons.

Augustine said, "It's good to get off the wagon. My back gets very stiff these days on those things." He pointed at the cart. They all smiled in sympathy, although Arthur and Merlin were young. They had heard the same from others of the age of about forty, and Augustine looked about that age.

Arthur said, "Come in, sir, and have some refreshments. You can then tell me your story."

They went into the main hall, where cold drinks were served, and they sat down in chairs around the fireplace. Fires were always lit in the castle even in summer, as it was always cold inside the stone building no matter what the weather was outside.

Augustine explained that he had been sent by Pope Gregory to the British Isles to establish the Christian Church in this country. The pope, Augustine told them, was the head of the Church in Rome, and he was appointed directly by God to advance the faith of Christianity. Augustine had arrived in Kent with a contingent of forty monks. He explained, "There have been a few converts in the past, but I am now required to formalize the church."

Augustine continued. "When I landed in Kent, the king there welcomed me but said I must stay in his kingdom. I founded the head church at Canterbury, and I am the first archbishop. My fellow monks have been touring the country for the last few years, establishing churches in many towns. Last year, we had ten thousand people baptized in the whole country, and the Pope was very pleased. Being baptized means accepting the faith of Jesus Christ. I would like your permission to preach to your townsfolk and baptize those who convert. There is, of course, no pressure. It is a matter of personal conscience."

"You say the king of Kent wouldn't allow you to leave his kingdom. So, what are you doing here?" said Arthur.

"He made a special dispensation for me as no one had been to this region."

"Very well, you have my authority. We have guest houses that you may use, and my attendant will show you to one."

Augustine thanked Arthur and left the room with the attendant. Then he and his monks were shown to a house for them to use.

Arthur turned to Merlin and said, "Well, what do you make of that?"

Merlin's reply was guarded. "It's a sign of the times, sire. Christianity will become worldwide. But so will many other religions. Wars will be fought over religion because every side thinks their religion is stronger than the other."

Augustine spent the next few days talking to individuals and holding meetings to advocate the teachings of Christ, the Son of God. In all fairness, no one could object to the teachings. All great religious men have similar teachings for the good of all. Merlin took an interest in these meetings as he wondered what the difference was in those days from 2019.

He concluded the teachings were much more basic then, more appropriate to everyday life as opposed to later in the life of religions, when all they did was fight against each other in the name of God, the same God. *After all*, he thought, *if there is a God, there can only be one.*

Merlin was sure Augustine meant well. He was a godly man, and Merlin knew one day he would be made a saint. At least he would be remembered in perpetuity, or at least as long as Christianity survived before being taken over by another religion. Who knows?

Augustine's preaching was successful. He had two hundred converts, and they were all baptized in the lake. Merlin had already been baptized all those years in the future. It all seemed strange to him when he thought about it. After a week, Augustine believed he had done as much as he could for now. He did leave one person, who was particularly interested in becoming a monk, in charge of his new church in Camelot, which one day would go by the name of the Church of Augustine, eventually St. Augustine. King Arthur gave him a house for that purpose. Before Augustine left, Merlin and Gwen had Aelfred, their son, baptized. Merlin thought, *It's not every day you have your child baptized by a future saint.*

The party left on their travels back to Canterbury, but they were going via Sarum. Augustine had heard that this was a major town in the area, and he wanted to set up a diocese there that would cover the whole district.

Merlin was always very busy in the daytime, organizing the defenses of the town. He looked forward every day to the evenings, when he and Gwen were alone and enjoyed each other's company. They had erected a small partition in their house so that Aelfred had his own area, and he was in his cot early. Although Merlin had a small battery for minimal light, he and Gwen were happy being alone and whispering their love to each other. Merlin had never anticipated such a love as this. He was now euphoric in his new life. Not having heard from Viviane lately, Merlin thought she must have been happy as well.

CHAPTER SIXTEEN

The settlers had come to Avalon gradually over the past thirty years. They had set up home in the areas around a town called Winchester, just on the edge of the district called Wessex. Winchester was an old town first colonized by the Romans. These settlers had come across the water from Northern Europe; they were rugged people, strong at fighting. In their previous regions, they had fought many wars. The truth is, that was the reason they left: they were kicked out.

They had settled in the southern areas of Avalon. Avalon was a general name; it had no defined area but covered most of the West Country, including Wales. At first, the settlers seemed to get on well with the locals. As more and more arrived, the locals felt that they were being overcome and losing their heritage. That, as it turned out, was correct because now, after all those years, the settlers ran the area. They had elected their king, and his name was Canute.

King Canute tried to be fair, but his nobles wanted to expand the kingdom. This had resulted in many small, local wars, but as the settlers were good fighters, they had always won.

Canute had had enough of fighting and was endeavoring to bring peace to his nation, discouraging it from any more wars, for the time being at least. Canute himself was advancing in years now, and he had spent all his life fighting. At the age of fifty, he felt as though he were eighty, and it showed in his face, which was scarred in all directions. His hair was now white, though it had been blond in his youth, showing his Germanic origins. He had two wives and four children who were now all fully grown and challenging him for the throne. All Canute wanted was to spend the rest of his life in peace.

His sons felt differently and wanted to push on with the wars and expand their domain. They had already spread their realm up to the borders with Camelot and wanted to go in and control that, too. Canute said, "No, we must now consolidate our holdings in the Winchester region, building up defenses in case of attack. One day, these people will attack us, and we need to be prepared."

He had won the argument for the last year. That was why Camelot had been spared a battle and been able to build up its defenses. Unbeknownst to the settlers, they had missed their opportunity. However, King Canute died suddenly. There was suspicion that he had been murdered by one of his sons, but nothing could be proved. The new council for the settlers decided to press forward with the expansion of their empire. They wanted a raid on Camelot to test its resolve. If successful, then a full-scale attack would follow.

Back in Camelot, everyone was pleasantly surprised that the settlers hadn't attacked during the winter. They knew it would come and soon, but they were glad of the respite to build the new outer wall. The wall was now advancing at a significant pace and would be complete within a month.

In three weeks' time, the wall was finished, the new ramparts had their hiding places, and another drawbridge and gate had been installed. That meant that any aggressor would have to break down two walls before they got into the town. The defenders had two opportunities for outer defense; maybe they could trap the attackers between the two walls and blow them up with their gunpowder.

Merlin had supervised the work of building the wall, and he was pleased. The arsenals were more protected as well as they were in between the two walls. Eventually, it was intended to remove the inner wall. This would leave more space to expand the town, but for now, it served better to leave the wall as it was.

There were about thirty houses and farms outside of both walls, including the one that Merlin and Gwen lived in. Aelfred was two years old now and beginning to walk. He was such a joy to Merlin and was now starting to play with Prince Cheadda. The day after the defenses were complete, King Arthur announced a feast for tomorrow evening, and the guest of honor would be Merlin.

The following day, the castle was dressed up with the finery. The grand feast was in the evening, and all the banners were displayed. The weather had changed that day: a storm had blown up, and it was raining. That would not stop the festivities, though. Merlin thought it was just like Christmas in 2018. There were music and dancing. The locals loved dancing; it was their only release from tedium. Merlin and Gwen were shown to the top table and sat next to the king and queen. After a sumptuous meal, the king stood up and called for silence. In front of him, lying across the table, was his new gold sword, Excalibur.

The king stood up and announced, "Ladies and gentlemen, this is a very special day. We come to celebrate Merlin, who has brought to our country so many wondrous things. We now have a double defensive wall to keep any intruders out, and we have archers and gunpowder."

At that time, a strange thing happened. The rain stopped, and it was quiet outside. The shutters were open to allow air in; suddenly, a whisp of light flew around the room. It stopped over Merlin, and a voice said, "I am very pleased with you, Sir Merlin." All of a sudden, the light was gone, and the room was quiet again. All turned to one another, wondering what had happened.

Arthur rose and said, "There is one other thing of a personal nature. Merlin, I have come to rely on you so much, and I have always called you friend. From now on, I would like to call you brother." He raised his arms.

Merlin was in tears as they embraced one another. He said, "Sire, I am so pleased. I have never had a brother before. I just hope that I can live up to that honor."

The merriment went on for a while longer. Music was plentiful from the players in town, who had reed instruments and drums. The dancing looked more like rock and roll to Merlin: no one worried about steps; anything went. The drumbeat was strong, like tribal music, softened by the recorder flute.

The girls were whirling around, enticing the young men to join them. The men were happy to oblige. Soon, couples joined up, and there was much drinking. Some men let things get out of hand, but the town guards also acted as policemen and kept things in order.

Merlin had always wondered why he was here, but now he knew.

The next few days passed by without incident, and the finishing touches were made to the new wall. Sentries were now posted to that outer wall first. Camelot was always ready for an attack.

The knights held their general monthly meeting; this was the first time they had used the new round table. Everyone was seated around it, with the king at the top; each knight had their own place with their name on it, including Merlin.

Arthur started off the meeting by saying to everyone, "Welcome to our new table, for which we must thank Sir Merlin." A small cheer went up, which Merlin acknowledged. "The only item on the agenda for today is the settlers and our reaction to them. As we know, they have encroached up to our boundary, and although we have and are developing our defenses, we must look at whether we wait for them to attack us, as they surely will, or whether we launch an attack on them. What is the consensus?"

All sixteen knights around the table, everyone except Merlin, made their comments. It was approximately half and half as to whether to attack or defend. The king said, "What do you think, Merlin? You are my trusted brother."

"Well, sire, my thoughts are that a bully, and that is what the settlers are, will always act like a bully. The only thing to do is to fight back as, in the end, you are forced to fight them in any case. In this situation, though, we have the advantage of having strong defenses and secret weapons. That will give us the advantage whichever direction we go. I believe that in the end, we will have to attack them, and at that time we will need the cannons. My advice would be to defend now and weaken them and kill as many as possible and then attack their town subsequently."

There were several nods of agreement now round the table. Arthur said, "Very well, let's have a vote. Those for defense now, followed by an attack later, raise their hands."

Thirteen hands were raised, including Merlin's. The king didn't vote – he didn't need to – and he said, "That's carried, then. We will continue as we are for the time being."

CHAPTER SEVENTEEN

In the settlers' town of Winchester, the new king was not prepared to wait. He had charged a party of twenty soldiers with the task of making the first attack on Camelot to test their reaction. The party set out on the four-day journey. They knew that Camelot sent out scouts every day to see if any opposing army was in sight. Before the attackers reached the outskirts of the kingdom of Camelot, they stopped and made camp discretely in a forest so that they were hidden. They then sent out a scout to check on Arthur's patrol. The scout came across the patrol quite quickly, without being seen, and hid behind trees in a copse.

When the patrol had gone past, the scout went back to the settlers' camp and reported that the patrol had not seen anything. They decided they would attack now before the Camelot townspeople knew what had hit them. It was a two-hour trip on horseback to Camelot, and they went as fast as they could. Just outside the town, they could see there were thirty houses. They were undefended; this was going to be the object of their attack: to destroy those properties and kill anyone who got in the way.

They came galloping out of the trees. The people in the settlement did not see them, but the guards on the outer wall did, and they raised the warning, but there was nothing they could do from that position. The archers were not on the ramparts; there had been no warning.

The attacking force raced to the houses, screaming and shouting abuse. At that point, the guards on the wall reacted again and shouted the alarm, but it was too late; the attack only lasted minutes. Waving their swords high in the air, the attackers brought the slaughter to the houses, riding through the settlement, slashing anything that moved with their swords, animals and people alike. Two dropped from their horses at each house, killing everyone inside and then setting fire to timber and thatched houses. Within minutes, the whole community was ablaze. People and children were running and screaming; the attackers showed no mercy. They had to be quick, cut and thrust and then leave within five minutes before soldiers could come out of the town.

Merlin's house was one of the first to be hit. The rider got off his horse, entered the house, and slashed at Gwen, who was sitting and feeding young Aelfred. The blade of his sword went through her neck, and she died instantly. Little Aelfred, not understanding anything, just tottered out of the house and straight under a passing horse. He didn't stand a chance.

Many houses were on fire now; people were lying dead on the ground, and many were reeling in agony. Bodies were trampled on by the speeding horses; blood mingled with the mud. Severed arms and legs were lying in the dirt. The enemy seemed to enjoy cutting off heads. It was carnage, all in five minutes. The guards from the town were coming out now, but they were too late as the settlers had already ridden off. Their job was finished.

Merlin, who had been in the castle with Sir Galahad, knew nothing of this. He rushed out of town as soon as he was told, not knowing what he'd find. He ran to his house and saw his beloved lying in a pool of blood. "What have I done?" he called out "I should have been here!" He couldn't even say goodbye to her; she was gone. He sank to the floor and wept. He screamed out, "Viviane, why did you allow this to happen?" There was no response.

The king was on the other side of town. When he heard the commotion, he raced to the scene, arriving a few minutes behind Merlin. He was devastated. His new brother was lying on the ground next to his beloved wife and holding his dead son. Arthur moved slowly toward him and touched him on the shoulder, at which Merlin lifted himself up. He was sobbing deeply, and they embraced. Arthur said, "I don't know what to say, brother. I am so sorry. No words can express my sorrow." Merlin just wept for several minutes.

Soldiers were now arriving, and Arthur said, "Come with me, Merlin. We will take you to the castle, and you will stay with the queen and me."

"Thank you, sire, but I must take Gwen and Aelfred to the new church." Merlin picked up Gwen, and Arthur took baby Aelfred. They carried them both into the church, laying them on tables in front of the altar. Merlin bent down and kissed them both. The new vicar gave his condolences and said, "We need to bury them both tomorrow. Bodies deteriorate so quickly; they need to go to God."

They left the church, and Arthur took Merlin into his private chambers, where the queen was preparing a room for him. They showed him in, and he asked if he could be alone for a while. They understood and left him, with Arthur saying, "We'll arrange for your belongings to be brought here." They had several of the castle servants collect Merlin's belongings and pack up all Gwen's and Aelfred's things.

Merlin lay down on the bed, still weeping. "Oh, God, how could you let this happen? Where were you, Viviane?" After two hours, he fell asleep in his grief. It didn't help when he woke up, though. It all came back, and his head ached.

He got up and went out for a walk, keeping away from his old house. He knew where he was going, but it was as though he was in a dream. He walked and then ran toward the lake, and once there, he sat on the bank. He was crying again, and he called out, "Oh, Viviane, please help me. I've lost Gwen and Aelfred. Please help me escape. I can't stay here now. I love Arthur, but I must get away."

Through his tears, he could see in front of him a ghostly figure rising out of the lake and coming toward him. She said to him, "Fear not. Gwen and Aelfred are at peace now, and your pain will go away in time, as mine did. I am sorry, but I could do nothing about what happened. It was fate."

"Take me away, please. I love Arthur, but I have to be gone now," said Merlin.

"Be patient a little more. There is one more task for you, and then you will see Gwen again."

"I don't think I can do anything now. My life is destroyed. All I loved has gone. It would be kinder just to kill me now."

"You must not think like that. I have developed your character to deal with situations like this. Be strong. Give it time. I know it is difficult, but you will come through it and survive," said Viviane, but she was worried for him. Had she given him enough strength for this ordeal? Merlin was her project; if he failed so did she, and she knew that she must leave him to sort his own mind out.

You will know when the time is right. Come back here then," she said as she vanished into thin air.

One more task, Merlin said to himself. *What on earth is that? I am no hero.* The Lady had calmed him a little, though; it was as if she had breathed fresh life into him. He had lost all he loved, but he knew he had to go on, and he would see both to say goodbye. Merlin pulled himself off the ground; he knew he must pull himself together. Taking deep breaths, he walked slowly back to the castle, where Arthur met him at the door.

Arthur said to Merlin, "Rest assured, I will bring havoc to these settlers and drive them from this country."

That night Merlin, went to bed thinking of the lovely evenings he had shared with Gwen, just making love talk. The maids had brought everything from Merlin and Gwen's house, and what little items they had were stored in the corner of the room. Merlin went to them and touched various items, remembering, deep in thought. At the very top was his calendar. He ticked off another day and turned it over. It said that he had been in Camelot for five years.

The settlers rode back to Winchester. They reported to their king that they had destroyed the outlying houses of Camelot and killed all the inhabitants. A cheer went up. "That means we must now go to Camelot with a vast army. They know we now mean business," said their king.

The next day, Merlin went to see the new vicar at the church. It might have been the old converted house, but it was very authentic. It had an altar at the far end and several rows of chairs. On the altar was a wooden cross, and in front were the bodies of Gwen and Aelfred on the table they had erected yesterday. The vicar said to Merlin that he was terribly sorry. He offered to give them a Christian burial. Merlin said, "Thank you, Father. I would appreciate that."

That afternoon, the funerals took place. It was a small affair, for the family only. Gwen's parents were there, and so were the king and queen. They all paid their last respects. Merlin wept all the way through, and Arthur comforted him, but he was crying, too.

The father said a few words and prayers over the bodies. He was reading from the new prayer book given to him by Augustine. Merlin and Arthur then carried the bodies of Gwen and Aelfred outside and laid them in previously dug graves. Ashes to ashes and dust to dust, the bodies were covered with earth, and then stones were piled up in a mound two feet high.

Chapter Eighteen

The next day, Merlin got into full work mode. It was the only way he could take his mind off what had happened. Everyone knew that the settlers would now attack in force, and preparations were finalized for the event. There were no houses outside of the town anymore. All the ruins were flattened so as not to give the advancing troops any cover. The king posted six men on permanent duty at the edge of his realm to get a warning when an attack was coming. Merlin now guessed that the forthcoming battle was the one that the Lady of the Lake had referred to.

He had made some bombs by filling glass bottles with gunpowder and adding a wick of oiled rags. Some were placed on the ground outside of town so that they could be set off with flaming arrows. More such bombs were made so that they could be lit by hand and then thrown at the attackers. There was now a multitude of arrows available for the archers.

The archers would be placed around the ramparts and battlements on both walls. All the knights, and anyone who could use one, were given steel swords. *We're as ready as we can be*, thought Merlin.

That evening, Merlin didn't feel like socializing. Everyone had already offered Merlin their condolences during the day. He had gone to his room early to be quiet and alone in his thoughts. There was a knock at the door, and when Merlin opened it, standing in the doorway was Arthur.

"Can I come in?" Arthur said.

"Of course, brother," said Merlin.

They spent the next two hours just chatting over the past, trying to keep off the subject of Gwen. Finally, Merlin said to Arthur, "Sire, brother, once the forthcoming battle is over, my purpose here is done. I wanted to stay here all my life with Gwen and with you as my brother, but that is not to be. I know now that I was sent here by the Lady of the Lake, Viviane, to bring you to the legend that you will be. Viviane is the ghost who appeared the other evening when you made me your brother. I come from a different century far in the future, and she brought me to you. You will be known as a founder of this great nation, a legend that will live for at least a thousand years. My task is done after this coming battle, and I must leave your town. My biggest regret now will be leaving you. I have never had a brother until now, but I will never forget you. I will take your memory with me, and I think that one day, I will return, but that will be out of my control.

"I want to wish you every success in the future. The things I have given you are far beyond this time period, so make good use of them. One day, our country will rule the world, but that is a long way off. You are in at its formation.

"On a personal level, you are my brother. Although I have shown you things from the future, I am grateful to what you have shown me and taught me about life. I think that is also why I was chosen to come here and not someone else. I know I am a better person now than when I arrived, but I am concerned at leaving Gwen and Aelfred without a gravestone."

There were tears in both their eyes. Arthur was astounded and said, "I always knew there was something different about you, Merlin. I thank you for all you have done, and I wish you everything that you would want for yourself. I, too, think that one day, you will come back here after I am gone. Please do not worry about the gravestones. It is too early now as the ground needs to settle. I will personally see to it on your behalf, brother.

"Like you, Merlin, I did not have any real brothers, which is why I wanted you as my brother. We have become very close over these years. I understand you have to leave, but you will always be my brother, and I yours." They embraced. Merlin felt his dream had come true; he now had a real brother.

They chatted as brothers do for the rest of the evening. Arthur was thinking about what Merlin had told him. He was a simple man and believed in ghosts and the like, so he accepted it. Finally, he said, "I am positive you will return to Camelot. I just know it in my bones. It may be after my death. I will not leave Camelot in my lifetime, but I will wait for you if I can. I have decided to be cremated on my death. I do not want Excalibur to be buried; it is too important to the nation. I will arrange for the sword to be hidden and guarded permanently until your return. At that time, you must take it and do what you think is appropriate."

"I will do that, sire, but how will the guard know it is me as opposed to a common thief?" said Merlin.

"Good point. Hmm. We will have a password, 'Milner.' That's Merlin rearranged. When he is old enough, I will tell Prince Cheadda all about you, fear not." They shook hands and embraced

"When the battle is over, I will be gone," said Merlin. Arthur left the room and went back to Queen Guinevere.

The next day, an envoy from the patrol returned to the town saying that the settlers were just entering the realm. They would be here in about a day; he estimated that there were three hundred men. The remainder of the patrol had hidden until the approaching army had passed. They would follow from a safe distance where they could not be seen. They intended to cause any havoc they could from behind once the battle commenced.

The day passed, and all Camelot knew that tomorrow would be the battle. All their lives depended on victory. Guards were on the walls all the time now. They had realized after the last attack that the wall must be staffed with guards permanently.

When Merlin rose the following morning, he knew that today would be his last in Camelot. He went around the room, seeing what he should take on his travels. He put on his finest clothes, which were simply a tunic top and pants. He made sure he had the best-quality shoes for walking, a pair of animal skin shoes with sturdy soles. He went through the drawers and found his old watch, which had stopped working two years ago as the battery had run out. He left it in the drawer, closing it again. *It's no good to me now*, he thought. That was all he needed, and he was about to leave the room when he noticed his calendar. He stopped in thought. Then he realized he must take it with him; it was his only tie to his own age if he was to be moved around time zones. He picked it up without further thought and left the room.

The guards on the wall could see a multitude of opposition soldiers spread out in front of them. The archers lined both walls and were ready to shoot as soon as they were given instructions.

All the archers could now shoot three hundred feet at least, but the enemy was still out of range for the time being. Half of the approaching army was on foot. Behind them, the others were on horseback with swords raised. Merlin, who was on the rampart, could see the settlers' king spurring on his troops.

The enemy started to move forward slowly, one foot at a time. As they took the step, an arm was raised, and a hail of loud abuse and shouting followed, all to scare the soldiers of Camelot. Behind were the king and a line of drummer boys thumping out noise from the drums. The noise was deafening even to Merlin, who knew he had the means to defeat the enemy. There was no offer to surrender, as was the custom.

These ruthless settlers wanted to fight; it was in their blood. On this occasion, it was decided not to use the cannons, as the archers should do the job required. Merlin thought privately that Arthur would need the cannons when he attacked Winchester at the next stage of the war. Both Arthur and Merlin were walking the ramparts, spurring on their troops, Arthur on the outer wall and Merlin on the inner.

Merlin told the archers to hold fire until the attackers were well within range. When they were two hundred feet from the outer wall, Arthur, who was standing on the outer wall, shouted, "Take aim. Fire at will."

A volley of one hundred arrows flew high in the air and then dropped, speeding up on the way down. Most arrows met the target of the walking soldiers, who had now started running and were yelling at the tops of their voices. The back row of soldiers was beating on drums. They were heading for the first drawbridge, which, of course, was up. Although they had helmets on, the arrows found chests and faces. Men were falling all around, tripping up those coming behind, which just added to the heap until the next volley of arrows hit them.

The archers, by now, had become very accurate with their shots. Some of the arrows hit horses, which was sad, but the horses were unharmed. They just reared up, throwing off the riders, who were then hit by more arrows.

The foot soldiers fared worse as a second and a third volley followed. The approaching army was now near enough for the archers on the inner wall to fire. The enemy now had two sets of archers shooting at them. They hadn't reckoned on these arrows showering on them as they had no knowledge of this type of weapon. They only knew hand-to-hand fighting, and they were suffering.

Merlin had himself become a good shot with the bow and arrow. From the rampart, he could see the king of the settlers, who had now moved forward and was within range. He was riding his horse at the back of his army.

Hatred overtook Merlin. "The bastard! He killed my beloved and my son!" he shouted, although no one was listening.

He picked up a spare bow from the floor, loaded an arrow, pulled back the string, took aim, and released the arrow. He watched it fly. He could pick it out even though others were traveling in the same direction; it was his arrow. He watched as it hit its target in the chest, a perfect shot. At the same time, he saw another arrow hit the king's chest as well. Merlin looked in the direction the arrow had come from.

It was from Arthur. He raised his bow in salute to Merlin, who, in turn, raised his. The settler king was still for a minute. Then he keeled over and fell from the horse. He did not move again. Merlin felt some satisfaction. "Take that, you bastard!" he shouted. The tide had turned; Camelot's army was now in control and bringing slaughter to the enemy.

Just then, Viviane appeared and stood next to Merlin; she smiled at him in a comforting way. "Well done, Merlin. Your strength has brought you through this." She looked into the crowd of soldiers coming toward them, and she picked out one man. She raised her arm and pointed at the soldier, saying, "I couldn't help Gwen, but that is the man who killed her."

From her extended hand, a flash of lightning left her finger and went to the soldier; he exploded in midair. Merlin said, "Thank you."

Viviane disappeared, saying, "I will see you soon. Come to the lake when you are ready."

At the same time, archers were lighting fire arrows at the ground bombs just as the approaching army was on top on them. The soldiers thought that the arrows had missed their targets and were happy. Then, below them, there was an explosion that blew horses and men into the air. There was by now considerable loss of life in the advancing army; the field was turning red with blood.

Twenty of the settlers got to the front gate, which was firmly shut, and the guards above them poured hot oil over the wall. The scolding oil burned the intruders, and then flaming arrows were rained down on the scalded men, and the oil was set on fire. Screams were heard as the men died in pain.

The front gate of the town was then opened, and one hundred infantrymen left Camelot, their steel swords raised and shouting abuse at the enemy. They met the approaching army head on, and the opposition quickly began to suffer. Fierce hand-to-hand fighting ensued, and the attackers were demoralized by the loss of their comrades.

Arthur's men were slashing with their steel swords at every soldier they passed. The settlers only had iron swords, which just broke after about three clashes with steel. Once the iron swords fractured, the holder was slashed to death. No mercy was shown; these settlers needed to be taught a lesson. No prisoners were taken; these settlers need to be eradicated.

Within an hour, the battle was over. Men died on both sides, but the settlers fared far worse; their army was demolished. Bodies lay everywhere. Helmets had come off, making it look like the wearer was buried under the earth. Arthur needed the settlers reduced in numbers for his planned counterattack on Winchester in due course. Not a single man of the settlers survived.

Arthur had left the rampart now and was on the battlefield, encouraging his men in the final stages. His soldiers collected around him and raised him up as they carried him back to town in victory.

Merlin had been watching all of this from the rampart; he was not a hand-to-hand fighter. It was his time to leave. He quietly climbed down from the wall once it was all over.

He left the town, walking along the side of the battlefield alone. He was saddened by all the death, but he knew this was the course of the future England. He didn't like goodbyes, and he had said this to Arthur. He walked to the site of his old house. It was now covered with blood, and there were six bodies lying around it. One was still moving, but he ignored that. He wept for Gwen and blew her a kiss. Then he carried on to the lake. He turned back to face the castle, and he could see Arthur being held high amid cheering. The citizens of Camelot loved their king. He had led them into battle, and they had won the day. Merlin also raised his arm to Arthur, who could see him now, and they both waved.

Merlin whispered, "Goodbye, brother, and God bless. I love you. I know I will return, but I don't know when." Tears were running down his face again.

Arthur was also moved by the crowd's response, but he was devastated at watching his brother leave his realm. He waved to him, saying, "I love you, brother."

At the lake, Merlin arrived and called out to Viviane. In the center of the lake, he saw her apparition rise out of the water, and with her was Gwen, carrying Aelfred. They came forth to him and stood on the bank next to him. Merlin cried at the sight of Gwen and dropped to his knees. She pacified him by saying, "Don't cry, sweetheart. Get up. I'm at peace now with our son. Viviane has told me that your tasks here are over now. You are young. Be free. You must forget me and live your life. Please don't blame her for what happened; it was destiny. We had a wonderful time together, but now you must move on. I will keep watch over you. I know you want a family, and you must have another in your new life."

Viviane said, "Well done, Merlin. Gwen is right; you have done all things asked of you. Besides that, you have learned much as well, and your life in the future will be significantly enriched."

"I loved you so much, Gwen. Take care of Aelfred. I will miss you terribly. One day, I will be with you," Merlin said to Gwen.

"Me, too," she replied.

Just walk straight forward, into me, and don't be afraid," said Viviane

Viviane turned into a bright light again, just as he had seen in the bank all those years ago, and he walked towards it and through it. The apparitions disappeared, but Merlin couldn't see that he had already gone.

CHAPTER NINETEEN

erlin landed with a hop and a skip on a dirt lane. All he had in his hand was his calendar. He had no idea where he was or the time period, but the roadway had been well trodden by many vehicles, horses, and cattle over the years. It was parched, and hoof prints were everywhere. The sun was high, so he guessed it was midday. In front of him was the direction he had landed, so he carried on walking that way. There was no one around, but it looked as though the road went into a forest in the distance. He assumed correctly that he had moved forward in time; the roads were now more established and used.

After about a mile, he was just on the edge of the woods. The trees were much the same, he observed. He could see a building on the left-hand side of the road ahead of him. It confirmed to him that he was in a much later period. The building was of stone, but it looked much more formal than the ones in his previous life with Arthur. The stones were cut square as opposed to being just piled one on top of another. It had a roof of slate tiles, and now there was a chimney stack with a clay pot on top. The windows had wooden frames with glass, the front door was ornately carved and stained, and the building had two stories.

As he got nearer, he could see it was a coaching house. Horses were corralled behind, and there were a coach and four horses parked in front. *Oh yes*, he thought, *this must be on a stagecoach route. Maybe it's Wells Fargo in the Wild West.* He liked the idea of cowboys and Indians. He knew how to ride now.

As he approached the coaching house, he could see a sign over the front door that said "Inn." *Not very cowboy like*, he thought, but the strange thing was another sign hanging on the wall. It had a face on it, and below was the name "Merlin." *It's a pub sign*, he thought, but he had never heard of a pub called Merlin. In fact, he'd never heard of anyone named Merlin other than himself. The sight of the word brought it all back to him; he was sad again. He knew he must get on with his life, but it would be difficult.

He was clearly not in the twenty-first century; he guessed it was the middle ages. He had decided he was still in England, so he went to the front door and opened it. Inside were four men sitting at the bar, drinking beer, probably from the stagecoach. There were several tables scattered around for passengers from the stagecoaches to eat at. The innkeeper was serving behind the bar, which ran down the whole length of the room. The floor was made of rustic wooden planks covered in straw. Merlin thought, *That would hide many creepy crawlies.*

"Well, hello, stranger. Where did you come from?" said the innkeeper in a very rural accent, knowing that Merlin wasn't on the coach and he hadn't heard the clip-clop of a horse arriving.

"Hello," said Merlin. "I've just walked from the next village down the road."

The innkeeper was immediately suspicious as he knew that there were no villages for miles, but this lad looked presentable, so he said, "What can I get for you, sir?"

Merlin said, "I have no money and was just passing and saw the sign that read "Merlin" and had to come in to find out more."

"Well," said the innkeeper, thinking he would do his good deed for the day. "if you will chop some wood for me out the back later, I'll give you lunch and pay you. We have some excellent roast pork today, which will be ready in ten minutes."

That's a clue, thought Merlin. *It means I am in England after the Norman Conquest if he said pork instead of pig meat.* "Thank you, sir. I'll be glad to do that." As the innkeeper poured him a mug of beer, he asked, "Can I ask you why the inn is called Merlin?"

The barman explained, "It's very strange. Merlin was the wizard to King Arthur. Arthur was the king of lower England, then called Avalon in the seventh century. Some say the king was the savior of the country, the start of the formation of this realm into one kingdom as opposed to before, when there were many small rulers."

"This inn was called The Green Man. That's a reference to a creature of the forest worshiped by ancient peoples, but about two weeks ago, I had a dream. In the dream, I was walking through the woods not far from here up the road." He pointed in the direction that Merlin had been heading. "I came across a lake. In my dream, a lady rose out of the water. I knew she was a ghost, but she was very lifelike and friendly. She told me I should rename the Inn 'Merlin.' I did ask her why, but she only said, 'You'll find out.' So, there you have it. Why do you ask?"

"Because my name is Merlin, too." *That's how they explained me saying I was a wizard*, thought Merlin.

"That is strange," said the innkeeper. He thought deeply and added, "That's what she must have meant. It was for you. You must have been intended to stop here. I wonder why."

The innkeeper left the room and returned in a few minutes with a thick slice of pork between two slices of bread.

"Thank you, and is this lake real?" said Merlin

"I think it was the lake that is about ten miles up the road in the forest."

"What's the name of the woods?"

"Well, you're not from these parts, then. This is Sherwood Forest, and Nottingham is about twenty miles along the road in that direction." He pointed. "And London is a three-day ride the other way."

Merlin finished his sandwich and went out the back to chop the wood. While doing that, his mind drifted to Robin Hood. *That would fit the timing and circumstances here.* He continued chopping the wood into logs for the use of the landlord in the winter months. Once completed, he went back into the inn and up to the innkeeper, who said, "Thank you. You've certainly earned your lunch today." Thinking that had been chosen to meet Merlin, he gave him ten shillings for his efforts.

They both knew that was far too much money for the job he had done. Merlin was grateful, though, and the innkeeper thought he was doing what the Lady of the Lake would have wanted. He was a very superstitious person, as many were.

Merlin walked up the road through the forest; it was now late afternoon, so he decided to stop as it was getting dark. He settled in under a tree and had a good night's sleep. He felt unexplainably safe; he was now used to sleeping out of doors and didn't worry about wild animals so much now. He felt confident that the lions would, by now, be extinct.

It was as though he had a guardian angel looking over him. *It must be Gwen*, he thought. He missed her desperately. Although he knew he had to get on with whatever life had in store for him, he missed those quiet evenings chatting in the darkness with Gwen. It was dark now, so he started talking to her as though she was with him. There was no reply, but that didn't matter; he just made it up. He often talked to himself, but it comforted him.

The next day, just as the sun was rising, he woke up and started walking north again. The food he had yesterday had sustained him, and he didn't feel hungry. He was well into the forest, although still on the roadway, when stagecoaches passed him in each direction. Neither of them slowed down, and if he hadn't jumped out of the way and behind a tree, they would have run him down. The coaches were very basic, just comprising bench seats in an open trailer pulled by four horses. As they rattled along the road, the wheels appeared very flimsy, especially considering the road was rough.

After an hour's walk, Merlin came across a large lake just off the road. He assumed it was the one the innkeeper had referred to in his dream. Merlin walked along the water's edge, and it was very peaceful, not a ripple in the water. He saw his face looking out of the water when he peered in. *I could do with a shave,* he thought. Although he had a beard, it had not been trimmed for several weeks. He found himself calling out to Viviane, and her name echoed down the valley, but there was no response.

He was sure that one day, he would have to return here, but how would he find it? He felt in his pocket and found a knife. *How did that get there?* he thought. *I don't remember putting it there.* It was just what he needed, though. He carved the name Viviane into a tree and added the word "help" below.

He continued walking north; he now had a bearing for the lake. It was on the Nottingham Road leading to London, just before you left the forest.

That should do it, he thought. *I can find it again.* He then thought about his name. Should he carry on using Merlin? He knew Merlin was an Old English name that people would recognize. Clearly, the legend of King Arthur was still well known, whenever this was, but Robert, he knew for sure, was a Norman name. He was aware that there was conflict in England with the Normans, especially after the conquest. He decided to continue using the name of Merlin. Besides, he liked it.

He had plenty to time to think while walking. He never met anyone; he had already concluded that this must be sometime in the middle ages. Sherwood Forest covered half the country and surrounded Nottingham. The names of Robin Hood and Kings Richard and John came to mind, but what was his task? Perhaps he had to do something about the Magna Carta.

He proceeded north towards Nottingham; the morning was progressing. A few more people were traveling on horseback along the road. They did not stop or even look at him either; they were as bad as the stagecoach, moving so fast that again, he had to jump out of the way or be killed.

Farther up the road, Merlin could see three riders coming toward him on horseback. They had some type of uniform on, but he stepped aside well before they got to him and moved into the trees to get out of their way. He could easily see them coming. Somewhere out of the trees in front of him came three arrows, the type that he had introduced to King Arthur. Merlin felt pride that his bow and arrows are still being used in this time that was years after he had left Camelot. He wasn't happy about them being used like this, though.

The riders were in a type of soldier's uniform, and the arrows hit each one of them in the chest, thump, thump, thump. As the men fell to the ground, Merlin thought he could have done with those archers in Arthur's day.

He kept on watching, not wanting to go out in case he got the same treatment. Four men came out of the trees, carrying longbows, the same type that he had introduced to Arthur. They went to the men they had just killed, removed their uniforms and any valuables they had, and then carried the bodies back into the woods.

The assailants came back for the horses, which were clearly still the primary method of transportation. Then they saw Merlin in the distance. He realized he had been seen and thought it was better to come out rather than to hide; he walked out, waving as in friendship.

He guessed these men were highwaymen. Merlin had nothing of value other than the few shillings he'd earned yesterday; maybe they would leave him alone. They approached Merlin, smiling, which relaxed him a little. They said to him, "Sheriff's men," pointing to what had just happened as though that made it all right. The three of them looked quite scruffy, with long hair and rather dirty. They were dressed in clothes that were not that dissimilar to those he'd seen in Camelot. "Where are you from, laddie?" said one of the killers in a broad Scottish accent.

"Well, I'm from London, heading north, but I'm not sure where I'm going." That seemed to satisfy them. *Perhaps no one here knows why they go anywhere*, thought Merlin. The three killers all looked at each other as though for guidance, and one said, "Why don't you come back with us? We live in the forest not far from here. There's a group of forty of us earning a crust doing this and that"

Merlin didn't know how to answer. He didn't want to offend these ruthless guys, so he agreed. He did think, *"This and that" must mean killing and stealing*. One of the men said his name was Will, and Merlin introduced himself. No one commented on his name.

After about an hour's walk leading the horses, they came across a clearing that had makeshift shelters around the edge. Standing in the center of the glade was an impressive-looking man just under six feet tall. He had the presence of a leader, a slim build, and was dressed in a bright green suit with jacket and pants; the crowning glory was the bonnet. Not something that Merlin had seen before, it fit snugly on the head but was pointed in the front. He had his hands on his waist, and his feet were shoulder-width apart. *That must be Robin Hood*, thought Merlin. *So, that's it, then. My task is Robin Hood. The Magna Carta would have been more acceptable*. Will introduced Merlin to Robin, but Robin was more interested in showing off his new suit.

"What do you think of this outfit?" he asked John.

"Well, I think I like it. Do I have to wear one of those? What color is that!" said John.

"The tailor told me it's called Lincoln green."

"Let's have a vote on it, men. do you want this to be our uniform?" Robin said to all the bandits.

A cheer went up; the men were happy to be given the opportunity to vote. Most of them put their hands up, signifying their agreement. Robin was pleased.

"That's it, then. Tomorrow, we will go to the tailors and order our new uniforms," said Robin.

Merlin's three companions on the journey explained to Robin that they'd met him on the road from London and had invited him to join them. After a while, other men arrived carrying the spoils of their trade. They all emptied their pockets into a large container. They were all highwaymen robbing passersby in the forest. They looked tough men and ruthless. It made some sense to Merlin now; it seemed his tasks were to form English legends.

At dinner, Merlin was introduced to the second in command, a man named John. He was as expected, a large man both in height and width, which made Merlin smile to himself. *The infamous Little John*, he thought. *He looks fierce.* John explained to Merlin that they had lost several men recently in battles. Others had left to get married and settle down.

Merlin thought he would rather be with them than against them, but he said, "I'm not a robber or physically strong, but I will stay with you for support if you wish."

John replied, "Well everyone here has to have a role. We're not a charity, you know. If that's what you want, you should try the Church!"

"I am a good cook," Merlin said.

John smiled and said in a deep voice, "There you go, then. Perhaps we can have some decent food in the future for a change. Tonight's food is rubbish." He laughed, looking at this evening's cook, who was turning red.

Merlin thought this must be the destiny that Viviane had planned for him. Maybe he must learn something as well.

That night, Viviane came to him saying, "You have come to the right conclusion, Merlin. You need to establish Robin Hood as the person you know of from your generation."

"Why didn't you say before, Viviane?"

"It is better that you come to the conclusion yourself. It strengthens your character and decision-making ability."

The next day, Robin arranged with his men to go to the tailor. In fours, they left to be measured for their new suits of Lincoln green. Four of them left, and the others arranged a roster. Robin then turned to Merlin and said, "You can come along with us today, Merlin, and see what we do."

So, Robin, three of his men, and Merlin headed off into the forest and back to the main road. Then they headed north towards Nottingham. Robin knew where he was heading; there was a recessed area that he used to ambush travelers. He could hide until it was too late for the passersby to see them.

Merlin stayed out of sight so he could watch what was happening. Robin held up every passerby, whether they were rich or poor. The poor seemed to be regarded as easy game because they were unarmed, like the rich people who had swords.

"Now you can see what has to be done," a voice said to him quietly.

Surprised, he turned to see Viviane sitting next to him on the branch where Merlin was hiding. "Hmm, I see what you mean," Merlin said.

"Yes, you have your work cut out for you, but it will be an emotional journey. Be strong."

This was certainly not the Robin Hood that he had heard of in the films and books. At the end of the day, they went back to their camp much the richer and very pleased with themselves—except, of course, for Merlin. This was completely against his beliefs. He felt disgusted with this, and several people had been injured in the robberies. This was not what Arthur had taught him. *Viviane, what have you gotten me into?* he thought. *This is worse than 2019.*

That evening, he took on his new role as the cook. The food was always simple, mainly stews of whatever meat was available, and there was plenty of game in the forest. Tonight, it was venison. Some of Robin's men had raided the king's forest and killed a deer for dinner. Merlin had to admit he enjoyed roasting the animal and eating it.

The next day, Robin said they must go to the priory to purchase some mead that the monks made. Robin said to Merlin, "Do you know about mead?"

"Oh yes," said Merlin, thinking about King Arthur's day again. That night, he lay under the shelter, and his mind drifted back to his Gwen. He felt depressed without her, but eventually, he got to sleep.

The priory was south of Nottingham. In the morning, they headed off in that direction. It took thirty minutes to get there. When they arrived, the priory was an old building of clay, brick, and stone built about two hundred years ago, with a roof in the style of an oast house. They knocked on the door and were let in by a monk. Even thieves respected the church, and everyone knew that.

They entered an anteroom. In walked a rotund friar of about fifty years of age. he was five foot six and had a round body and face and very little hair; his bald head shone like a beacon. He was wearing what Merlin could only describe as a brown dressing gown tied with an extended length of string around the middle. Merlin smiled. He knew who this was.

The friar had the appearance of a kind, fatherly figure. His smile was welcoming, but he didn't look as though he was very worldly. The truth was the opposite, although he didn't let people in on that secret. In his youth, the friar had attended the Sarum Cathedral School in Old Sarum, founded in 1091. The friar had attended in 1160. Saint Osmund, the Bishop of Salisbury, founded the school; he was the first cousin of King William the Conqueror.

He had been a good student, studying archaeology and history. His teachers were very surprised and disappointed when the scholar decided not to pursue his studies and take up a life in the church instead. They tried to talk him out of it; they told him he would be giving up so much, that it would be a waste of his great brain, but he would not change his mind. He said he had a visitation and had to follow it.

Robin negotiated with the friar as to the price of the mead. Once the agreed, the friar said, "It will be ready for you tomorrow. We are right out of stock now. Can you send back your new recruit tomorrow?" He knew all of Robin's men by sight and had not seen this one before.

Robin agreed, and Merlin said, smiling, as they were leaving the room, "I know who you are. You're Friar Tuck."

"That's right, my son, and I think I know who you might be." But the friar said no more. They stared at each other knowingly, except that Merlin was not sure what the friar knew.

The next day, Merlin was back at the priory. He had brought with him his calendar, though he wasn't quite sure why. He needed it to be kept dry, and the priory seemed the best place. Friar Tuck met him at the doorway and said, "Welcome, my son."

"Thank you, father," replied Merlin.

Tuck showed him into the reception area with its comfortable settees, and they both sat down. "There's room for me on your chair," said Viviane who could only be seen by Merlin.

Tuck said, "Firstly, please call me Tuck, like everyone else. I was expecting someone to come to me, but I had no name. We don't get many strangers here. What is your name?"

"It's Merlin."

Tuck was suspicious. He had a questioning mind, although he had expected Merlin at some time, but was this the real one? Tuck had had a dream the other day. An angel had appeared to him saying that Merlin would come to see him. Merlin would have a task, one that he would have to work out for himself. He would, however, need Tuck's help and advice as he had traveled a long way in time. Being an intelligent man, Tuck didn't know whether it was just a dream or a visitation.

In the morning, he thought carefully about it; he knew Merlin, the compatriot of King Arthur, would have been dead for at least five hundred years, although in truth, there was no documentation of any of it.

Here in front of him was someone claiming to be Merlin: coincidence or what? Tuck said, "Merlin had a son. What was his name?" He knew not many people would know the answer. The look on Merlin's face gave it all away. It had dropped inches; he looked devastated. Without waiting for a reply, Tuck said, "I am sorry, son. I shouldn't have asked that."

Merlin said, "I understand, Tuck. It is all very difficult to believe, I know. My son was named Aelfred, and he died at the hands of the settlers."

Tuck said, "I had a dream a while ago that someone called Merlin would come to me, and I had to make sure it is really you."

Viviane was smiling at Merlin. "It's all in the plan."

"When you had your dream, did the angel come out of a lake?" Merlin asked.

"Yes, she did. She rose out of the water."

"That would be Viviane, the Lady of the Lake. In my real time, I was getting into bad company. She saved me when I was in trouble with the police, and she transported me back in time to create the legend of King Arthur. I think she was also forming my character at the same time. When my task was over with Arthur, she transported me here, but she hasn't told me what my task is."

"Interesting," said Tuck. "I should say I schooled at Sarum, quite near to the site of Camelot. I studied archeology and spent many days in Camelot, so I am aware of the legend you created, and it developed further after you left. The angel told me you would come to me for a purpose, but she did not say what, which is why I asked you to come back; we have plenty of mead in our cellars. There are strange things that happen in life, and I am a religious scholar, but you were alive five hundred years ago, and yet you look only about twenty years old."

"I know. I don't understand any of it myself. I'm twenty-five years old now, having spent five years with King Arthur. All I know is that the Lady of the Lake, who was a real person once, transported me. I hesitate to say this, but I will as you are a man of the cloth. She has now brought me on to here. What year is this?"

"All in time. Tell me your story," said Tuck.

"The Lady of the Lake is named Viviane. She was with me in the time of King Arthur and is sending me through these time warps. She does not tell me what I must do. Can you please help me?"

"I will certainly try to help you, my son. I think she is also developing your character. You said in your real time you were getting into bad company." He was a goodly priest, enjoying his calling.

"Yes, I was caught in a robbery."

"I have always befriended Robin in the hope that one day, he would reform into a righteous person, and I think I have been chosen to help you as well. Why don't we sit down and see if we can work this conundrum out," said Tuck, who thought he had the answer. "Firstly, to help me work things out, what century are you really from?"

"The twenty-first, the year 2019," said Merlin.

"Wow, that's another thousand years on," said Tuck, almost in disbelief. "This must all be very strange to you. You may think it is hard for me to believe as a Christian. I take the view that if our Lord ascended into heaven, then anything is possible, and perhaps we should not think why too much."

"Thank you," said Merlin. He felt very comfortable with Tuck.

"Let me tell you what's going on. The year is 1193, and King Richard is on the throne; he is off on the Third Crusade to win back Jerusalem from the Muslims. He has not been in this country for more than six months in his entire reign. Richard left good men in charge of things here before going to war. However, his brother Prince John has taken more control than was intended. He has sacked the people Richard left in charge and put his people in their place.

"Richard is, of course, a Norman. There is still a lot of bad feelings with the Normans; they have taken all the lands of the previous owners. The king owns all the property of the country and gives sections of it to the lords of the manor who run the estates. He, in turn, leases it off to farmers and the like. King William the First instructed the preparation of the Doomsday Book. That itemizes every piece of land in the country."

"I know about that. It's called the feudal system," said Merlin.

"They give names to everything in time, don't they!" said Tuck, laughing. "The towns are all run by Norman elected men. Nottingham is a case in point. We had a good person whom King Richard had left as sheriff. Prince John got rid of him and put in the present man, who is hated by everyone. He is a hard, corrupt man who believes in ruling by force. He takes extra taxes from the people and keeps the money for himself."

"Not like Arthur, then. He was a good man. Before I left, he made me his brother and knighted me. I felt deeply honored. I miss him a lot," said Merlin.

Tuck continued. "The outlaws in the country, of which there are many in Sherwood Forest, fight the sheriff's men at every opportunity."

"Could that be it, then, to fight the sheriff? By the way, it's strange you say Richard isn't liked as a Norman, because, in the twenty-first century, he is held in the highest regard. He is known as 'the Lionheart.'"

"Interesting. Maybe that's because of the Crusades. He is a real fighter, and even to this day, the English are warriors. It's in our nature, you know. You should remember that all the conquerors of Britain have been fighters, Romans, Angles,

Saxons, Jutes, Vikings, and Normans, so that must have rubbed off somewhere. However, I don't think you're here to fight the sheriff. Neither you or I are built for that. Those men always get their comeuppance in the end. By the way, how did you know my name?"

"Oh, you are famous in the legend of Robin Hood."

"Ah," said Tuck, "that is good to know, but maybe that's it. Tell me what the legend says."

"Well, Robin Hood is the son of an Anglo-Saxon; his real name is Robin of Loxley. He had his lands taken from him by the Normans, who evicted him following the death of his father. Doing the only thing he could, he became an outlaw in Sherwood Forest. He plays havoc with the sheriff of Nottingham, is a firm follower of King Richard, and he steals from the rich and gives to the poor. In many ways, he has similar principles to King Arthur."

"That's interesting," said Tuck. "So, Robin comes out well in all his antics, then. The Robin Hood we know today, if it is the same one, is nothing like the one you describe. He steals from everyone and is the son of a tinker, but maybe that is the answer. I think we have to make him into this hero."

"I had that thought as well," said Merlin.

"By the way, the name Hood refers to all highwaymen, so called by the cloak they always wear. When you live in the forest, you need warmth, and the head is the greatest loser of heat in the body," said Tuck.

"I was taken back to Arthur to bring him up to a certain standard to build England. I gave him some of the discoveries of the twenty-first century, but I was careful not to alter the course of history. I left a couple of artifacts with Arthur, and I wonder whether they survived."

"No, you probably formed it. Who knows what would have happened if you had not been there? As for artifacts, none are surviving that I know of."

"There is one member of the legend that we haven't mentioned, and that is Maid Marion," said Merlin

"Ah, "said Tuck, "Maid Marion is part of the legend, is she? Well, let me tell you about her. She is the daughter of an Anglo-Saxon lord. He still has his lands; no one quite knows why. Certainly, the sheriff of Nottingham has been trying his hardest to get them, and her for his wife. She is the ward of King Richard, and he won't allow it for some reason, but of course, the king is now out of the country. It is ruled by his brother John, who is unlikely to have the same thoughts. Robin is very keen on her, but of course, she is way outside his level of expectation."

"Interesting," said Merlin. "That's certainly in the legend. Marion becomes his girlfriend. I can't remember whether they get married or not, but maybe she is our link."

Tuck said, "You and I have to work out a plan for how we can bring all of that about." On that, they shook hands. "By the way," said Tuck, "there is one thing I should tell you that you may not know. It is the law now that everyone must attend church on a Sunday morning. The reason for that is that each Sunday, notices are read out in the church. It is the only way the crown can keep in touch with its citizens to keep them in touch with progress."

"That certainly is different than the twenty-first century, when not many people go to church at all. In that case, though, I will come to church this Sunday. I don't suppose Robin does, does he?" said Merlin.

"No, he doesn't," said Tuck. "Do you like living in the forest?"

"Frankly, no, I never did like camping."

"Well, we are a priory here, and one of the duties is to keep beds available for passing vagrants. You would be welcome to sleep here. Also, many of the farmers give us clothes for the passersby. Looking at yours, I think you would qualify. Come with me." Tuck led Merlin to a closet full of shirts, pants, and some quality leather shoes. Nottingham was the center of the leather shoe trade.

Merlin said, "Thank you, Tuck. I would like to take you up on your offer of accommodation, at least on rainy nights. There is one other thing. One of my problems with moving around in time zones is keeping a note of my own age. I have developed this calendar to record the days and years as they go by. Can I leave it with you for shelter, please?"

"Certainly. You must keep some kind of calendar. Otherwise, you will lose touch with yourself," said Tuck. "Leave it with me; I'll see if I can work out something for you that will be more robust than a plank of wood."

Merlin chose three sets of clothing and two pairs of boots for his own use and purchased the mead for Robin. They then said their goodbyes, and Merlin went back to Robin's camp. On arrival, he said that Tuck had offered him accommodation at the priory, which he would like to accept if that was all right with Robin. He would still offer any help he could to Robin's community.

Chapter Twenty

𝕯ays went by with Robin and his men doing the same things, robbing anyone in sight and fighting any of the sheriff's men who were brave enough to show their faces in Sherwood Forest. The sheriff had tried on many occasions to clear the highwaymen out of the forest; it covered most of central England. It was an impossible task, though as his foe kept moving around.

Tuck was spending much more time now at Robin's camp. He knew where it was, although, when he first arrived, Robin said, "How did you know where we were?" \

Tuck said, "I have special contacts with him up there, my son," pointing to the sky. Robin laughed. The truth was that many locals knew where the camp was.

Tuck said, "It's time you moved on to a new site." The friar was spending more time with Robin now as he was being thrown into this legend and needed to help Merlin. He saw it as part of his calling.

"What can we do for you, friar?" said Robin.

"I just came for a chat with your new guy. There may be a convert there, but while I'm here, I'd like to discuss something with you."

"Go on then, friar."

"As you know, Lord Howarth has been spared from losing his property. The Lady Marion runs the estate now that her father is getting too old. They only have one farm under their control, which is why they could keep it. The sheriff is now beginning to come down hard on them; he is after that farm for himself. I have heard that he is going to take it by force. Would you be prepared to protect them and fight off the sheriff? There is no financial gain in this, but you would get a lot of prestige locally, and you would score many points in the eyes of Marion."

Merlin had overheard this, and he knew where Tuck was heading. He waited for Robin's response, which came in a couple of minutes. "You know how to get to me through the heart, don't you, friar? You know I'd do anything for Marion, and anything to kill off a few more sheriff's men. Okay, do you know when the sheriff is going to act?"

Tuck was relieved the first battle over. "Well, my understanding is that it is tomorrow at midday."

"We'll be hiding in the trees soon after dawn; I know the spot well. I spent many a day in my youth in those trees, waiting for Marion to come out, but she didn't have eyes for me," said Robin, laughing but with a sad face.

The friar left the camp, smiling at Merlin but not before whispering to him, "I think I have the answer to our calendar problem. I'll see you at the church on Sunday."

Robin noticed that Tuck, although he'd said he wanted to speak to Merlin, hadn't done so other than the whisper he'd made as he left. Robin wondered what that was about.

"See you on Sunday?" said Robin to Merlin. "Are you going to church?"

"Yes, I am. It's the law here, you know," Merlin said sarcastically.

"Well, you know what you can do with that law, but don't forget you are the cook for Sunday lunch," joked Robin.

Robin arranged with John to be in the trees with six men at dawn the next day. John was an enormous man. Robin said, "I think we should call you Little John."

That's more like it, thought Merlin.

The next morning at dawn, the eight of them, including Merlin, left the camp for the house of Lord Howarth. Merlin wasn't expected to fight, but Robin said it would be good for him to see what happened. As they approached the house, the farm was just down the road. Robin guessed the sheriff would go directly to the manor house to demonstrate his strength, so he placed his men in the trees around the front of the property, the ones he had used all those years ago. Their one advantage would be surprise; there was no way the sheriff would expect this. Robin had never performed an act of compassion in his life; he even surprised himself.

Merlin had climbed a tree as well, away from the fighters, and sitting next to him was Viviane. She said, "You seem to be settling in well with Robin Hood. We can watch what happens from here. You might enjoy this piece of fun."

Merlin thought, She's getting very friendly now, but he was sad. He still desperately missed Gwen, and seeing Viviane again only made it worse.

At midday, six riders plus the sheriff rode into the front courtyard. The sheriff got down from his horse, walked to the front door, and thumped on it. The manor house was an old building built to the exacting standards of its day, with Roman columns at the front, but now it looked very tired.

Lord Howarth was behind the door; he was now a frail old man of seventy-five years. He looked much older: his hair was white, and his whole body had shrunk. He had once been a wild young man, six feet tall, but the years of fighting for his country had taken their toll. He was frightened about what would happen to his only daughter, Marion, when he was gone. Next to the front door was a sword lying on the table, but the truth was he could hardly lift it, let alone swing it in combat.

He didn't open the door, nor did he invite the sheriff in as expected. The sheriff shouted through the door, "We are taking your farm! you have forfeited it because you will not show allegiance to Prince John. He has seized the throne due to King Richard being away on the Crusade." That was an exaggeration, but he knew it was the plan. That would be put into effect next year if King Richard did not return for whatever reason Prince John could concoct.

"You can't do that," Lord Howarth called back. "I am a peace-loving citizen and loyal to the crown and King Richard." The sheriff's patience had gone. He thumped on the door again with the palm of his hand, shouting, "Let me in!"

At that moment, an arrow came from the trees and went straight through the sheriff's hand, pinning it to the door. He yelled in pain and could not move it. With his other hand, he loosened the arrow from the door. He was now free and stepped sideways, taking cover behind a tree. Taken by surprise, the captain of the sheriff's men jumped off his horse, thinking that this must be a lone raider as no other arrows had come from the woods.

He went to the sheriff and broke the arrow above the back of the hand so that he could pull it through from the point. The sheriff let out another yell as the arrow went through his hand again, but at least it was gone. His thoughts were now on getting away.

More arrows came flying out from the trees, and they slammed into the backs of the five soldiers who were still on their horses. Six more arrows followed, and the soldiers fell to the ground. Robin was chuckling and saw that the sheriff had moved behind the tree, but it did not cover him completely. His right-hand shoulder was sticking out, so he released another arrow with a careful aim. The arrow slammed into his arm and blood poured out; the sheriff moved sideways in pain. The tree was not wide enough, and another arrow hit him in the other arm.

He and his captain then scampered over to their horses. Jumping on, they rode off, zigzagging in case any more arrows came. The captain lagged slightly, and two more arrows were shot and landed in his back. The five soldiers on the ground were still. Robin was laughing and said, "I enjoyed that. Let the sheriff get away. We'll get him another time."

Viviane said to Merlin like a sprite, "I told you that you would enjoy it." She was trying to cheer him up. Before disappearing, she said, "You need to work on Robin and Marion!"

Robin, John, and Merlin went over to the house, and Lord Howarth had now opened the door. Marion, who had been standing behind him, came out. She was an extremely attractive young lady. She was twenty-five years old and had long red hair, which showed her Viking ancestry. Her hair went halfway down her back, and she wore a small white bonnet on top of her head.

She had a long, flowing red dress on that matched her hair. She went over to Robin gracefully, moving across the ground as though she was floating. Robin was now on the ground, and she said to him, "I cannot thank you enough for what you have done, Robin. It has been many years since you and I played as children. Although we grew apart when you got older, I have often thought about you." She didn't know that Robin had watched her from those very trees in later years. She noticed a new man was standing next to Robin, but she didn't say anything to him. "We don't have anything to give you, I'm afraid. We live hand very much to mouth here."

Robin suddenly felt pride, a feeling he'd never known before, and he said, "You don't owe us anything. Just to look at your beautiful face is all I need." He took the money bag from his waistband. "Here, take this. It may help a little, and I'll see what I can do for you in the future."

Marion was taken aback and didn't know quite what to say, so instead, she bent forward and kissed him on the cheek. Robin blushed.

As she went back inside, John said, "I have never seen that happen before."

"Nor have I, and I have to say I enjoyed it. We'd better get back to the forest," said Robin, who didn't think the Howarths would have any further trouble with the sheriff, at least for the time being. As Robin marched off into the forest, Marion was still watching him. She thought, *It was a long while ago that we were friends. I think I must keep a closer eye on him.*

Merlin had been watching all of this and thought their plan was beginning to work well. *We now need a few more events to establish Robin as a do-gooder.* He said to Robin, "I'll go to see Tuck and tell him how we got on. I'll spend the night at the priory."

He left for the priory. Tuck was expecting him and was waiting in the doorway.

"How did it go?" said Tuck.

"Fine. Five soldiers were killed, but one got away injured. The sheriff fled with two arrows in his arms, but he'll live. The other soldiers won't. Marion kissed Robin on the check, and Robin gave her a purse of money."

Tuck beamed. "Excellent," he said. "We now need to arrange a few more charitable deeds."

"Can I spend the night here, please? It will be good to sleep in a bed for once, and it looks like rain later."

"Of course you can, as I said before. Come with me, and I'll show you to your room. Before I do that, however, let me show you the device I have had made." Tuck left the room and returned with a contraption of wires full of wooden balls on a wooden frame.

Merlin looked at it with interest.

"It's an ancient device called an abacus. There are three wires the top. One represents each day, the second one represents months, and the third one years. For your purposes, to keep a record of your age, I suggest you use the lunar month of twenty-eight days. That way, there are thirteen months in a year. I think it is mainly the years that you will be interested in. Each ball is tight and shouldn't move, but if they do, then you will need to secure them better."

There were only ten balls on the bottom rail, so Merlin said, "That's just what I need, and I suppose after ten years I restart the process again."

"Yes, that's it. All you need to do then is to record the number of ten-year periods."

Merlin thanked Tuck for his new device and took it with him to his room; he was pleased to get into a bed that night. He lay in bed in the darkness, thinking of Gwen. He imagined her body lying next to him; he could feel her breasts resting on his chest, and his body was aching for her. It helped, and he soon fell asleep, dreaming of making love to her.

The story of Robin Hood helping the Howarths was spreading through the community. Nothing happened here without the whole town knowing it. Robin Hood was starting to become liked in the neighborhood. The sheriff got back to Nottingham and received medication for his injured arms. He had decided that he would not pursue the farm any further. He would turn his attention in other directions to try to improve his finances.

Price John had appointed the sheriff, and John was now effectively in command of England, which was not a democracy; the king was supreme. One of the duties of the sheriff was to collect taxes and send them to London. The amounts were all laid down except that this sheriff added ten percent as his share.

The sheriff had tax collectors going around to all the farms for that purpose. Those men were hated, as they always will be. Taxes were collected every three months, and it was coming up to that time now. It had been a bad harvest that year due to the rains in July, so money was very tight for the farmers. There were no excuses as far as the taxman was concerned. The tax was assessed on the property, not the income of the farm.

Robin had heard of all these difficulties in the past. He was now taking an interest in such matters after the debacle at Lord Howarth's home. Tuck had come to see him and filled him in on what was happening. With Tuck, in his buggy, was

Maid Marion. Robin was taken aback but pleased, and he said to Tuck, "If it will help, we will be at the collection points and stop the collections. We could just steal it from the collectors."

Tuck said, "Well, that might work, but there are many collection points. Frankly, if you succeeded, the sheriff's men will only come back later. I am a man of religion, but if I were you, I would attack the convoy once it heads off to London through the forest with all the tax money on it. That way, the farmers wouldn't be part of the robbery. You have control of the forest in any case. You could, if you felt so disposed, return the money to the farmers."

"Father, I think you and I are changing positions," said Robin.

"No, but these people need help, and I believe that you're the man to do it," Tuck replied.

"Okay, Father, when are the collections due to take place?"

"Starting next Monday and all the week."

"Do the farmers have the money to put up now?" said Robin.

"It is arranged through a community fund that I am administering," said Tuck.

Robin realized he had been set up here, but he was happy to go along with it. His men had excellent resources and didn't need the money on a day-to-day basis. Robin said, "Right. Will you let me know when the money is to be transferred to London?"

At that point, he turned to Marion, saying, "It's good to see you again, Marion."

Marion said, "I thought I'd take the opportunity of coming over here with the father to say hello." She got down from the buggy, and Robin and she spent time just walking around the campsite, reminiscing, while Tuck spoke to Merlin.

"It was a wonderful thing you did for us the other day with the sheriff," Marion said to Robin. "Dad has gotten timeworn now, and he can't cope with officialdom anymore. I must do that now. I don't know if you are aware, but the sheriff has wanted me to marry him for some time now. I keep telling him no, but he is persistent. I can't stand the man."

"You know I have always had a soft spot for you ever since our childhood, but I realize you are far above my station in life," said Robin.

"Well," replied Marion, "I wouldn't say that so much nowadays. In years gone by, that may have been the case, but now my father has no standing. As for me, I have no interest in status; it's all about love and happiness. Why don't you come and see me sometime?"

"I'll certainly do that, Marion, and you know you will always be welcomed here at camp. Although we do move around occasionally, Tuck will always know where we are."

They had walked the whole field now and were back with Merlin and Tuck. Merlin said, "It's good to see you two together. You make a good couple walking like that."

Robin smiled and kissed Marion on the check. Little John, who was nearby, said, "That's the second time I've seen that," and he patted Robin on the back. Robin and Marion blushed.

Robin turned to Tuck, and trying to change the subject, he said, "Don't forget to let me know when the taxes are to be transferred to London."

"I will," said Tuck, feeling very pleased with himself, and he left the camp with Marion in his buggy.

Tuck said to Marion, "He's a good man, really. You know, Merlin is here to develop Robin's character, and he's doing well. I'm helping out where I can." Tuck was becoming a matchmaker.

Viviane circled the field, looking on with pleasure.

Chapter Twenty-One

Over the weekend, the farmers all got together and met at the priory. The priory, like all churches in the country, was the general meeting place for the citizens of Nottingham. It was used for many purposes; they even took animals to church on Sundays to be blessed. Some of the farmers had fared better than others over the summer. Those growing crops had not fared as well as the cattle farmers because of the wet weather this year.

They calculated the total of the taxes needed, and they each put in sums that they could afford. A tally was kept by Friar Tuck so that once Robin returned the monies, they could redistribute it correctly in the amounts that each had put in. One of the first community funds in the country was set up.

The priory covered the small shortfall. The priory had resources of its own, earnings from the sale of mead and beer, as well as their own crop sales. It also ran a farm, producing all the food it needed and selling off the excess, which was considerable. Also, when wealthy men died, they often left money to the church in the hope of getting a better place in heaven. The priory benefited from not having to pay tax.

Even the Normans thought they needed to keep on the right side of God.

The significant risk was, of course, that the farmers were putting all their trust in Robin Hood, the outlaw, and they weren't entirely happy about that. They had no alternative, though. Also, they had to provide for the ten percent that the sheriff took for himself. They all knew he did that, but there was nothing they could do about that either.

On the Monday morning of the tax collection day, the sheriff called his two collectors into his office for instructions. The sheriff had evil eyes but, being tall, a significant presence. He had very dark hair and brown eyes, and he had a scar on the left-hand side of his face, the result of an encounter with a do-gooder many years ago. It made him look ferocious, and today, he felt it, as he always did on tax-collection day. He loved this time of year as it increased his personal coffers. He was now forty-six; the scar had never gone, but he thought it made him look more dangerous.

He regarded himself as a businessman, conning the inhabitants of every penny he could. His collectors entered the room, and he instructed them to go to each farm in turn. "Don't forget to collect the extra ten percent for me."

They set off later that morning. The first farm they reached, the farmer had sufficient money to pay the tax collectors. They were very surprised; they had gone to work that morning, expecting trouble. They knew it was a bad harvest for some, the rains having come late in the season. They moved on to the second farm and then the third, and so on. It was the same story each time.

The collectors couldn't help thinking these people must make more money than they let on. One said, "I'll let the sheriff know; maybe he'll increase our percentage. He might be able to pay us more then."

This is a hard job at times, they thought, *but not today.*

By the end of the week, all the taxes had been collected and placed in the large safe at Nottingham Castle. The castle was in the center of town, on high ground surrounded by a rocky escarpment, difficult for an adversary to attack, particularly from the rear, which had the sheerest drop. The sheriff knew he had only to defend the front. Being new, what he didn't know was that there was a secret entrance from the rear. The ousted sheriff certainly wasn't going to tell him.

Through his spies, Tuck learned that the taxes were to be moved on the forthcoming Wednesday. It was a full day to London by horseback, and that would involve several changes of horses. Pulling a wagon full of heavy gold coins, it would take at least two, perhaps three, days. That meant the coach would be setting off at daybreak. The sheriff knew that once they were out of the forest, the troop should be safe. Tuck went to see Robin to advise him of the arrangements.

"It's all up to you now, Robin. Don't let me down, will you? There are a lot of people depending on you," Tuck said.

"Don't worry, Father. Will you give us your blessing before you go?"

"I most certainly will." Tuck was shocked and pleased. He thought, *Maybe there is another convert here.* He gave them his blessing with the sign of the cross. "May the Lord go with you, my sons," he said, and he returned to the priory.

On Wednesday morning at daybreak, the patrol set off from Nottingham Castle. There were six soldiers and the captain in front; behind them came the wagon carrying the money, pulled by six horses. Bringing up the rear were six more soldiers. Arrangements had been made for three changes of horses along the route. All the soldiers were equipped with swords and protective clothing. They had crossbows and darts with them, but they were not practical to use from horseback.

The plan was to go through the forest as quickly as possible. The horses would be fresh at that stage, and they believed that would be the most likely place for an attack. Towards the end of the forest, the first change of horses was to take place, at the Green Man, now renamed The Merlin Inn.

The orders were that if they were attacked, they must immediately stop and circle the money trailer. Then, using the crossbows, they must protect the money at all costs, including their lives. They knew, however, that their crossbows were no match for longbows. The Anglo-Saxons had been using that weapon since the time of King Arthur. The crossbow was a close-range weapon.

Robin had selected a convenient spot for his ambush. Firstly, it was at one of the most southerly spots in the forest. He'd calculated that would be best because, psychologically, the enemy would think they were safe at that distance and become sloppy. Secondly, the horses would be tired by that time and would be looking to be changed. It was about two miles on the Nottingham side of the coaching station where Merlin had arrived. Everyone thought horses were stupid, but they knew the important things, like where the coaching inn was.

He chose the ideal spot, very secluded and heavily wooded, surrounded by his favorite oak trees. It was just short of the coaching station, but not near enough that anyone from there could see what was happening. Robin had to make sure no one would see anything. He anticipated the entourage would arrive at about eleven in the morning.

He took twenty good men with him, and ten were distributed in the trees overlooking that part of the road. A high tree had been felled to lie across the road, blocking it. There had been a few passersby on horseback, whom Robin ignored, and they raced off as fast as they could, knowing what the fallen tree meant.

The other ten men went back one mile toward Nottingham; Robin had told them that once the soldiers had passed, they should cut down the medium-sized tree that had already been cleared of branches. The procession would then be prevented from returning to Nottingham.

The soldiers had left Nottingham shortly after seven o'clock in the morning. They were limited as to the speed they could travel due to the weight of the money wagon, which got stuck in the mud caused by the recent rains every few miles. They were getting about eight miles per hour in some places, much less in others. Three hours later, they were beginning to feel happier, thinking they were nearly out of the main danger area. They were, however, getting sore butts and were ready for the horse change, which was not far off now.

The captain who led the procession turned a corner and could see the tree Robin had felled about a hundred yards ahead. He stopped the procession and sent the rear six soldiers up to the tree to investigate. It was possible that it had fallen in the recent heavy winds, but he was not optimistic.

He stayed back for the remainder of the procession and waited. The advance party got to the tree. At that time, the captain could hear another tree being felled behind him. He knew this was trouble.

Simultaneously, a volley of ten arrows was sent down on the advance party. This was followed by a second volley. All arrows found their targets, and six men fell to the ground.

Three stayed down, dead, the other three just managed to get up, but Robin's men were on them in a flash, picking up the fallen swords, which were run through the three soldiers before they could collect themselves.

The captain had seen this disaster, and he turned his smaller troop round and attempted to head back north. The second fallen tree halted them. Again, a hail of arrows came out of the trees. The remaining six soldiers and the captain were dealt with in the same way as the first group. Robin's men stripped the soldiers of their uniforms. Robin had a collection now of about thirty uniforms back at his camp. He knew that one day, he would have to attack the castle and the uniforms would come in very useful.

The bodies of the soldiers were placed in the wooded area to feed the animals. The uniforms were placed in the money wagon. They then removed the second tree so that the road back to Nottingham was clear; Robin left the other one tree for someone else to move.

Robin was very pleased with the operation. He then drove the money wagon back to the priory.

Tuck said he was delighted and would see to the redistribution of the taxes to whom they belonged. He emptied the cart and took the spoils into the priory; he had to be careful, but as with all priests in those days, they had a secret hideaway in the cellar. He stored the money and added the uniforms to the pile he already had. Robin and his men sank back into the forest with the wagon, which was set on fire once they were a long way from the priory.

Tuck called upon the farmers to give them the good news. They arranged to come that evening to collect the cash; they were still short of the ten percent that the sheriff kept.

But their taxes were officially paid, so at least they were happy for now.

Back in Robin's camp, Merlin thought, *Well, I haven't done much in this exploit to satisfy Viviane. Was all that I had to do, make Robin more humane?*

Robin decided that it was time to move the camp. They had been there for a month now. Tuck had found it quickly, he'd said, so maybe the sheriff could, too.

The sheriff was always sending out spies to see what information could be picked up. He was sure that some of the surrounding peasants – that was what he called the farmers – must know where Robin's camp was. His trouble was that although they were not particularly fans of Robin Hood, they hated the sheriff with a vengeance. It was the lesser of two evils as far as they were concerned.

On this day, however, the sheriff had appointed a new spy. He couldn't keep using the same ones as they were recognized by the locals and avoided. Today, Mort arrived in town, was paid two marks for the day, and was told to go south of town to The Crown pub just on the edge of town. The sheriff's captain told him, "Have a few drinks and see what you can find out about the camp of Robin Hood. Take care; they'll kill you in a flash if you ask the wrong person."

Mort was a wandering jester, and he looked the part in his diamond-patterned pants. He played the ukulele and sang songs to earn a few pennies. His favorite song was about King Arthur, but he had many. To make two marks a day was special for him, although he wondered whether he should have held out for more with this danger. He rode out of town on the London Road until he came to The Crown pub. He found it easily by the picture of a crown swinging on a board in the breeze at the front of the building. It was a converted house, like the coaching house, The Merlin Inn, but smaller.

He tied up his horse outside and went in. The pub was busy; it was late afternoon when the farm workers were going home, stopping for a drink on the way. No one drank water for fear of typhoid; beer was weak but healthy otherwise, and better to be drunk than dead. Mort went to the bar, introduced himself, and ordered a beer. He drank it down in one go. He was thirsty and ordered another.

The atmosphere hadn't warmed up yet. These were the workers turning out from the fields. The real action wouldn't start for another two hours yet. Then hardened drinkers would arrive, but the two barmaids were setting the scene, two young girls in their twenties. There was only one requirement for the barmaids: they had to be large-breasted. Clothes were loose, and the more bosom they showed, the more the landlord liked it – no, demanded. The girls were available for dancing at a cost, and if a breast fell out, so much the better. That would be much later in the evening.

For now, next to Mort was a local farm worker just off the fields, also drinking beer. They toasted each other. He was a young lad of about eighteen, and he'd just finished his day's work. Like all the young, he thought he could drink more than he was able. They got into a conversation about the area. Mort explained he was passing through and didn't know anywhere.

The youngster, named Richard, said, "In that case, be careful where you go. This area is plagued with highwaymen."

"Thanks for that, but how do I know where they are so that I can avoid them?"

"They are all over the forest, but don't carry any money if you go further south. Nottingham is safe. The sheriff keeps it so, but he has no idea where Robin Hood is. He's the leader," said Richard

"Well, you seem to know a lot, Richard. Do you know where they hang out?"

"Oh, yes, but it would be more than my life's worth to say where."

"Here, have another drink, Richard."

"Thanks, I will."

Mort bought him a large jug, which Richard demolished in a matter of minutes, and he was now getting quite woozy.

"About Robin Hood's camp, if you told me where it is, I would give you five marks," Mort said. Five marks was a lot of money, more than Richard would earn in a year. Silence prevailed; he was apparently thinking about the offer.

"How about if we make it ten."

Richard wasn't hesitant anymore. He agreed immediately, but he wanted the money up front.

"Okay, be here in an hour," Mort said, and he left and went back to the sheriff's captain, saying, "Give me fifteen marks, and I'll get you the camp location today."

The captain agreed, and he handed over the money. The captain thought, *He's bound to have added his bonus, but it will be worth it for Hood's location.*

Within the hour, Mort was back at The Crown. Richard was waiting outside, having sobered up somewhat and now regretting what he had said. He wanted the money, though; ten marks was a fortune. They both set off on horseback into the forest. Richard explained, "We must take care. We cannot go right to the camp." They rode down the road about three miles; Mort had to remember where he was going and retain some landmarks in his mind. They turned off the road to the right at a huge, ancient oak tree and then rode another mile. Finally, Richard stopped.

He said, "The camp is another mile down this road on the right-hand side, but we cannot go any nearer. We may have been spotted already. You won't see Robin's men; they hide in the trees. No, don't look," he said as Mort was starting to turn.

Mort said, "Okay, you've earned your money. Let's go back." They set off and parted at The Crown, at which point Mort gave Richard his ten marks. Richard thought, *Well, I don't have any allegiance to Robin Hood, and I need the money.*

Mort then went back to The Crown and had another drink. It was warming up now; fellow drunks were getting tipsy, and the barmaids were loosening up. Everyone had plenty of full glasses, so the girls came around the front of the bar and did their show, playing up to the men. Only men went into pubs then. The girls were dancing, showing off their bodies.

So, the evening went on, but Mort thought he had seen enough and left. He rode back to the castle and told the captain what he'd seen and exactly where the camp was. The captain congratulated him and said, "The sheriff will be well pleased with you. If he catches Robin Hood tomorrow, he will no doubt give you a bonus in addition to the one you've taken already." They both laughed.

CHAPTER TWENTY-TWO

𝕿he next morning was a wet day. It had been raining all night, so the ground was muddy, and the skies were full of black clouds. Robin's men were soaked through and cold to the bone. They had some shelter with makeshift tents, but the rain still came in. It was one of those storms that made it hard for anyone sleep. Most felt miserable this morning. Robin had intended to move camp that day, but they had all gotten together and decided to postpone it until at least the rain had stopped.

The procedure in the camp was that every morning, guards were posted in the trees around the camp. Guards were also in surrounding trees for about a mile away from camp, which had to happen no matter what the weather was. They knew that an attack would come in daylight – attackers had no light, and the bushes were thick – so at night, they knew they were relatively safe.

That morning, the guards were posted in the trees as usual. They also had a system of watchers along the road to Nottingham. That was the direction any adversaries would come; the warning sign was a system of arrows being fired toward the camp.

Soon after daybreak, the sheriff sent out a detachment of thirty soldiers to find Robin's camp, with Mort guiding them. Mort had arranged a further ten marks to show them the way, but he made it clear he was not going into the fight. He would leave before they were at the camp, and he'd made that quite clear to the sheriff. "I'm a musician, not a fighter," he had said.

They rode off along the road to London, entering the forest. It was then that the first of Robin's men saw them. Once they were past, he fired an arrow at the next watcher. He then shot an arrow at the next, and so on.

Eventually, one arrow landed in the center of Robin's camp. Everyone looked at one another, saying, "We've got about ten minutes." They took to the trees, with the others already there.

The detachment of soldiers rode up to the ancient oak tree, and Mort said, "We need to turn right here. The camp is just over a mile further on, but I'll leave you here as agreed." Mort rode back up the road to Nottingham, feeling good about himself and a little richer.

The captain then slowed down the troop to keep the noise down. They needed to keep their eyes open for the camp, which they knew was near now if the informant had been arcuate. They traveled slowly along the new road, scanning the trees, not seeing anyone. But Robin's men were there, and they were watching the progress.

Robin's men knew the rule was don't act until the troop gets near enough to the camp. That way the rest of the men could take them on in battle. It made no difference if the soldiers found the camp now. Robin was about to move anyway. Once the camp had been discovered, they should have run yesterday. *No, let's have some fun today,* thought Robin.

Merlin had climbed one of the trees, and he sat on a solid branch to keep out of the way. The forest was thick at this part, so hiding was easy. Alongside him came Viviane. She said, "Best if we keep out of the way of this fracas. Robin and his men can handle this fine."

As the sheriff's troops got near the camp, Robin's outlying men saw them going past. They got down from the trees and were quietly following the force through the trees. The captain suddenly caught sight of the camp in the distance, about one hundred and fifty yards off. He indicated to his men to spread out. Robin, who was sitting in a tree just over the captain, sensed from the attitude of the captain that the camp had been seen.

Robin pulled back his bow and fired an arrow at the captain. It hit him in the arm; Robin thought, *I only missed because of the rain!* But it was the signal for the battle to commence. Arrows rained down from the trees. The soldiers were off their horses in seconds, but they now lacked the advantage of surprise, which was with Robin.

Half of the soldiers were hit by the first volley of arrows, which either killed or maimed their targets. Robin's men continued firing arrows, but the rain and the cold were affecting their shots. The bows were wet, as well as the arrows; even so, they were silencing many soldiers, but there were still more left. Robin's men decided to come down from the trees.

They had to collect the swords of the fallen men. Robin's men didn't have swords of their own, although they knew how to fight with them. Clashes were now happening all around the field. Slowly, Robin's men took over the situation; it was brutal, and blood was staining the wet grass, now turning it from green to red. There were only a few soldiers left, and they started to run away. Robin let them; he was going to move camp anyway, and he was more concerned now about the injuries to his men. One had been killed, but three had injuries that needed attention.

Out of the soldiers, twenty were dead. Five were injured so badly they wouldn't last the day as there was no real medicine available, only herbs, and the remaining five had gotten away.

Robin and his men collected all their belongings. The bulk of them set off to a new campsite that Robin knew of on the other side of Nottingham. They would have to take a long way around to avoid Nottingham. Robin and Merlin had set off to go to Friar Tuck with the three injured. They could ride, and Robin thought their injuries were not life-threatening.

When they arrived at the priory, Tuck was outside, tending the garden. He saw them coming, and he looked around to make sure no one else was there. Robin said to Tuck, "We had a visit from the sheriff's men this morning. We came off best, but three of my guys were injured."

"Let me have a look," said Tuck, inspecting the injuries. He was not a medicine man, but he had a little knowledge. He said, "I think they'll live, but they need rest. You need to leave them here." After a moment's thought, he added, "We are away from people here, but if there are any troops around, they will have to hide in the basement, where I have a hideout."

"Thanks," said Robin. "You are a strange one, but it is appreciated, and you did say yesterday that we should move, so we are gone now."

"Don't tell me where, just in case the sheriff's men come here, but come and see me in a few days."

They left the three men with Tuck. Robin and Merlin rode off to the new campsite, which the others had set up by the time they got there. When they arrived, the rain had stopped, but three of Robin's band were coughing and sneezing. Merlin said to them, "It looks as though you three have caught a cold."

They looked at him blankly, not knowing what a cold was. Merlin stopped short at that point as he realized that they did not have did not have the common cold in 1190. They recovered in three days' time.

At the end of the day, Robin said to Merlin, "That was a close thing. Glad to have you with us, Merlin."

Merlin thought about that. *I've done nothing yet. Perhaps it's spiritual.*

The next day, Merlin thought he needed to bring Marion back on the scene. She didn't know where Robin' camp was now. Merlin wasn't too sure himself, but he decided to go to Marion and bring her back. He knew the general direction of Nottingham, and he rode off, leaving a trail so he could find his way back.

After an hour, he arrived at the manor house of Marion's father and knocked on the door. Marion opened it. Surprised, she said, "Hello, Merlin. I have got the name right, haven't I?"

"Yes, that's it," said Merlin. "I wondered if you would like to come back to Robin's camp with me. He had to move as there was an attack from the sheriff."

"Oh, thanks. I'd love that. Come in and wait while I get changed."

Marion went upstairs and came down in fifteen minutes; Merlin was at the bottom of the stairs, watching her come down. She was wearing one of the new Lincoln green suits that Robin had chosen for his men. She looked ravishing;

Merlin loved the way the pointed cap looked on her, with her long red hair hanging down behind. He said, "You look beautiful."

"Thank you," she said. I'll ride over with you. "Do you know the way?"

"Yes, I left a trail to follow."

They set off. Merlin was able to pick up the trail easily, making sure he destroyed the markers as they passed. Merlin thought, *I must get one of these green suits.* They arrived at the camp at midday. Robin was surprised to see Marion but delighted to see her in his new suit. He told her she looked lovely, and they spent the rest of the day riding in the forest. Merlin planned to bring the two of them together, knowing that a good lady would temper Robin's brutality.

Before it got dark, Marion said, "I'd better be going home before it gets dark. I know the way."

Robin said, "That's fine, but I'll ride halfway with you to make sure."

At the halfway point, they said goodbye to each other. Robin thanked her for wearing the suit and confirmed it suited her. They parted with a kiss, a somewhat stronger one this time, in private.

CHAPTER TWENTY-THREE

After four days, Prince John was concerned that he had not received the tax money from Nottingham. He sent out his envoy to the town. The road had been cleared by then, and the envoy changed horses at The Merlin Inn. He rode into town and up to the castle gates, demanding access, which was given. The prince's envoy was always welcome in Nottingham as the sheriff wanted to keep in the prince's good books.

The envoy demanded to see the sheriff and was shown into his office.

"Where are the taxes from Nottingham? Why haven't they arrived in London?" demanded the envoy in his most annoying voice. The sheriff looked at him, surprised. It was true that his guards had not returned yet, but that was not surprising; when they went to the big city, troops always let their hair down.

"A force of twelve men left the castle to come down to London last Wednesday in the morning. The men haven't returned but are no doubt drunk somewhere in your city," said the sheriff with a little sarcasm.

"Well, they didn't arrive," said the envoy. "They must have been intercepted in the forest or somewhere on the way."

"Impossible. There have been no such reports. They can't just disappear into thin air."

"Well, you had better investigate. Have some soldiers go through the forest on that road and see what they can find out. This is your responsibility. That's what you are here for. Prince John will not accept ineptitude," said the envoy as he strutted around the room with authority.

"Very good, sir. I would except for the fact that two days ago, I had a location for these highwaymen called Robin Hood and his merry men. I sent out thirty soldiers to arrest them, or more to the point, kill them. It's not worth the time or expense of a trial. Only three returned."

"So, are you saying you don't have enough men now?"

"Regretfully, that is about it, sir, but I will arrange for the investigation. If you need me to go after Robin Hood, then you need to arrange for me to have an army sent up from London," said the sheriff, not expecting a positive response.

"Prince John is so concerned about this. I will make the arrangements that you require. In the meantime, I want you to send out a scouting party to investigate the road. I will sit down at the end of this interview and write a letter to the prince requesting the troops. Can you provide a rider to go to London? He can go with your scouting party as far as the end of the forest."

"Very well, sir," said the sheriff.

He organized a scouting party to investigate the road but was not hopeful of finding anything. If there had been a holdup, he knew the attackers wouldn't have left any trace. Bodies disappeared very quickly in the forest due to natural animal feeding overnight. The sheriff had to comply, though, and the envoy advised him that he would await their return.

Six men had the task of riding the road toward London. A seventh would go with them and beyond, to London, with the letter for Prince John. The offending stretch of the road was about fifty miles long, which would take about three hours to ride at speed. The men couldn't do that speed; they had to do it at walking pace as they needed to see the countryside in detail. They decided to walk the length and pull the horses. There were stretches where they could travel faster as the sides were open, but much of the ground was in the trees.

After four hours, they came across the spot where the attack had happened. At least they hadn't seen any highwaymen, who, of course, had now moved to the north of Nottingham. The area was cleared, but they could see where two trees had been felled. In the bushes off the road were the remains of the naked bodies of the killed soldiers. The bodies had been mutilated by animals and were now mainly bones. The soldiers decided they would move the bones to the edge of the forest and bury them in a mass grave.

There was no other evidence to be found. They traveled on to The Merlin Inn and spoke to the innkeeper; he confirmed he had seen nothing on that Wednesday. He had, in fact, been waiting for the soldiers to arrive to change the horses, for which he had made special provision. He would be sending an account to the sheriff for payment, he emphasized to the captain, but he knew he wouldn't get paid. The men then rode back to Nottingham at full speed, while the seventh rode on to London. They did not want to be out in the forest at night in uniform.

They relayed their findings to the sheriff and the envoy together. The envoy said, "Prince John will not be happy with this; you are in charge here to keep the peace and protect the countryside. If you can't do that, then you will be replaced."

The sheriff expressed his most sincere apologies and promised that nothing like this would happen again. It was a promise he knew he couldn't keep, but again, he stressed he needed the army for assistance.

The envoy left the next morning for London. Robin had been watching the road constantly yesterday. He had come back south of Nottingham because this was the most lucrative route for travelers. He had seen the soldiers yesterday and guessed what they were doing, so he'd thought it best to let them go. Today, he saw the envoy from Prince John riding past, and he felt adventuresome. He swung out of the trees, landing in the envoy's path, and drew his bow, indicating that he stop or be shot. The envoy stopped as he did not want an arrow through the chest.

"Time to hand over your purse, sir," said Robin. The envoy was not a fighting man and decided he'd better comply. He threw down his bag to Robin, who said, "Now you may pass on your way, and give my compliments to Prince John," and he spanked the horse's butt to make him gallop.

"You'll regret this!" could be heard from the envoy as he rode off. Robin laughed out loud.

Upon the envoy's return to the Tower in London, Prince John was fuming at the loss of his taxes. He even took it out on the envoy by slapping his face with his jeweled glove, which brought blood to the man's face. The messenger always got the blame.

Back in Nottingham, the sheriff was beginning to panic. He knew he had a cushy number at Nottingham, aside from having to deal with Robin Hood. He had an easy time of things and had earned considerable money through his extra ten percent taxes and other extortions of the citizens. Being in the center of the country, Nottingham was a very productive area. It was also the center of the lace and shoe trade in England, but he knew he had to rid the area of this Robin Hood.

Robin, on the other hand, thought that he had to rid the town of this corrupt sheriff, and he was formulating a plan to do so. His first objective was to get back the ten percent that the sheriff had kept back of taxes.

There was the annual Great Summer Fair being held in three weeks' time. It was a day of fun and laughter, with sideshows, contests, and performers, and the height of the show was an archery competition. Robin was undoubtedly the best shot in the county, but he was also well known to the authorities. If he entered, he would be recognized. That was his intent, and while he was escaping, Little John and the other Merry Men could attack the castle and get back the remainder of the tax money, which would be held in the castle safe.

The problem was how to open the safe without a key. Robin was talking this over with Merlin, who said, "Does gunpowder still exist from King Arthur's day?" Robin looked at him with a blank stare. "So, you don't," said Merlin. "Let me tell you a story. There was a helper in King Arthur's day who invented a black powder called gunpowder. It exploded when lit, especially in a confined space. Does any of this ring a bell?"

"No," said Robin.

"Okay, do you know where Camelot is?"

"Well, yes, I believe so, if it ever existed. I've certainly never been there, but the rumor is that it is on the other side of Salisbury. If it existed, it must be in ruins now."

"Can we go there? You may find it interesting if things are still intact."

"All right, we'll set off tomorrow."

Today was Sunday, and Merlin, as agreed, went to the priory to morning service. There were about thirty people in the church, which meant it was almost full; most were there because it was a duty. Some were very religious. The service was conducted in Latin. There was only one Christian denomination then, Catholic. Merlin managed to find a seat, which happened to be next to Marion, and they exchanged hellos.

When the psalms and prayers were completed in Latin, Tuck shifted to English for his sermon.

He was readily aware that Merlin was in the congregation. He first read out the government notices that there was no news yet as to the return of King Richard. He was still being held prisoner in Germany. He then started his sermon proper, which on the spur of the moment changed and became directed at Merlin.

"I would like to talk to you all today about the path of life. All of us must travel that road, which can have many twists and turns. Then there are the crossroads. Which way should I choose? That is a good question," he said in a very caring manner.

"In many cases, it is up to us to choose the right option. Occasionally, we do not have a choice; the route has been selected for us. We must go down that road whether we like it or not. When that happens, my advice can only be to do the best you can and hope that things will become apparent in the due course of time. Remember, God moves mysteriously, and we have to comply with his wishes.

"Don't always question yourself. Spend your energy doing rather than thinking, and remember that there is always light at the end of the tunnel. On that note, God bless you all."

Most of the congregation thought, *What on earth was all that? I work all day clearing up the farm. What crossroads does he mean? My life has not changed since the day I was born.*

One person in the Church thought differently.

Marion said quietly to Merlin, "I wonder who Tuck was referring to in the sermon? It has to be a new attendee; all the regulars would not know what he was talking about." She looked at Merlin suspiciously.

After the service, Tuck stood at the exit door and shook hands with all the parishioners as they left. The last to go was Merlin; Tuck shook his hand as though he were taking vibes from him. Merlin said, "Thank you for your sermon. I felt it was directed at me. Robin and I are going to Camelot tomorrow. There are some things I need to collect." He did not want to be specific in public.

Tuck was concerned. He knew that trip would be traumatic for Merlin and he would need some spiritual and feminine guidance. Tuck thought about it for a moment, and suddenly, he became a real father and said, "I think I must come with you both; this will be a tough trip for you mentally, Merlin. If you don't mind, I will also ask Marion to come. You might need female company."

Merlin was relieved to hear that. He had worried about going back to Camelot after only five months of leaving, even though five hundred years had passed in time. He wasn't sure whether his mind would cope with it. He said, "Thank you, Father. I would appreciate you being there."

"Wait for me, and I will come back to see Robin with you. We can take my wagon, but you'll have to guide me, as I don't know where the new camp is," said Tuck.

They rode off together in Tuck's horse and wagon. Tuck didn't like walking more than he had to. When they reached the camp, Robin said sarcastically, "You found us all right, then."

"Of course, my son. I told you I have guidance from above." Tuck got down from the cart, smiling. "That is the reason I came. I should go with you both tomorrow to Camelot. I will bring Marion with me. Without going into details now, what we find there will be a struggle for Merlin to come to terms with, and he may need our help."

Robin said, "Tuck, you know you are always welcome, whatever the reason. For my part, I would love to have Marion with us. We leave from here at sunrise. As you are south of us now, and that is the direction we are going, we will pick you up mid-morning from the priory."

"I'll be there," said Tuck, and he turned the horse and said goodbye.

Merlin had moved off into the group, but Robin watched as Tuck rode away, thinking, *I'm sure there is something different about Merlin. Tuck must know more than he is letting on.*

That night, Merlin was sleeping at Robin's camp. He'd fallen asleep quickly. Usually, he would lay awake for an hour or so. In the night, Viviane came to him in a dream, saying, "Tomorrow, you are going back to Camelot. There are things you will see that will upset you. Be aware and rely on the advice of Tuck. He is a good man, and the female company will help, too. Keep up the good work with Robin; it won't be long now."

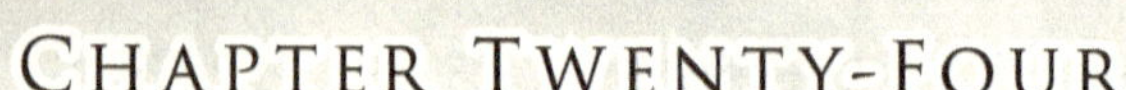

Chapter Twenty-Four

In the morning, Robin and Merlin headed southwest, leaving Little John in charge of the camp. Merlin had said they needed a horse and wagon, so they took two, one for the three riders and one for supplies. They rode down to the priory, where Tuck was waiting outside with Marion.

They all greeted each other, and Robin said, "I hope we haven't kept you waiting long."

Tuck said, "No, my son. God's work cannot be rushed."

To Marion, Robin said, "It's good to see you again," and he kissed her on the cheek. Marion got on the wagon in the front, next to Robin, leaving the rear for Tuck and Merlin.

They spent the rest of the day traveling and chatting about nothing important. Tuck did ask, "What we are going to Camelot for?" The reply was, "Gunpowder." No response from Tuck.

Marion had never been to Camelot, and she said, "I didn't know it actually existed. I thought it was all legend."

"Oh, no, it exists all right," said Tuck.

"Do you know what gunpowder is, Tuck?" said Robin, emphasizing the word "you."

"Of course. It is a black powder, which was the original name it went under, and it's used for causing explosions. It was discovered by the Chinese a thousand years ago."

"How would you know that?" said Robin

"You may think I'm a simple old priest, but that is not the whole story. It's true I am that priest, but I haven't always been so. As a young man, I was very well-educated, learning about everything in heaven and earth. I know, for example, that gunpowder in this country was introduced about five hundred years ago in Camelot. It has been used in the far east for a lot longer." Tuck was smiling at Merlin. Robin was completely perplexed at this revelation.

Viviane suddenly flew in and sat on Merlin's lap, as there was no other room. Tuck was familiar with Viviane – she had appeared to him before – and she was visible only to him and Merlin.

"I am concerned for Merlin. This will be a very emotional journey for him," Viviane said to Tuck.

"I realize that, which is why I came, ma'am," said Tuck.

Surprised, Merlin said, "I can feel your body against me."

"No, what you can feel is my energy. I am highly charged, and that warms the molecules in your body, which move faster, and you feel that as heat," said Viviane. "Take care, Merlin. Be strong." With that, she flew away. Surprisingly, neither Robin or Marion had heard the conversation.

They arrived at Stonehenge at lunchtime on the second day, having spent the night in a tent. It brought back happy memories to Merlin, and he wanted to have a good look around before they moved on. He saw that the stones were still there, but they were not used anymore. He imagined the banners streaming down from them. He pictured Sir Galahad riding his stallion against Sir Lancelot in the joust; it was so fresh in his mind.

Tuck interrupted Merlin's thoughts, explaining that this site was a very ancient temple, used by the Druids, who were sun worshipers. Tuck said, "The stones were transported from about three hundred miles to the north of here in the Welsh hills. There are no records of that, only the stories that have been passed down. It has always made me wonder why they would bring the stones so far when there were plenty nearby. They must have had a reason, probably spiritual. More importantly, how did they transport them that distance over two thousand years ago?"

Merlin was fascinated with that story. He, of course, knew the stones came from North Wales from information in the twenty-first century. He realized that the past generations knew a lot more than the later generations gave them credit for. That was why Tuck had told the story.

However, it was evident to Merlin now that the ancient day ceremonies that he'd seen here five hundred years ago were no longer held. The stones were crumbling in parts, and others had fallen. He wondered why: was it an earthquake, or had people taken them down? He was now happy to move on; he depressed himself with his thoughts.

Robin was not too sure where exactly Camelot was, but Merlin knew it was west of where they were. Tuck confirmed that, saying with a smile, "It is about a two-day ride from here."

Merlin suddenly realized that Tuck had been to Camelot before.

"There's one thing I will say," said Tuck. "We are all about to see things that are best forgotten once we leave

Camelot." Merlin knew exactly what Tuck meant, but Robin and Marion had no idea.

Eventually, after the two-day ride, they came across Camelot, or what was still left of it. There were the two outer walls still standing, but they were both crumbling away, and the internal one was partly down. The drawbridges were gone, rotted away, and had been replaced by earth and rock walkways. There were no cannons at the entrance anymore.

Merlin could see from a distance that much of the interior of the town had fallen into disrepair. All the houses were gone, probably used for building materials in other villages. There was no one living here now. At the sight of it all, he felt sorrowful. It brought tears to his eyes, and his travelers sensed it. The town that he had helped to establish was falling down.

They parked the cart outside of town. Getting off, Merlin wondered, *What happened after I left? I'll never know, or will I?* He suddenly realized he was standing on the spot where the settler army had been lined up across the horizon. It had only been a few months ago to him, though over five hundred years in real time, and hatred once again took him over. This journey was harder for him than he'd imagined. He took a deep breath to calm down, and his thoughts turned to Tuck. *He has to know more than he has said. Maybe he will tell me shortly.*

Merlin saw the small church. It now had a large stone cross outside, but it was the same building. It was the one building that seemed to have been maintained. Marion just looked on in amazement; she said, "It does actually exist, then, but it is crumbling. That's so sad." She looked to Merlin and could see his thoughts were far away and there were tears in his eyes.

"Why don't you have a look around for a while on your own, and I'll look after Merlin," Tuck said to Robin. Robin, too, now realized there was more to this trip than what was being told, so he agreed and went exploring. They left the wagons outside of the crumbling town for safety and walked in.

Tuck said to Marion kindly, "Please come with us." They went over to the church.

Merlin said, "Thank you, Father. I feel comfortable with us being here together, but I don't want to go into all the history with Robin."

"That's fine. Some things are better left unsaid," said Tuck.

Tuck went inside the little church and said a few prayers, leaving Merlin and Marion outside. This was a spiritual place for him, too. There were thirty graves around the entrance now. Merlin found the two he wanted: Gwen's and Aelfred's. He was crying intensely now; tears were running down his face. He dropped to the ground, prostrate over the grave of Gwen. "I love you so much. I don't know how I can live without you," he said.

It all seemed so unreal to him; he was looking at the ancient grave of his dear Gwen, who, to him, had only died less than a year ago. How could his mind cope with this?

Arthur had kept his promise; most stones were five hundred years old and weathered badly. The writing had almost worn off, and Merlin couldn't come to grips with the fact that it had only been months ago to him. The graves of Gwen and Aelfred appeared new when he considered it, but it didn't occur to him why.

He raised himself off the ground and kissed the tiny gravestones that Arthur had made after Merlin had left, as he'd said he would. The ground had to settle before the stones could be added, Arthur had explained. He missed Gwen and Aelfred so much.

The writing carved onto Gwen's headstone said: "Here lies Gwen, wife of Merlin, brother to King Arthur." The other headstone simply said: "Aelfred, son of Merlin and Gwen." Merlin rubbed his finger along the markings on the stones; he was saying a little prayer of his own as Tuck came out of the church. He thought his finger was warming up from rubbing the stone; perhaps he imagined that.

"Oh lord, why did this have to happen? We could have had such a good life together. I love you, Gwen, and can't bear being without you. Please help me, my love."

Marion, who was standing behind Merlin, could see he was severely affected by what he has seen, although she couldn't understand what was happening. She went to him and put her arm around him. He turned to her, and they cuddled like brother and sister. Merlin was crying, and Marion was comforting him.

She realized the graves he was looking at were important. "It's okay," she said. "Just let it all come out." All this time, Viviane was flying around overhead, keeping a watch over Merlin. She knew this would be traumatic for him, and now he needed real affection and not that of a ghost.

Tuck was pleased he had brought Marion with him. He knew Merlin needed a woman to caress, and he said, "Have strength, Merlin. Let's say a few prayers together."

Tuck is a wonderful man, thought Merlin, *such a help. He knows just what is needed to comfort people.*

After ten minutes and a few prayers, they all left the area together. Marion said to Tuck so that Merlin couldn't hear, "Whose graves were they? They were very old except the two."

"Well, that's one of the things I spoke of before about forgetting what we see here, but in all fairness, I will say they are the wife and child of Merlin," said Tuck.

"But...our Merlin?"

"There is only one Merlin, Marion."

"Merlin was a wizard, wasn't he? So that means he has lived for all those centuries."

"It's complicated. I'll tell you the story when we get back to Sherwood. For now, just go along with things," said Tuck. "Just remember many strange unexplainable things happen in heaven and earth."

The part of Camelot that Merlin needed was, of course, the arsenals. Walking to the main city walls and breathing deeply made him calm down somewhat. He had a job to do, and he had to get on with it. He climbed the steps up the wall he had been on in that last battle six hundred years ago. It was crumbling badly now, but he thought he was on the spot that he'd shot the arrow that had killed the settler king. Beside him appeared Viviane. "You are making it hard on yourself. It does not pay to dwell on the past," but she looked out with satisfaction at the position of the soldier she had killed, the one who had murdered Gwen.

Merlin looked down; the arsenals were both intact, just the way he'd built them in between the two outer walls. The entrance paths were full of earth, but Robin had joined him now, and they managed to clear them and entered. As Merlin feared, any remnants of gunpowder had gone, but he noticed when they had arrived at the town that the dung heaps that he had initiated were still there all these years later.

They were not the same ones, of course, as Camelot would have gone on for many years after his time and new ones been installed. The dung had washed away almost, but there were still the deposits of saltpeter underneath; in fact, after all these years, they were ripe.

Robin had rejoined them now, and they removed the top layers of the dung heaps and collected up the saltpeter. They had brought a barrel with them, and they filled it with much more saltpeter than Merlin had expected.

Merlin explained that the saltpeter had to be mixed with sulfur and charcoal to form gunpowder. He walked past the site of his old house, and he had a few more tears. It was completely flat now, and nature had taken over. He knelt on the ground and kissed it. He did not know why, but it helped him to do that.

He wondered what had happened to Arthur's sword Excalibur, so Merlin and Tuck reentered the town and went to the castle keep while Robin and Marion walked around the town. Marion didn't mention what had just happened.

The keep was crumbling as well but was in better condition than most of the other buildings. They entered, and there were no tapestries hanging now. The building looked sad, and so was Merlin. His face was long and drawn.

Merlin couldn't believe what had happened. It seemed a different life, which he decided it was, a life that had gone and could not return. He had been thinking to ask Viviane to move him back to Arthur's day, to before Gwen had died. That way, he could move her away from the danger.

Just inside the castle, on a chair, was a young man of about twenty. He was dressed as a farmer. He looked bored and was glad to see anyone. He got off his chair and stretched his legs.

He must have been here for some time, thought Merlin. *I wonder why.* He said, "Hello. You look tired."

"I am. I've been here three hours. Time goes so slowly," the young man said.

"What are you doing in Camelot? There is no one else here."

"My name is Cedric; I am one of the guardians of the sword Excalibur."

The words of Arthur came back to Merlin: "I will arrange for guards for Excalibur until your return, Merlin, after my death." Merlin was surprised that Arthur had remembered. These poor people had been guarding the sword for five hundred years. This was a very emotional day for Merlin; he was glad to have Tuck with him. Tuck noticed Merlin's distress again and held his arm to steady him; he had started swaying.

"Well, your duties are complete, Cedric. I am Merlin."

"You would be surprised how many people have said that over the last five hundred years. If you are genuine, you will know the password and the name of your wife and child," said Cedric.

"Yes, the password is 'milner.' My wife's name is Gwen, and my son is Aelfred," said Merlin.

Cedric was relieved his task was over. "Oh, thank God. My village's duty is over, then."

Merlin asked how all this had been arranged. Cedric replied, "My village is about a mile to the east. King Arthur charged our chief at the time to guard the sword and to maintain the church and your family's graves. The village young people have been doing that in six-hour shifts ever since. The gravestones of your wife and son are renewed every fifty years. That is why they are newer than the rest."

Merlin was staggered, but Tuck did not look surprised, which was noticed by Merlin, who gave him a strange look.

Cedric took them over to a wooden door that had not been there in Merlin's day. He pushed it open.

Inside it was a small room, no bigger than a cupboard really, but on the floor, carved out of the stone, it read: "Here lived King Arthur, the first King of All England." No date was written. Merlin wondered why not, but he said a prayer for his brother. In the wall above the stone was another small wooden door in perfect condition, as though it had been built yesterday.

Merlin opened the door. Inside was a box. He took the box out and opened it. Inside, wrapped in an oilskin, was a sheet of parchment. It was still intact, but he unrolled it very carefully. The writing was just legible. It said:

Written by Scribe Matthew on the
instructions of King Cheadda

To Merlin on your return to our lands. My father told me all about you and how you saved our lands from the settlers.

After you left, my father heeded your advice. The settlers were very much weakened by their attack on us. They had lost most of their fighting men, including their king, and Father went with the full army and the two cannons to what was left of the settlers at their town of Winchester. After the town had been bombarded with the cannons for a day, they surrendered without a fight, which pleased Father as he did not like killing people.

Any settler who gave allegiance to my father could stay. If they didn't, then they were exiled. Most stayed, and our realm was then extended as far as London. On his return to Camelot, my father immediately ordered two more cannons to be made from our mines in Cornwall.

My father believed you were a wizard and would one day return. He asked me to write this letter to you for your return if we ever left Camelot. The country will always remember you for bringing the inventions you did that helped to unite many of the kingdoms. Unfortunately, the alchemists couldn't remember the procedure for making what you called electricity, so that has been forgotten for future generations, but we still produce salt and gunpowder. My father lived for another forty years after you left but has passed on now.

The day before he died, he knew the end was coming and asked his servants to carry him down to the lake and leave him there alone. They collected him later in the day. I spoke with him that evening, and he had become very peaceful in his mind. He said he had seen the Lady of the Lake, Viviane, and she had spoken with him, but he didn't tell me what she said, and he died peacefully that night. Mother had died ten years earlier. I think the Lady of the Lake, Viviane, had something to do with you, but who am I to know these things?

I am king now, and I will endeavor to carry on as he instructed me. I had always discussed with Father about moving the capital to London now that our country had progressed and grown so much after you left. He always said I should not move to London until after he had gone as he was waiting for you, his brother, to return. I carried out his wishes, but we are now all moving to a small village to the west of London called Windsor. I intend to build a new town there. It is an ideal spot on a river called Thames, which we will build a castle alongside. The four cannons have been given new steel wheels and will go with us. The river at Windsor goes into

London, giving us easy transport there. I will, of course, take with me the bust of my father that you made, and it will be given pride of place.

My father was cremated after his death. A boat and pyre were made. The round table you made for him was too large to move to London, and there are now too many knights to sit around it. I thought it was fitting that it should be cut up and used for the pyre. He was placed on top, there was a ceremony at the salt flats site that you prepared, and the pyre was lit. The boat was pushed out to sea. It burned for two hours and then sank into the sea very gracefully. It was very touching, just the way he wanted.

The sword Excalibur you gave him is in the case behind this box, and he asked that Camelot be left as a shrine to him and you. He arranged to have guards to protect the sword as he knew you would return one day, and on his deathbed, he told me to tell you that he had erected the stones on Gwen's and Aelfred's graves. These, too, will be renewed as necessary, as he promised, and hence this letter. Please replace the letter when you leave for future generations, but you are free to do what you consider appropriate with the sword.

Signed with an X,
King Cheadda

There was a large X at the bottom of the letter. Tears were now streaming down Merlin's face, and he knew he had to pull himself out of this depression. He rolled up the letter and put it back in the box for future generations as requested. He thought that the sword was part of England's heritage and must be handed over to the present king for safekeeping.

Merlin wanted the sword to form part of England's crown jewels, so he removed it from its hiding place. It was in perfect condition after all these years, but then it was made of gold and jewels. He held the hilt, raising it in the air, thinking that Arthur had held the hilt just the same. He loved his brother.

Merlin felt a hand on his shoulder; he had forgotten about Tuck in his deepest thoughts. Viviane was standing behind them both, admiring the sword that she had charged with energy all those years ago.

"Take strength in the letter, Merlin," said Tuck. "You were right. The sermon last Sunday was directed at you. You must be out of your mind wondering what it is all about. My only advice to you is what I said. Just carry on. Things will all be clear eventually, and you have undoubtedly formed the future of England already. How many men can say that in their lifetime?"

Merlin then realized that Tuck had been here before and read the letter, which explained a lot. He took great comfort in his friendship with Tuck; he was now sure that Viviane had sent Tuck to him to help him get through these tough times.

Merlin sealed up the opening with stones as the original wooden door had rotted away. He turned to Tuck and said, "You knew all of this, didn't you?"

"Yes, my son. I was here as a young man during my studies at Sarum School. I specialized in history, which brought me here many times. I was learning about all the things you gave Arthur. I found the gunpowder interesting; it was ingenious the way you made saltpeter. I met the guardians every time and got very friendly with them, and they trusted me. Being an impetuous lad of twenty, I wanted to see Excalibur. Of course, I wouldn't have touched it.

"I arranged to be here when they were changing guards, and the two of them went outside for a brief time. I took the opportunity to enter the cupboard. Finding the letter, I read it and put it back. I did not get a chance to see the sword before they came back. I can see it now, though; it's magnificent.

"Reading the letter made me decide to take up the cloth. I realized you are a time traveler, and if Arthur knew you'd be back, then I did too. I knew then that you would need my help if I were still alive at that time. I was a significant scholar in those days, but I gave it up because I now had a calling. My advantage was that I had the choice. You didn't."

Before they left, Merlin said to Cedric, "I would like to come back to your village to see your leader. Will you please wait for us? We will drive you back."

"Certainly," said Cedric, thinking, *That will save me a walk.*

Robin and Marion had rejoined the two of them again and said, "There are salt flats over at the coast."

Merlin said, "Yes, can we go and see them."

It was a short ride in the wagon. Merlin stood at the beach, surveying what was in front of him. The kilns were gone, just a pile of rubble on the ground, affected by many a high tide at various times over the last five hundred years.

The salt flats, although visible, were of no use now. Nature had taken over and was leveling the ground back to the beach. He looked to the sea, wondering at what point the pyre boat had been released. He said another quiet prayer to himself and bowed his head, saying, "Goodbye, brother. I love you." Tears were running down his face, and Marion comforted Merlin again.

Merlin said, "Just one more spot I must see, the lake."

They all walked down to the lake, which meant nothing to Robin; Tuck guessed this was the spot where Viviane had appeared to Merlin.

The area had completely changed now. The edges of the lake were maintained in Arthur's day, but not now; nature had taken over. The surroundings were now heavily wooded. Merlin could see the river went off in the same manner, but the area looked completely different. He looked deeply into the water, and he willed Viviane to reappear. Nothing happened, though. What did he expect? He said, "I think I've seen enough. Can we head back to Nottingham now, please?"

Tuck said, "Yes, let's do that." Robin was completely confused by all that was happening, but he just went along with everything. Marion was beginning to guess. As they left Camelot, they picked up Cedric, and he directed them to his village. He led them to the village elder's house, knocked, and introduced Merlin to the elder, who immediately bowed.

"There is no need to bow to me, sir," said Merlin.

"Oh, yes, there is, Merlin. You are the brother of King Arthur. That makes you royalty," said the elder.

"I wanted to thank you on behalf of my brother and myself for what your village has done over the years. You have done an incredible task, but it's over now. I think we should let the graves decay on their own in the future."

"I will do whatever you say, sir, and may I say God bless you in your tasks," said the elder. It seemed to Merlin that everyone knew his tasks except him!

They left the village, and on the way back to Nottingham, Merlin said to Tuck, "I think that has cleared my mind somewhat. Camelot is five hundred years old, and I believe it should be left in peace now to fall back into nature. I do not intend to return here anymore."

"I think that is very wise," said Tuck. "There is no question that you have developed from all these experiences. It is time for you to move on in your life once we have sorted out the Robin Hood legend."

Viviane was pleased to hear that, too, although she knew that would not be the case.

"By the way, have you ever heard of the bust of King Arthur?" Merlin asked Tuck.

"To be honest, no, I haven't. If King Cheadda set up a court at Windsor, that's interesting because William the Conquer built a castle at Windsor. William may have put his castle in the same position as the previous one. That's common for kings. In that case, the bust might still be in the king's treasury. If we get the opportunity, we should speak with King Richard."

"I'll certainly do that if I can."

It was a slow journey pulling the wagon back to Nottingham. Tuck was driving, and he avoided Stonehenge this time, but he called in at Sarum. He knew the bishop and a teacher here from his school days and wanted to speak with them. Merlin had been here in the year 600 and enjoyed looking around again to see how it had changed in those five hundred years.

Merlin decided it hadn't grown much; it was clearly still very busy, although the new town of Salisbury nearby was taking precedence. Tuck went to his meeting with the bishop and the teacher, who was now in his eighties. He was a single man. He had been engaged to be married when he was twenty years old to a very attractive lady. Sadly, she'd caught the plague in one of its appearances, which had happened every twenty years or so. There'd been no cure, and she'd died a horrible death. He'd never gotten involved with a lady after that.

He remembered Tuck well. It was he who had tried to get Tuck to change his mind about leaving school and going into the church. "Was it the right decision, Tuck?"

"Oh, yes, sir. I have just found my vocation has been proven right." Tuck told him the story of Merlin. He still called the old teacher "sir" out of respect.

The teacher intently listened to Tuck's story of Merlin. They were both amazed, and Tuck said him, "Do you see now why I had to leave school at that time and wait for Merlin to return? He needed my solace, although, at the time, I had no idea what my task would be, or indeed, whether he would return in my lifetime."

"That applies to most of us, Tuck. God bless you. I don't suppose I will see you again, but thank you for coming to me and telling me all this. I can die in peace now," said the old teacher.

Robin, Tuck, Marion, and Merlin met up to continue the trip back to Nottingham. Tuck said to Merlin, "I did find out from the bishop that they intended to move the church diocese to the new town of Salisbury and build a new cathedral, which would have the largest spire in England, but as always, money is a problem, so the building has been put off for the time being."

After three days, they were back home in the forest. As they dropped off Tuck at the priory, Merlin said to Robin, "Do you mind if I go in with Tuck for a minute? I need to speak with him." Robin said he would wait outside with Marion.

Merlin went in with Tuck and said, "Can I give you Excalibur for safekeeping? I will give it to King Richard as soon as we are able for him to add it to the crown jewels."

"That's fine," said Tuck. "Safer with me than in the forest!"

"I also wanted to thank you for your company on that trip; it was so traumatic for me. I can't really accept that I was with Arthur only a few months ago. It was devastating just being near Gwen. will I ever get over that?"

"I am sure you will. You are a young man, and time is a great healer. Don't rush; just let it happen. I am so pleased to have been able to go with you. I know now that my vocation in life is to see you through this time. I realize the angel I saw was Viviane. God bless you, Merlin."

Merlin left and went back to Robin. Marion stayed with Tuck, and he told her the rest of Merlin's story. He impressed upon her that it was better that they didn't discuss these matters in public.

When they got to their camp, Robin told his men what had happened. The saltpeter that they brought back was mixed with the other two ingredients, charcoal and sulfur, both of which were readily available. Merlin gave a demonstration of its power without wasting too much, and Robin was very impressed, just like Arthur had been. Merlin set up piles of dung to make more saltpeter for the future.

Chapter Twenty-Five

The sheriff was livid. His men had allowed Robin Hood to steal all the taxes, although he had no proof. No one else would have the nerve or the capability of doing so, and the sheriff was above the law anyway and didn't need proof. *I must rid myself of this pestilence*, he thought.

His lieutenant said, "We have the archery contest coming up soon. We all know that Robin Hood is the best shot in the area. He'll be so confident. His ego is a different league. He will attend, and if we lay a trap for him, we'll have him in our grips."

The sheriff thought about it carefully. "Okay, perhaps you are worth your keep. We'll use the green at the far side of town, away from the castle, where the summer fair is held. There are some old caves up there that we can put our soldiers in to surprise him. Yes, I like it more and more."

So, the contest was set up, and posters were put up around town proclaiming a summer fair and archery competition, not that many people could read, but word always spread like wildfire, and gossip was rife. As anticipated by the sheriff,

Robin's ego would not let him turn down the opportunity of the contest, although he rightly guessed it would be a trap.

Robin called a meeting of his followers. Merlin had heard of this contest in the twenty-first century, although he didn't know the outcome, and neither could he say. Robin said, "It is bound to be a trap. We are well aware of the green. There are a lot of caves around to hide an army. We could use that to our advantage. We have gunpowder, and the sheriff doesn't. I want to make a double attack. Half of us will be at the contest. The other half will raid the castle for the taxes that the sheriff has kept back, which we will then redistribute back to the farmers. With such a large force at the contest, the castle will be left undefended except by a few."

Everyone thought that was a great plan. Robin would be in the competition, so he designated Merlin to lead the attack at the green, as he was familiar with this gunpowder, while John would lead the attack on the castle.

Robin had been away for some time at Camelot with Marion. Now that he had been back for several days, he was missing her. He felt she was having an effect on him; he was now very careful only to attack the richer passersby on the road to London. He had even started to give money away to the poor.

Today, he was on his way to see Marion. She was always at home these days. Her father was now becoming incapacitated, so she had to look after him as well as the estate. When Robin arrived, she was pleased to see him, and she took him to see her father, who was grateful for the help Robin had given them those weeks ago.

He said to Robin, "I'm getting old now. I don't think I've got long to live. I'm worried about Marion. She needs a good man to look after her."

"Don't be silly, Father. I'll be fine," Marion said, embarrassed. "Anyway, you've got many years yet."

Robin and Marion spent the rest of the day chatting about what they had both been doing in Camelot.

"Marion, if I can be of any help to you in the running of the estate now that it is too much for your father, then please let me know. There's no charge," said Robin.

"That's not like the Robin Hood I have heard of," Marion said as a joke.

"I think you're right; I don't know what is happening to me."

Marion told Robin that the sheriff was still pestering her to marry him and she was holding him at bay. She added, "I don't think Dad would worry who I married as long as I married someone."

"How about me?"

"How about that?" she said with a glint in her eye.

That gave Robin some hope. Even as a child, he'd always wanted to marry Marion. He had been involved with other women at times, but nothing serious. Robin told Marion that he would enter the archery contest and that he had a plan that would upset the sheriff.

"Don't tell me what it is. Then I can't say anything accidentally," said Marion.

At the end of the day, they kissed in an embrace that took the breath away from them both. Robin rode back to the camp feeling elated.

The next few days, they surveyed the green in detail where the archery contest was to be held. Behind the green was a small wood. Beyond that were two caves going deep into the hillside. No one knew how they were formed, but they were ideal for hiding an army. Robin had to admit that.

"The problem is always in setting off the explosion. You need a wick of some kind," said Merlin. In his last life, he'd used a flaming arrow, and that was a real possibility here, especially as these men were expert archers. He wondered whether he could come up with a fuse that would work and be easier to use. To fire an arrow on the spot was hit and miss; a fuse would be better.

He explained his idea to Robin, who said, "Good luck with that, but if it doesn't work, we can resort to the lighted arrow." Merlin spent the next week preparing several types of wicks soaked in oil plus some gunpowder. By the end of the week, he had produced a wick that would burn for two minutes before setting off the explosion. He was content with that, and Robin approved the demonstration.

He had also prepared a gunpowder paste and wick for Little John to use at the castle. Merlin explained to John that he must press the paste into the lock and surrounding area on the safe and then cover that with clay to seal it in. He would then have two minutes to leave the area once he lit the wick.

They decided that they needed more gunpowder than they had, so Robin and Merlin went to see an alchemist that Robin knew of in a local village, someone who would keep quiet about the purchase. They asked him whether he had any potassium nitrate, also known as saltpeter. He said, "I do. It's a new ingredient that is just coming in from Europe, where it has been found to occur naturally." Merlin was delighted because this would be of a better quality than what he had, and they purchased all the alchemist had. He also realized he didn't need his dung heaps anymore, and he thought the trip to Camelot had not been necessary – or had it. It at least allowed Merlin to see Camelot again and help his mind to cope with the past.

Merlin said, "We have two options, either we bury the explosives in the ground and explode them once the soldiers are in the cave, which would trap them inside, or we blow them up as they leave."

"Why not do both?" said Robin

"We could, but some would get out with bad timing."

"Well, let's make the gunpowder and see how much we have."

So, for the next week, they mixed the gunpowder up and made bombs out of old, small whiskey barrels. The week before the contest, excitement was growing in the camp. Robin gambled on the sheriff using the caves; there were no straightforward alternatives. Robin, Merlin, and three men went to the caves at dusk a few days before the contest. The area was in the countryside, and no one lived nearby; it was deserted.

They dug four holes at the spots Merlin chose at the entrance to each cave and buried a bomb in each. Merlin had to guess at the size of the bomb, but he had allowed for more powder than he thought necessary just to make sure.

Merlin didn't want to fix the wicks until the day before the contest in case they became dislodged. Lighting them was still a problem to be resolved. They stood back and admired their work. When they got back to camp, they knew they had to come up with the answer of how to light the fuse. Merlin was concerned about firing a lighted arrow, as seeing it fly would alert the troops too quickly.

Merlin thought that the area of the caves would be densely populated on the day. It should be possible for him, who was not known to the sheriff or his soldiers, to stroll around with a lighted taper. They settled on that, and the day before the contest, Merlin went back to insert his wicks into the four bombs.

"Why don't you wear one of the soldier's uniforms tomorrow, the day of the contest?" Robin said to Merlin. "That way, you can merge into the crowd, especially as there will be soldiers around. They won't suspect you. They have many soldiers coming and going all the time, so a stranger will not be noticed."

"Good idea," said Merlin, and he went over to the priory, saw Tuck, and asked him for a uniform. He collected it and took it back to camp.

The next day, John set off for the castle with half the men. He left early so that he was at the edge of town shortly after daybreak. He and his men sank into the background. Two troops of ten soldiers left the castle, heading in the direction of the contest green. John smiled; everything was going to plan. An hour before the competition, the sheriff and his entourage left the castle, traveling in that direction as well.

In the meantime, Merlin had put on his uniform. It was gray with green flashes, and he felt very proud; he had never worn a uniform before. He set off for the green, and when he arrived, it was already full of stalls.

At the green, there were stalls selling household goods, food, and homemade utensils, pots, and pans, really everything you would expect at any summer fair. Then there were the stalls that had games. Hoopla was familiar, throwing the hoop over a gift on a table; if it landed flat on the table, you won the gift.

There was an early form of a coconut shy. No coconuts, though, but they used large apples instead, which smashed quickly, but that added to the fun. There were acrobats, jugglers, and tumblers; they were always popular. Minstrels sang of the exploits of a King Arthur.

Darts were the rage, using a wood board with chalk markings. The site was very colorful, with flags, banners, and bunting all around the stalls and on the edge of the trees. *This is just like the jousting field in Arthur's day*, thought Merlin. There were stalls with cattle and sheep in grids, geese in another, and even swans.

Merlin had walked right around the site, and the soldiers were just beginning to arrive, entering the caves. Robin, too, had arrived early and watched the soldiers deployed, but he was out of sight. At midafternoon, there was now a large crowd of people to watch the archery contest. These events were well attended. There was no other excitement in middle age England.

The crowd was moved back, and three large bullseye targets were erected at the end of the field. The targets consisted of a three-foot diameter disc of straw covered with the bullseye painted on an animal skin fixed to straw. They placed the targets two hundred feet from the shooting line. Merlin knew from his past that was an easy distance for a good archer.

An awning had been erected for the sheriff to sit under. He had just arrived to watch the contest, and he took the cheers, or was it boos, from the crowd, probably a mixture of the two. Merlin was a little surprised to see Marion sitting under the awning with the sheriff. So too was Robin, but he took it in his stride. He knew that the sheriff wanted to marry Marion, but he was feeling jealous. He was aware that Marion had to play along with the sheriff. Otherwise, he could make life difficult for her. That made Robin more determined to get revenge.

The sheriff raised the flag to start the festivity in his usual brash manner. Robin was keeping back at this stage, and the sheriff began to wonder whether Robin had taken the bait. The first three rounds saw twenty of the contenders leave.

There was still ten left, which was whittled down to four. Robin suddenly appeared, unannounced, out of the audience. The sheriff had never seen him face to face and could not do so now because Robin had his hood up. The sheriff guessed this had to be Robin Hood; he could sense it. "Now I'll have him," he whispered to himself.

Merlin was already mingling around the entrance to the caves. He knew exactly where the bombs were, and there were a lot of people around. Merlin guessed some were sheriff's men not in uniform. He discretely held a lighted taper in his hand, and he waited for Robin's signal.

Merlin was surprised, however, that most of the soldiers were saluting him as they passed. He wondered why, but then it dawned on him: he had chosen a captain's uniform. "Oh, shit," he said. Now he was just drawing attention to himself. There was nothing he could do at this late stage other than bluff it out and salute back. Most of the soldiers were now in the caves, which took the pressure off.

The contest was now down to Robin and one other for the final shoot-off. Although Robin couldn't see the sheriff directly, he knew the sheriff would wait until the last shot. Robin's opponent shot first, and his last arrow and hit the bullseye in the center. Robin knew that the only way he could win was to split his opponent's arrow. Otherwise, by ancient rules of archery, his opponent would automatically win as he had shot first.

Robin took a deep breath. This had to be accurate. He took aim. He also knew that the moment he shot the arrow would be the time that the sheriff would act and call in his men from the caves. He shot his arrow and watched it fly, getting nearer to the target, and then he heard the split. He had broken his opponent's arrow in two and won the contest.

Robin immediately reloaded an arrow and fired it up high over towards the caves, which was the signal for Merlin to light the fuses.

Merlin, in his captain's uniform now, marched over to where he needed to be and lit all four fuses without anyone taking any notice. No one knew what a fuse was for anyway. He quickly moved out of the way, taking cover. The sheriff had already sent off his lieutenant to get the troops from the cave. By the time he arrived, there were four enormous explosions, which brought down the hillside around the entrance to the caves.

At that stage in the confusion, Robin and his men sank into the background and the forest. Merlin joined them, and they could see people trying to dig out the men from inside the caves. The sheriff was once again livid that this outlaw had foiled his plan. He, too, was exiting the green; he didn't want to hang around with explosions going off or for Robin Hood to get him. He even left Marion; he was no gentleman. Merlin couldn't get his uniform off quickly enough. The general populous scampered away from the scene when the explosions went off, leaving the central green area clear. Robin went over to Marion, who was still sitting under the awning.

"Well, your boyfriend left you in a hurry," he said with a little sarcasm.

"Oh, please don't say that. You know I had to come with him. He's too powerful to say no to," Marion said, glad that Robin was showing jealousy. "Will you please take me home?"

Robin was glad to do that; he put her on the back of his horse, and she put her arms around his waist. She was glad to be able to bury her head in his back and hold him tight.

CHAPTER TWENTY-SIX

Back at **Nottingham Castle**, which was in the center of town on top of a steep, rocky hill, John had chosen the secret entrance at the back of the castle, up through the rock-face tunnels from the bottom of the hill. This entry had been used for a quick exit many times over the centuries. Today, it was to be used by Little John to gain access to the castle.

At the bottom of the hill was a house built of stone. It was unused, but it housed the entrance to the pathway up to the castle. John and ten men entered the building; at the back was a door. When opened, it led to a dark passage that had been hewn out of the cliff surface many years ago. It gradually wound its way up the hillside, and at the top was another door, which John carefully opened a small crack, just enough to peer in and listen. All was quiet on the other side.

John pushed the door open, and the men all entered the castle. Then the door was carefully closed so as to not give away how they had entered the castle. It was supposed to be a secret; at least, this sheriff knew nothing of it. The last sheriff didn't tell the new one about it as he was sacked. He had, in fact, said to himself at the time, "I hope someone comes up the tunnels and kills this sheriff."

Once inside, they could see the castle was almost free of soldiers; nearly all been had assigned to the archery contest. John worked his way up to the room where he knew the safe would be; he had been here twice in the past. Before he became an outlaw, he was a soldier for the previous sheriff. That sheriff was a good man, not like this one, and John was well trusted.

They arrived at the office, and he sensed there was someone inside. He couldn't hear talking, so he guessed there might only be one person. John turned the handle and kicked the door open to make a noise; that way, he would take the inhabitants by surprise. John had been right: there was only one person inside. He rushed forward with his knife in hand, grabbed the guard around the neck, and slashed his throat. The guard sank to the ground without a sound.

John pushed him aside and went to the safe. Merlin had given him the paste made of gunpowder stuck together with gum, along with the clay to place over it. It already had a wick attached. He pushed the paste into the lock and around the outside, covered it with the clay, and lit the wick. He then had to rush out and close the door before the explosion. It was a little excessive, but the lock smashed to pieces. John went back inside, leaving the other men to guard the outside. The blast would surely bring soldiers any minute. The door swung open, and he removed the bags of cash.

After three minutes, six soldiers came along the corridor. When faced with ten burly men with knives at the ready, they backed off. John came out carrying three bags of gold coins. They went out the same way they had entered. No one else was around, and they made sure the door to the tunnels closed properly.

Outside was John's man with the eleven horses. They got on and promptly rode off, just before the sheriff, who had left the green in a hurry, came around the corner. He had missed them, and John's crew were back in the forest within minutes.

When the sheriff entered the castle, he heard what had happened, and he had a fit; he slapped the man who told him and had him arrested. He fumed as he went into his office and found the money gone from the safe, his money now, not the kings!

He looked at the state of the safe and was amazed at what had happened to it. *How is that possible?* he thought. Later in the day, he learned that his soldiers at the contest had been dug out of the caves with only one loss of life. Did he care, though? No. All he cared about was his money.

He swore that he would lead an expedition into the forest to rid himself of Robin Hood. He sent an envoy to Prince John in London with another request for more soldiers to fight Robin Hood. "The man who stole your taxes," he told the prince in his letter. The prince was sympathetic, especially since his money was involved and this was the second request.

He needed the taxes for the release of King Richard, who had been captured by the Duke of Austria on his return to England after the Crusade, unless, of course, he siphoned it off first. John wanted to become king himself, and the Normans were ruthless leaders. They'd mostly killed off one another, which would be their downfall in the end.

Prince John sent a platoon of one hundred men to Nottingham. They had strict instructions that if the sheriff did not produce the goods, he must leave the country quickly before being executed. The sheriff took that threat seriously.

When Robin and John got back to their camp, there were grand celebrations. No men had been lost, and they had the money from the sheriff. They took the money to the priory and Friar Tuck to distribute it to those who had paid their taxes. In fact, they realized there was more money here than was due the farmers, so Robin said, "We'll keep that back and distribute it to the poor."

The farmers were over the moon, Robin's prestige had risen, and Merlin thought that his job must be nearly done. Merlin took the opportunity to bring his abacus calendar up to date. He realized that this was a much better device than he'd had before and went to Tuck to thank him once again, and he took the opportunity to spend the night at the priory, which had a comfortable bed.

Robin had at least one more job to do, and that was to rid the townspeople of this sheriff. Robin's scouts on the main road from London counted one hundred soldiers riding in procession along the way. They immediately went back to the camp to report.

When the soldiers arrived at Nottingham, they set up a campsite outside of town as their barracks. The town inside was too small to accommodate such a large extra number of soldiers. The captain reported to the sheriff, who said he was very glad to see them. He offered to put the captain up within the castle, but the captain declined, saying he would rather be with his men.

The next day, they met to draw up a plan. "The forest is very extensive, spreading from Leicester to Sheffield. It is dense in parts and not in others," the sheriff told the captain. "Robin Hood must be in one of the dense parts.

We would have found him without help had he been in the clearings." The truth was that he moved around frequently and sometimes was in the clearings. From now on, while the additional soldiers were in town, he would only inhabit the wooded parts.

So, a plan was formulated to divide the whole forest into a grid system and tackle each part and then move on. They started doing that from the north, just south of Sheffield and working down.

Robin had lone spies out to watch what was going on. It was easy for one man to be going around on his own; it didn't raise any eyebrows. They were stopped a few times and asked what they were doing. The soldiers did not know the district, so the spies were able to say anything. The scouts reported back to Robin on what the soldiers were doing. They had divided up the forest into ten-mile-square sections and were going through one at a time. It was working; anyone caught in the area was questioned. If there were more than six people together, they were interrogated more vigorously.

Robin said, "They will be here in about three days. We are going to have to act." In this case, Robin thought a tactical withdrawal was the safest option. They packed up all their belongings, making sure that there was no evidence of a camp, and they walked to the east, out of the forest, keeping in small numbers so as not to raise suspicion in the local inhabitants. They circled the soldiers to get behind them, where they had already checked. It was a game of cat and mouse.

The important thing for now was to keep away from such a large force of soldiers. By the end of the week, the soldiers and their captain were getting tired of this ineffective method of finding the enemy. The captain had guessed what Robin was doing, but his hands were tied. Another three days, and they had been through the entire forest in detail. They had found nothing that looked even remotely like a camp. He had to admit that they had been outsmarted.

"It's a hopeless task," he told the sheriff when he returned to Nottingham. "Guerrilla warfare is always impossible to deal with. You have tried a trap, and that didn't work either. My orders have just come through that my men need to go back to London. An attack is expected from rioters demonstrating against Prince John. We need to leave tomorrow." In the morning, the soldiers were seen leaving town, heading down the London Road.

Robin and his men cheered as they saw the soldiers leaving the forest that day. "Now we can get on with the issue of getting rid of the sheriff," said Robin. However, he sent spies to make sure the soldiers were leaving to go to London.

Robin planned to get reinforcements from other towns in the neighborhood. There were many villages where the men were fed up with the sheriff and prepared to form an army to oust him. Robin toured the district, calling for recruits for an army that would storm the castle from different sides. He came away with a list of two hundred men. Half of them would go north of town and camp in the forest and would be led by John. The other half would come to the south with him.

The sheriff had decided he wanted to be married. He preferred it to be Marion Howarth, but if that was not to be, he would choose someone else. He would give Marion one last chance. He rode over to the Howarth manor house and knocked on the door. He was allowed in this time as he was alone and it seemed he was coming in peace.

He was shown into the sitting room, where Lord Howarth was resting. The sheriff treated it very much like a business deal. He said, "Good morning, my lord."

Then, to Marion, he said, "If you marry me, you will be well looked after. I will leave your father and farm intact. Otherwise…"

Marion's father interrupted and said, "My daughter will marry whomever she chooses and not for any reason to do with me. Marion, I forbid you to marry anyone you don't want to. I have had my life. I served the late king and was proud to do so. You must do as your heart commands. We will take our chances in the world if necessary when King Richard returns. I am sure he will help us."

The sheriff took one look at Marion, and he could see the venom in her eyes. He then looked at her father and said, "So be it. I will leave now, but beware. It will be King John, not King Richard." He left without waiting for any response.

CHAPTER TWENTY-SEVEN

Two years ago, in another country far away, the King of England, Richard, son of King Henry II, was fighting a war against General Saladin the Saracen in Palestine for control of Jerusalem. It was the Third Crusade, with contingents from all over Europe fighting in the name of Christendom. Although all the Christian troops were fighting on the same side, they mainly fought their own battles under their own command. This was because they did not get on with each other and hurled insults at one another at every opportunity.

Although Richard was successful up to a point, he had won back many towns along the coast of the Mediterranean, but not the primary objective, Jerusalem.

It was, like always, a glaringly sunny morning under the heat of the sun that scorched the sand underfoot. There was no wind today; it was very still. Richard was astride his white horse, dressed in heavy fabric armor, his sword raised high in the air as he rode at the head of his three thousand troops, who were on foot and spread out to his left and right, three deep.

Opposing him were the forces of Saladin, at least five thousand men waving their swords in the air and screaming in the language of the Turks. The two armies moved forward toward each other. When they were four hundred feet apart, they stopped. It was all textbook stuff.

Richard turned to his troops and said, "We have to destroy the enemy this day. God is on our side; the nonbeliever must be annihilated. We will be victorious today, and then it is on to Jerusalem. God be with you all."

Saladin was no doubt saying the same to his troops, except they already had control of Jerusalem. Both leaders turned towards the opposition and shouted, "Attack!" in their respective languages. All the troops moved toward each other and met in the middle with hand-to-hand fighting. Swords could be seen clashing against each other, and the sound was intense. Blood was spilling; soldiers were dying on both sides. The carnage went on for two hours until the loss of men on both sides was so great that Richard called his troops back. Strangely, Saladin's men didn't follow; if they had, they would have finished the job off properly, but maybe they had had enough too. Richard said to his aide, "Jerusalem is not going to be ours today."

At the end of the day's fighting, Richard was getting tired of this mission; he had lost men through the battle and disease, which had been a real problem. He had fought here for three years now and needed a break. Many soldiers had been replaced by new recruits, noblemen coming out from all over his realm of England, Normandy, and Aquitaine. It was the thing to do; the first son was the heir, and the second would go to the church. Now that the church was at war, that meant the second son would fight in the Crusade. The truth of life never changed.

The new recruits coming out from England were advising King Richard of the situation back home, that his brother John was taking more and more control. Apparently, he was building up to take over the throne by any means. John was hoping that Richard would be killed in the battle.

Although Richard had left reliable people in place to run England on his behalf, John was sacking them, or perhaps killing them, and then putting in his own people to replace them, people he had control over.

Effectively, he was taking over the throne in Richard's absence, and possession was nine-tenths of the law, particularly when the king might be killed in battle, as so many were. That was the prognosis for English kings.

This distressed Richard. He knew that it was only his mother, Queen Eleanor, who would safeguard things. He couldn't leave everything to her, although she was probably one of the most powerful women that English history had ever known.

Richard and Saladin had come to something of an impasse in the fighting. Richard had gained a strip of land along the coast of the Mediterranean Sea but not his prize of Jerusalem. He decided to have a meeting with Saladin and propose a truce. At Saladin's tent, under a white flag, they met and signed a treaty for a three-year truce. That gave Richard time to go back home and resolve matters before coming back and resuming fighting again.

Things were very civilized in those days, so it seemed: access to Jerusalem was given to any pilgrims wanting to go to worship. "I wonder why Saladin was so cooperative," was said many times then and since.

With the war going on for many years in the region, towns were set up along the coast, and ports were built for supplies to be brought in from Europe. There was very little food in the Palestine area, which was basically a desert. Everything needed to be shipped in.

At the end of 1192, King Richard, his batmen, and five of his officers set off from Accra on the Mediterranean Sea, heading west towards Italy. They couldn't sail the direct way home, through the Straits of Gibraltar, because navigation was not good enough for such a small ship at that time. He had to choose a route landing in modern-day Italy, a hostile country to Richard then. Italy was split up into many smaller kingdoms in those days.

They had found an old sailor whose boat they had hired for the trip; it was a vessel about fifty feet long with a single sail and places for ten rowers, five on each side. The boat was of the Greek trireme type; it had the old seafaring captain dressed in his uniform of white blazer, navy-blue pants, and his captain's cap. He had the customary bushy white beard.

He assured Richard that the sea would be calm and the weather perfect for this time of the year. He said he knew the weather like the back of his hand.

They set off one morning at nine o'clock, and the sea was calm, as it was for several days afterward. The captain had agreed that it would be comfortable if they sailed from island to island each day and stayed on land overnight. That way, they could take on supplies as well at each island. For the next five days, they sailed to Cyprus, Rhodes, Crete, and Zante.

Then they headed up the Adriatic Sea, and they spent two days at Corfu to rest for the last part of the journey and to take on extra supplies. This would be the last stop before their final destination near Venice. Richard was concerned at having to go that way as Venice was hostile to him.

They set off after the rest, heading northwest, but after three hours, the weather was starting to close in, the sky was clouding over, turning gray, and the wind was getting up. The captain left the sail up for the time being, and the rowers were steadying the boat on the course the captain wanted, which Richard thought was just the direction of the wind. The wind built up more, nearing gale force now, and the captain took down the sail. They were just relying on the oarsmen to keep the boat going in the right direction; luckily, it was a northwest wind.

They were now on the open seas, and there were no islands in that region. It was been unlikely that they could have made it into a port anyway. They would have been smashed on the rocks; they had to wait the storm out as best they could, not that anyone got much sleep. The sea was rough now; six-foot waves were lashing the boat, coming over the bow and sides. The sailors were bailing out the water as fast as possible. They were used to these seas and were not affected by seasickness, unlike Richard and his men, who were suffering badly and heaving over the side for hours. No one was eating.

After two days of this ordeal, the captain said, "We are getting over the worst. The wind is slowing down somewhat." That didn't help Richard and his party, though; they were still ill. At least they were heading in the direction of land, somewhere around Venice; they had no chance of steering in this raging storm. After another day, the rain had subsided, and the captain said they were west of Venice and should see land by tomorrow.

"How do you know that?" said Richard

"Because I have traveled this way many times."

The storm was abating now, and the wind had calmed down. The sea was still rough, though. The captain said, "It will be like that for several days now."

The next day, someone shouted, "Land ahoy!"

The passengers were so glad to see land. They were still sick, and they knew it would not clear until they reached shore. The boat could now be steered, and within two hours, it was bumping up the sandy beach where the captain had chosen to land. Richard had previously told him he must not go into a town as he feared for his life. Once at the beach, Richard and his party got off the boat. The captain had already been paid, so he set off in the boat again, having told Richard that Venice was to his left. He could see the conurbation in the distance.

Richard and his officers went to the grass behind the beach and just lay down. Although it was only late afternoon, they all fell asleep due to exhaustion and sickness. They did not wake up till the morning, when Richard told his officers that they must now split up to get back to England. Together, they would be too conspicuous; this was hostile country. It was agreed that Richard and his batman would head off to Venice first and the others would follow tomorrow.

The problem was that during the crusades, Richard had fallen out with many of the generals who came from the areas that he would now have to travel through, but he had no choice. The pope had decreed that anyone fighting the Crusade on the side of Christendom must be allowed home freely without encumbrance. Richard would not rely on that, though. The pope was one thing, but he would not be there to save him on the day.

Being a Norman, and due to his Viking ancestry, Richard was very feisty and had made many enemies. One of them was King Henry VI, the Holy Roman Emperor, not to be confused with the pope. Henry was also the king of Germany.

Having landed near Venice, Richard and his batman went there first, and the two visited a brothel. Unfortunately, through habit, his batman always called King Richard "sire," as would be expected. The king had told him during their travels back to England that he must not do so, but he could not get out of the habit, and once at the brothel, he called the king "sire."

This was picked up by soldiers of the duke of Austria, who were also at the brothel, and they then knew that this must be King Richard, who was known to be on his way back to England. Richard had made an enemy of the duke of Austria in the crusade. Three of the soldiers, knowing that their master would be pleased to capture Richard, got together and went upstairs with three girls as decoys.

The batman was sitting outside the room being used by Richard, on guard. As the soldiers got to him, they grabbed him and put a chloroform pad over his mouth. The batman was asleep in seconds, without a sound. The girls were paid off, and the batman was laid on the floor.

The three of them then burst into the room. Richard was in bed with a prostitute, and he, too, was chloroformed before he knew what had hit him. The batman was left where he was, but Richard was carried out of the house, laid in a cart, and driven off to the soldier's camp, where he was handed over to their master, the duke of Austria.

He was subsequently taken and held prisoner in the castle at Durnstein in Austria. Eventually, he was handed over to King Henry VI in Germany, where he was held prisoner in various castles. He ended up at Trifles Castle, near the border with Luxemburg, no doubt being moved around from time to time to stop any attempt at a raid by the English.

King Henry demanded a ransom of one hundred and fifty thousand marks. This was a staggering sum, but Richard's mother, Eleanor of Aquitaine, was a wealthy lady. She was the wife of the deceased King Henry II of England, Richard's father. She had vast wealth in Aquitaine and managed to raise the ransom in time, much to the annoyance of her other son, John, who had effectively assumed the throne in England in Richard's absence and liked it.

Eleanor was a member of the Ramnulfid dynasty of Aquitaine and southwestern France before marrying Henry II of England. It was a business marriage, as so many were with royalty. Henry II wanted more land in France. Although her husband was dead now, she still had considerable wealth and influence in Aquitaine.

She arranged for an envoy to go to Aquitaine, collect the money, and transport it on the very dangerous journey to meet the German contacts. Carrying such a vast sum of money, secrecy was essential. The envoy, by hook or crook, managed to get through to King Henry and pay the ransom.

Richard was released and started his long journey home. He dressed not as a king but as an ordinary traveler. He didn't want to be taken prisoner by anyone else on the way. These were still not friendly lands as he had to go through France, and Richard was also about to go to war with King Philip, king of France. These were dangerous days.

Richard eventually made his way to Calais in France by horseback. England had ruled Calais since the Norman Conquest. From there, he sailed across the English Channel to Dover.

During this time in Nottingham, Robin had talked with Merlin as to what they needed to do about the sheriff. They both knew that King Richard was out of the country somewhere in Europe. Merlin had heard at church – he went every Sunday now – that King Richard was on his way home from the Crusade but had been taken prisoner and held for ransom. Prince John was effectively in charge. Robin said, "I think we should appeal to John's mother, Queen Eleanor, in London for help getting rid of the sheriff."

Merlin agreed, saying, "I think so, but it would be better if I go as you would not be well received. I'm not sure that I will either, but it's worth a try." That was agreed, and the next day, Merlin set off for London. He was given safe escort through the forest by Robin's men. They then said goodbye, and it was a further three-day journey down to London.

Once at London, he went straight to the Tower on the Thames. The Tower had been built by William I after the conquest of England in 1066 to impress upon the locals that the Normans were here to stay and meant business. Everywhere the Normans built castles or churches, of which there were many, it was done to show their strength. The buildings were intended to stand for millennia, which they thought their power would last. The Tower was William's London home and palace.

Merlin went to the outside of the building; he was amazed at how grand it looked. Of course, he had been to it many times in the twenty-first century, but then it had been dwarfed by the other buildings. Here and now, though, being new, it overpowered everything.

He went to the main gate and asked the guards to see Queen Eleanor. The guards just laughed. "You must be joking. You think you can just turn up and ask to see the queen? I think not. Be on your way."

Merlin did not object. Withdrawal was the thing for the moment. He left and went to a local inn and spoke to the innkeeper; he knew that landlords knew everything. Merlin said, "I need to see Queen Eleanor. Is there any way you know how I could do that?"

"Yes, sir. She walks past here every day in the afternoon with her entourage. She should be going by within in the next hour. I take it you're an outsider. Once you've seen her, you might want to inspect the new bridge they're building further down the road. It will be unique, wide enough to have shops on both sides of it. It's only in the initial stages now, but you can see the size of it."

"Thank you very much, sir. Can I have a beer, please? I'll wait outside. I may well walk down to see the new bridge." Merlin did want to see that; he knew about the bridge, which would continue being used until the 1800s.

Merlin went outside with his beer and sat at the table and waited. During that time, he wrote a letter explaining the problems at Nottingham. Eventually, he saw the queen, and about ten men and ladies with her, coming down the road toward him. As she got near to him, he stepped out to speak with her. The queen did not speak much English, only French, unbeknown to Merlin. He said to her, "Ma'am, I have to talk to you about King Richard," at which point her guard jumped in front of her and held Merlin at bay.

The queen ignored him and moved on, but Merlin pushed the letter into the hand of a lady in waiting, who smiled at him and moved on.

Merlin found some cheap lodging. Before going there, he walked along the Thames and saw the new construction of the bridge. It wasn't so significant, being only twenty-six feet wide, but by the standards of the day, it was large. He knew the bridge would see amazing history over the years to come.

Merlin returned to Sherwood Forest the next morning and relayed his tale to Robin. He said, "I wasn't very successful, but I have left a letter for the king. I don't know whether he will receive it."

"Let's hope that works, then. Either way, you have done what you could. Thank you," said Robin.

That night, Merlin went to sleep at the priory. He almost had a private room there now; he was the only person using it. After his evening prayers, Friar Tuck went to see Merlin in his room. he said, "I've been thinking more about the abacus calendar. We need to get you a pouch for it if you are going to move around in time zones. It's important for you personally to know your age relative to yourself. Come back tomorrow night, and I'll work something out."

"Thanks. I do like sleeping here anyway. It's much better than camping!" said Merlin.

The next day, Tuck set about having a leather pouch made that the abacus would fit into tightly so that the balls did not move about when the abacus was transported. By the end of the day, Tuck was pleased with the result, and when he gave it to Merlin, he was delighted.

"That's just what it needs. Thanks, Tuck. You have been a godsend to me," said Merlin.

"A godsend indeed, Merlin. All those years ago, I knew I had a purpose in life, and you turned out to be it."

Merlin now had his calendar. He knew he was twenty years old on arrival with Arthur, and he'd spent five years with Arthur and, so far, two with Robin Hood. That made him twenty-seven. *I'll soon be an old man*, he thought.

Having landed at Dover, Richard rode to London. After such a long journey, he was very exhausted and somewhat relieved to be back home again safely. On arrival in London, he was acclaimed king again by all. Even John was forced to acquiesce, and Richard was, in fact, recrowned, the only English king ever to be crowned twice. He planned to return to Europe and fight more wars with the French this time and subsequently return to Jerusalem to finish the job with Saladin that he had started.

He took a month to sort out some of the mess his brother had made in his absence, the appointments he had made for favors. He heard of the situation at Nottingham, which was a paramount city. He was shown the letter that Merlin had left with the lady in waiting, and it concerned him deeply; he decided to visit Nottingham before heading back to France.

The king had been told that there was an outlaw in the region who lived in the Sherwood Forest with a band of highwaymen. Lately, he had transformed himself into a guardian angel who protected the weak and ordinary folk against the wrath of the sheriff. While he had stolen the taxes due to the king, Richard was sympathetic. He knew John had used taxes for his own benefit. However, he wasn't quite sure that the stories were true, and like all men of power, he was a skeptic.

That night, Richard went to bed early, having devoured a whole bottle of wine by himself. In the night, Viviane came to him in his slumber. Sitting at the end of his bed, she said, "Sire, there have been troubles in Nottingham while you have been away. There is much unrest in the district concerning the sheriff; you would be advised to go and see for yourself."

The king was half-asleep, in between the conscious and subconscious minds, but he was aware and able to speak. "And who might you be, madam?"

"I am Viviane, commonly known as the Lady of the Lake."

"Are you, now? That's King Arthur's time, isn't it? I thought that was all myth."

"Oh no, sire. Do I look like a myth? The stories are all true. Some have been exaggerated over time, but the essence is correct. I have placed Merlin in Nottingham; you may recall from the myth that he was at Camelot. He is trying to transform Robin Hood into a hero. He may need your help." With that, Viviane faded into oblivion.

By that time, Richard was completely awake, and he whispered to himself, "I'll have to investigate this."

None of the news of King Richard's return had gotten through to the outlying towns yet. There were many rumors, of course; they were plentiful every day. Robin was planning his attack on Nottingham Castle to oust the sheriff once and for all. He had no way of knowing that King Richard was back and was coming to Nottingham.

T̄he sheriff gave up on his plans to marry Marion; she wasn't going to change her mind, and he knew it. Marriage was difficult enough without starting it badly, so he turned his mind to his little black book with all the other candidates. He spent many hours thinking about each. He liked that one, but could he marry her? No. Would he like children with that one? Definitely not; they would look like the mother-in-law.

In the end, he settled on a girl named Lady Caroline Devon, daughter of Lord Devon. *Yes, she would be a good catch. Her father is lord of a castle in Sheffield. If I lose the job here, I can run the family estate*, he thought. *Yes. I like that.*

The sheriff knew Caroline quite well; they had met socially on several occasions. Romance had never been discussed, though, but now was the time. He sent a messenger to the castle in Sheffield, asking Caroline if she would meet with him on a personal matter. That was a general introduction then, and she knew it.

Caroline was a plain girl, twenty-five years old, but she did have a lovely smile that made her face beam. The sheriff knew she came from a good family; that was the most important thing. However, she was not attracted to men, and most men weren't attracted to her. She was, according to her father, now getting to the age where she needed to find a husband promptly. Although, on the face of it, they appeared to be rich, it was old wealth, and the money was beginning to run out.

Lord Devon would be happy to palm off his daughter on any unsuspecting gentleman, particularly if he had money. He was thinking of his old age as well. Wealth came from favors from the crown, usually from battles fought. That was how Lord Devon's ancestor had acquired his wealth, but the current lord was no fighter; he preferred tending his garden.

When Caroline received the invitation for a liaison from the sheriff of Nottingham, she was delighted, and so was her father. Caroline immediately sat down and wrote a note to the sheriff saying she would be happy to meet him with a view to discussing personal matters, as he'd put it. She added she was aware he couldn't leave his official post, so she would be pleased to come down to Nottingham Castle a week from today.

The messenger returned with the note to Nottingham. The sheriff, in turn, wrote a reply saying how much he relished the idea of Caroline staying at the castle and that he would prepare rooms for her and her maid. The note was sent back with the messenger, who was getting tired of riding back and forth to Sheffield, but it was his job.

In seven days' time, Caroline, with her small entourage and a large trunk full of clothes, arrived at Nottingham Castle. The sheriff was out on business that day, and the castle wardrobe keeper showed Caroline and her companion to their rooms. They were appreciative of the time to unpack and settle in before the sheriff returned.

For the next seven days, the sheriff and Caroline courted. They got on better than the sheriff had anticipated, which surprised and pleased him. By the eighth day, Caroline was wondering whether anything would come of this liaison. She hoped so. That evening over a quiet meal for the two of them, the sheriff proposed marriage to Caroline. She gleefully accepted, which made the sheriff think, *Is she too eager?*

The next day, the sheriff and Caroline rode to her father's castle in Sheffield. The weather was kind to them that day; it was sunny. It had been raining the last three days. The sheriff thought it was a good sign.

They went in to see Lord Devon, and with a glass of sherry wine, the sheriff asked Lord Devon for permission to marry his daughter. He was, of course, delighted at the news, which he had been waiting for every day last week, but being an experienced gentleman, he was careful not to be too overjoyed. He delved into the sheriff's prospects and wealth. The replies he received were, of course, all lies, but they suited Lord Devon.

By the end of lunch, Devon had given his permission. The sheriff said, "I realize you would like to have the wedding in your castle here, but being sheriff in such an important town as Nottingham, I request that it take place there."

Lord Devon was delighted to save all that cost, but he pretended to agree out of necessity and with sadness. Caroline's mother would have loved for her to be married in Sheffield, but she had passed five years ago.

That was it; a date was fixed seven days from today. The sheriff said he would arrange for a marquee to be erected on the green for the wedding breakfast, and the whole town would be invited. He added, "You will, of course, stay at the castle for the celebrations. The wedding will take place in the parish church of St Augustine on High Street."

The couple headed back to Nottingham to make all the arrangements. That evening, the town crier walked through the streets of Nottingham, stopping at his usual places. He shook his handbell, saying, "Oh yeah, oh yeah. 'Tis six o'clock, and all is well. Richard Wells, sheriff of this town, announces his marriage to Lady Caroline Devon next Monday at eleven o'clock at the parish church of St. Augustine on High Street, and afterward, a grand breakfast feast will be held for all the town at the green, where a marquee will be erected. God save the king. Oh yeah, oh yeah."

Word soon got around town; everyone loved a free feast, and the sheriff didn't give much away usually. Merlin had been in town and heard the arrangements. He headed back to Robin's camp, but on the way, he stopped at Marion's house. She was delighted to hear the good news that the sheriff was getting married. That meant he would not pester her anymore. Her father was well that day, and she said to him, "Do you mind if I head back with Merlin to see Robin?"

"No, not at all. Enjoy yourself. You don't get out enough. Come back tomorrow. I'll be fine tonight," said Lord Howarth.

They rode off to Robin's camp. Robin was also delighted to hear the news. *One fewer contender for Marion*, he thought. He wanted to hear all the plans for the feast, saying, "We all must go. Marion will, of course, have her own invitation. We can go as townsfolk."

"Very risky, Robin. You may be recognized. We don't want to interfere with our battle plans for the castle attack," said Merlin.

"Hmm," said Robin, in thought. "I know. I'll grow a beard; seven days will do the trick." They all laughed but agreed it might work.

The campfire was dying down now; time to go to sleep. Marion looked up at Robin. He got up and held her hand, leading her to a quiet corner just outside of camp. He made a bed of blankets, and as they laid down and looked into each other's eyes, a feeling of wellness erupted over them. They made tender love that night, all night.

Morning comes early in the summer months as the sun rises early. Robin rode home with Marion, and they kissed tenderly before he left. Pinned to the front door was an invitation to the sheriff's wedding. Robin said, "See you there."

Merlin had gone into Nottingham. No one knew him there, so he was able to walk around unnoticed. He went to the green and saw that the marquee had been erected. It would hold at least one thousand people; it was huge. The top table was installed, and various tables were dotted around.

Merlin spoke to a workman, who told him the top table would seat the town dignitaries and family of the bride. The groom didn't have any family. The townsfolk would stand around and use the tables as a buffet. Merlin was impressed.

He continued, going into town for the next few days to see the progress. Each day, more and more bunting was being erected in the streets. Flags were flying the Cross of St. George, the red and white flag of England. The marquee was now fully laden with silverware, and oil lamps were on each table for decoration. A bar had been set up to serve wine and beer.

Tomorrow was the big day, and all was arranged. Robin had grown his beard, as had many of his men. Merlin looked at Robin and laughed, saying, "Marion won't recognize you now." He had a goatee.

The next morning, Marion and her father went to the Church of St. Augustine half an hour before the wedding. The church was full of the invited guests. At eleven o'clock, the bride and groom arrived on a brightly decorated carriage, and the marriage took place. All went well. Outside was a line of carriages to take the invited guests to the green.

The service was short, and by midday, all the guests were in the marquee and had drinks in their hands. Merlin, Robin, and his men all arrived separately so as not to draw attention, and they mingled with the crowd. Marion was seated at the top table with her father, and Robin gave her a wave, which she discretely returned.

In walked the sheriff and his new bride, and everyone seated stood up and clapped the couple to their seats. For today, at least, the town was prepared to celebrate with him. The townspeople always hoped a good man might escape from him, but Robin knew better. After the speeches and toasts, everyone started to enjoy themselves. Robin was now with Marion and her father; they all seemed to get on well. Lord Howarth wanted Marion to be settled down before he died. He knew that time was fast approaching.

Merlin looked around the tent, taking it all in. The townsfolk were enjoying the free drinks and dancing to the band. He noticed there was one stranger who didn't look as though he fit in with the locals. He was a tall man, very well dressed and dignified, and he seemed to be on his own, walking from party to party, chatting casually but informally. After half an hour, the stranger left the marquee; Merlin followed him, curious as to who he was. The stranger walked over to the horse corral, and he picked up his horse, a large white stallion of at least eighteen hands, and rode off.

Merlin went back to the marquee. The drinking was getting out of hand in some circles; when it's free, people will always drink too much. The locals loved dancing, and some were tiring from that and the drink. One couple went back to the table after a dance, somewhat tipsy. Now every table had a lighted oil lamp on it. Unfortunately, one couple knocked into a table as they danced, and the lamp fell over. The burning oil spilled out over the tablecloth, which immediately caught fire. Flames were leaping up five feet into the air within no time.

Panic set in with the guests, who were packed into the marquee. Everyone stampeded toward the exits. In doing so, other lamps were knocked over, and soon, the whole tent was ablaze. Everyone on the top table had evacuated behind them and were safe. Merlin rushed over against the crowd to get to the top table. He pulled off a large tablecloth. Robin had seen Merlin and followed him. He, too, pulled off a tablecloth, although he wasn't sure why.

They both left the tent from the rear and came around the front to where the clothes of several people had caught fire. Merlin spread his tablecloth out, indicating to Robin to follow suit. Merlin made the flaming people lie down, and he rolled them up in the cloth. That extinguished the flames. Robin did the same, and within moments, they each had saved ten people who would otherwise surely have burned to death. Passersby also threw water over the burned people to cool them down, as well as over the marquee, or what was left of it.

Sadly, though, not everyone was saved. The fire very quickly burned out, and once the tent had gone, ten badly burned bodies were left in the center. Robin went to Merlin and said, "That was a neat trick you just played. What was it all about?"

"Well, fire needs oxygen, or air, to burn. If you cut off the supply of air, you extinguish the flames," said Merlin.

"I'll remember that one. It can be very useful around a campfire. We often have clothes catching fire from the embers."

Everyone was now leaving, glad to be alive, and the sheriff and his bride had gone. Robin made sure that Marion left with her father, who was suffering from all the excitement. It was a sad ending to what had been a good day for the Nottingham residents before the fire. Merlin turned his thoughts to the stranger. *Who was that?*

CHAPTER THIRTY

The next few weeks passed quietly after the fire at the wedding, the bodies of those who died were buried, and the town was getting back to normal. The sheriff was his old self again, although the townsfolk liked his wife, their animosity towards the sheriff had returned.

Robin reverted to his original plan and started to assemble his army to attack the castle. One hundred men north of Nottingham and one hundred to the south. Both contingents would live in the forest for two days to prepare; John was to lead the northerly unit to take charge of the attack on the front gate of the castle. The other contingent to the south would be under Robin's control, and they would use the secret rear passageway for access. Merlin was assigned to Robin to accompany him, as he might have more experience as a leader of soldiers.

Merlin had made a hundred grenades, comprised of a bottle that was filled with gunpowder leaving a wick out of the top and sealing it. The wick could then be lit, and the grenade was thrown, it would explode in one minute. He also filled a number of bottles with a highly inflammable oil that could be thrown as incendiary devices. If a flame could be sent in by an arrow, the oil would burn and set fire to the surroundings.

They intended to burn the castle down and all who were in it. Robin was concerned, however, about the men held in the castle dungeons. He didn't know how many there were, but the rumors were there were hundreds. He planned to release them first, and that would give him more helpers.

Robin had to make sure the sheriff would be in the castle at the time of their attack, so it was decided to do it at first light. Merlin had now concluded that this might be his final act in this adventure and that after this battle, he would head south to the lake to see if Viviane appeared.

Robin and Little John agreed on a day for the attack; John would deal with the main entrance to the castle from the north, while Robin would use the secret rear entrance up the rock face from the south. Robin would then go to the dungeon to release the prisoners. As usual, Merlin didn't want to take part in the fighting but would go along with Robin to advise.

Robin had decided he would wear a soldier's uniform so that he could get around the castle at first without the real soldiers knowing. He said to Merlin, laughing, "I won't make the mistake of wearing a captain's uniform, though. That is reserved for you." Merlin sniggered in contempt. They did have a problem, though: how would the two armies time their attacks together?

Merlin came up with the solution. "We need to get all the church bells to ring at the appointed time. I'll go and see Tuck. He can start the bells ringing, and then other churches can follow the lead."

"Good idea," said Robin, and Merlin left the camp to see Tuck.

The friar was pleased to be part of the operation. "Leave it to me. I'll see the other clergymen and make arrangements."

On the eve of the appointed day, both armies got into position. John was a mile into the woods to the north of town, while Robin was a mile to the south. They were both agreed that no one must be seen until it was too late for the sheriff to act, and timing would be crucial.

That evening, King Richard was staying with the lord of the manor at Mapperley, a small village not far from Nottingham. He wanted to have access to Nottingham incognito to investigate the situation. He had another visit from Viviane, and she said to him, "Sire, you should be at Nottingham Castle tomorrow just after sunrise."

The king, who was half-asleep, said, "Madam, why should I be doing that?"

"Because the answer to all your queries will be seen," said Viviane.

"Why are you telling me all this?"

"Because I am doing your job for you. You spend all your time at war in countries that are far away, and yet you leave your own country in the hands of your brother to ruin and use to his own advantage. Your fellow countrymen are left to their own devices and doing your work for you. That leaves me, the ghost of a poor country girl, to take up the reins on your behalf."

The king was astounded. No one had ever talked to him that way. He was at a loss for words, but he realized that what the ghost was saying was true. Viviane left in a huff. "Men!" she whispered to herself.

The next morning, while the townsfolk were asleep, both of Robin's armies moved forward into their start positions. As the sun rose over the horizon, Tuck started ringing the priory bells, and within seconds, church bells were ringing all over Nottingham.

"What the hell was that about?" the sheriff asked his wife as he woke up from his sleep.

Robin, dressed in his uniform, went into the old building at the bottom of the rear tunnels, waiting for the signal from Tuck. Robin and Merlin climbed to the castle top. Robin's men followed them up; once everyone was upstairs in the castle, they came across a patrol of four men doing their rounds. Robin and three men hid behind columns while Merlin and the remainder of the men kept well out of sight.

The four-man patrol was being very casual, not expecting any trouble. No doubt they were half-asleep, but they were in for a rude awakening as they passed the columns. Robin stepped out in his uniform, and the real soldiers acknowledged him, at which time he produced his knife, and his three men sprang out from their hiding places with knives in hand. Each knife sank in where it was required, with a hand over each soldier's mouth to prevent any sound.

The four bodies were dumped in a large cupboard. Robin knew he had to act quickly now as, when the patrol didn't return, the game would be up. He was aware that the dungeons were downstairs, so he and Merlin rushed down the nearest stairway. Halfway down, there was a door on the left marked "Arsenal." Robin opened the door to find a room full of weapons, mainly swords but also rows of daggers and large knives. He quietly closed the door and descended to where six prison cells contained at least fifty men, many of whom were asleep.

There were two guards outside who were also asleep on the floor. Robin moved quickly, and they were silenced with his knife and never woke up. Merlin, who was standing at the bottom of the stairs, could hear the sound of men coming down the stairway. He quickly said to Robin, "Psst," indicating someone was coming.

The guard was being changed. Two new guards came into view, and they were fresh and awake. Seeing their compatriots on the ground, they rushed over to them and turned over the bodies, revealing the blood-stained clothing. Robin was immediately out of his hiding place and on their backs while Merlin went to pick up the cell keys, which were on the waistband of one of the dead guards. While Robin was fighting, Merlin opened the nearest cell, and ten men came rushing out and quickly wrung the necks of the soldiers.

Robin took a deep breath and whispered, "That was close."

Merlin released the other prisoners from the cells. They were exhilarated and noisy. Robin said, "Quiet, men. Don't warn the castle we're here. The armory is halfway up the stairs. Arm yourselves, and we are going to take over the castle and get rid of this sheriff once and for all."

All the men let out a quiet, "Aye aye." They all went up to the armory and collected an array of swords and knives. Robin quickly removed his soldier's uniform, revealing his Lincoln green uniform underneath; he didn't want one of the prisoners attacking him by mistake. He led everyone up to the main floor to join his other men.

At the front entrance of the castle, on the higher level, John and his contingent of men had been waiting for the church bells to ring. The castle had a large wooden gate at this level. John threw several of Merlin's incendiary devices at the gate, and lighted arrows were fired to ignite them. The fuses of six grenades were lit, and the grenades were thrown at the entrance. The gate splintered and was burning strongly now. "Another few minutes, and we'll be in," said John.

The noise had woken all of the castle's inhabitants; guards were rushing around, heading to the front gate, where the explosions were coming from. They hadn't realized there were already one hundred and fifty men on the loose, rampaging through the castle.

Robin and his men were picking off the confused guards as they ran around. No prisoners were taken. Several of Robin's men were hurt in sword and knife fights, but more of the soldiers died. The ex-prisoners were particularly brutal; they had been incarcerated so long that hatred had overtaken them, and they applied much more force on the guards than was necessary. No one was spared. All the soldiers were slashed with the swords and any other weapon available, and blood was pouring out of their wounds. Merlin was surprised at the dexterity of the prisoners especially after being in prison for so long.

The castle guards had started firing crossbow darts through the latticed front gate but had to move back from the heat. They did manage to kill a few of the attacking force, but John was now inside the castle, as the gate had burnt down. Fierce fighting lasted over an hour. John's men were firing arrows at the guards with longbows, which were much more efficient than the crossbows, and the guards were eventually totally overwhelmed. Robin and his men had now linked up with Little John.

The attackers were now in control of the castle approach area; only the keep was in the hands of the sheriff, who had a personal guard of twelve soldiers. These were the elite soldiers, and Robin knew they would be the hardest to overcome, but time was on his side. He made sure the remainder of the castle was his and there were no stragglers left behind.

He estimated that at least fifty of the guards were dead, and ten prisoners had been captured. He had also lost ten men, and he went back to the center of the castle by the keep. From a window, the sheriff could be heard saying, "If you go now, you will be allowed to live. Otherwise, the king will hunt you down like the criminals you are."

A voice behind Robin said, "Who speaks in my name?"

Turning, Merlin saw the massive white stallion three feet away from him. He had to look up, and on its back sat a tall man in a soft white vest. It was embroidered with three rampant red lions. He had dark pants, and to the right side hung a sword in its scabbard. He was a rugged man and appeared weary. He had been in many wars, as evidenced by the scars on his face, and he wore a small golden crown on his head. No one in the castle had seen the king before, but all knew who the stranger was and bowed low.

This was King Richard at his finest; Merlin also realized that this was the stranger who had appeared at the sheriff's wedding. The word had gotten around that something was being planned: Richard had been determined to be at the castle today.

Viviane could be seen only by the king as she was flying around the keep. She said to him, "Glad you made it, your majesty. Exercise your authority." The king just smiled.

Neither Robin nor Merlin had ever seen King Richard before, but the insignia of three rampant lions on his chest and his shield told them that's who he was. The king did not speak English, so everything he said was through an interpreter. "Sire," said Robin, bowing, not sure what the king would do.

Merlin was standing next to the white stallion, who held his head high in a regal manner. The horse looked down at Merlin and suddenly lowered its head, as though bowing to him. Merlin took hold of the horse's bridle to steady it while the king got down. The horse was feisty, but Merlin breathed into the horse's nostril, and the horse bowed his head to him. The king stood still, smiling in amazement, and through his interpreter, he said, "And who might you be? I have never seen my horse act in that way to anyone before."

"I am Merlin, sire."

"Ah, that answers a lot," said the king

The king called up to the window, "Are you the sheriff? I have been told of the troubles at Nottingham, which is why I am here."

The sheriff, realizing who this was, said, "Sire, I'm so pleased you have come to save me. My castle has been taken over by these criminals."

"We'll see about that. You may come down now, but you will be under arrest until I resolve this matter."

The sheriff and his wife came downstairs and out of the door. He bowed before the king, but the king said, "Arrest him. I want to get to the bottom of this."

The king turned and took in the scene; there were now about a hundred and fifty simple folks who had stood up to officialdom in the form of the sheriff. *That took a lot of guts*, thought the king, *but why was it necessary?* He stood back and walked around Merlin, looking him up and down as though he were a freak. Merlin became embarrassed. The king said, "You don't look as though you come from these parts. My horse seems to recognize you, but Merlin is a very famous name, and there is a spirit that thinks I should listen to you."

Merlin was surprised. Would this king know about Arthur? "In what way famous, sire?"

"Well, there was another Merlin in this land five hundred years ago who served the king at that time, King Arthur, the man who united England into one country."

"Yes, sire, I know of whom you mean." Merlin was amazed that a Norman king would know the story of an Anglo-Saxon king from five hundred years earlier.

"I have had several dreams about you, Merlin, on my way back to England and since. I dreamt of a lake, and out of the lake came a ghostly woman. She said to me that when I got back to England, I would meet someone called Merlin and that I should listen to what he had to say. She went on to say that you had helped another king of England become a legend to his people and that one day, I too would become a legend. Because of that, I had better listen to you. I will set up court in the castle. Be here in one hour."

The king's entourage set up a courtroom in the main hall. There was a long table at the head of the room with five chairs behind it. There was a single chair to one side for witnesses and then a collection of chairs for the public. In an hour's time, the hall was filling up. Robin, Little John, and Merlin sat in the front row. A messenger had been sent to Friar Tuck, Lord Howarth, and Marion to come to the castle for the trial of the sheriff. Friar Tuck was seated behind Merlin, and members of the public, including some of Robin's men, filled the rest of the room.

The sheriff was brought into the room, tied at the hands, and he sat opposite the witness chair with an armed guard behind him. Once all the seats were full, the main doors were closed and locked.

At that point, the king entered the room. Everyone stood and bowed, and someone shouted, "Three cheers for the king! Hip, hip hurrah!" which was repeated three times by the crowd. The king acknowledged this by raising his hand and giving the royal wave.

The king sat down, and all followed suit. He said, "During my period away fighting for the Crusade in the advancement of Christianity, my brother Prince John took on my role as king of England and Normandy. It is told to me that John has abused his position and caused much hardship to my people, which I will not tolerate. Nottingham is a central part of England and a vital town. I would like to hear what you, the people of the town, think."

Lord Howarth and Marion arrived outside. The guard at the door said, "Sorry, sir, but the hall is full now, and the king has ordered the doors closed."

Lord Howarth said, "Please send a message to the king that Lord Howarth is outside and begs entrance. I have matters to raise at this inquest."

"Certainly, sir. Please wait here."

The guard entered the room and went to the king, saying, "Excuse me, sire, but Lord Howarth is outside, asking for admission."

The king rose and said, "I apologize and interrupt the proceeding for five minutes while I attend to a matter outside." A mumble went up around the room.

The king left the room and saw Lord Howarth and Marion standing there. He said, "Lord Howarth, it is a pleasure to meet you. My father, King Henry, told me of your battles with him. He respected you and was always glad to have you at his side. This must be your daughter, the Lady Marion."

"It is indeed, sire, and thank you for your kind words. We came this morning because I have information about this sheriff," said Lord Howarth.

"Then you are welcome here, sir. We will make room for you. Please come in," said the king.

They re-entered the room; the king asked two people in the front row if they would kindly move for two important guests. That was, of course, a polite order. No one would dare argue with the king; your head was at risk.

Having taken their seats, the proceedings continued. Several members of the audience stood up and made their comments. They were all along the same lines that Prince John had taxed them into poverty. He had imposed men such as the sheriff on them, who were unscrupulous and making money personally.

The king then called on Lord Howarth to speak. Howarth began to stand up, but the king said, "Please stay seated."

"That is very kind of you, sire, but I know my duty." Howarth stood up, resting his hands on the back of the chair in front of him. He related the story of how the sheriff had tried to take over his estate by force only four months ago. "If it had not been for Robin Hood and his followers interceding, I would now be a prisoner in this castle, and I don't know what would have happened to my daughter." The king glared at the sheriff, who looked down at the floor.

The king graciously thanked each person who had spoken, and after hearing from six people, he realized that the stories were all the same. The sheriff had been sitting quietly through all this; he knew his turn would come. The king turned to Merlin and said, "I would now like to hear from you, Merlin. What is your take on the situation here?"

Merlin stood up. "Sire, I am not from around these parts. I was sent here by another, whom I believe you have been in communication with, to resolve issues of which you have already heard from the inhabitants. There is outrageous corruption in the region, led by the sheriff sitting over there. He has collected taxes, which is his responsibility, but he has added a personal tax on top, without authority. He has usurped his power to evict people from their properties so that he can take control of them.

"I feel strongly that the sheriff's personal fortune should be examined. It will contain considerably more than would be expected based on his salary from the king's coffers. I would also like to say that Robin Hood here has been helping the local inhabitants through these bad times. Although he has taken the castle by force today, this was an act against the sheriff and not against the crown.

"There is one other matter I would like to deal with, sire, that is not relevant to this trial, but since I have your attention..." He moved to Friar Tuck, who was carrying Excalibur wrapped in a cloth.

He took it from Tuck, saying to the king as he unwrapped Excalibur, "Sire, this is the ceremonial sword of King Arthur, presented to him by another with the name of Merlin. I would like you to place it with the crown jewels of England. This sword is an item of royal jewels from the first King of England for the future prosperity of generations to come."

Merlin handed the sword to the king and bowed. The king unsheathed it and said, "This is a beautiful item and of much historical value. I will see it is preserved in the vaults for future generations to enjoy." A gasp went up from the crowd.

The king said, coming back to the court case, "That was quite a speech of damnation, and what is your relationship to Robin the Hood?"

"Sire, when I came to Nottingham, Robin led a band of highwaymen living in the forest and robbing all passersby, whether rich or poor. With a little help, he has become a person of good character. He has fought the sheriff on many occasions to protect the people, including, I will admit, stealing Prince John's taxes and giving them back to those affected. The charges were extortionate and unreasonable.

"Robin has now become something of a hero locally," he added for strength. "Sire, one day, mark my words, Robin Hood will become a legend in his own right, like yourself."

Those last words impressed the king. He did not know who Merlin was, but the Lady of the Lake was apparently involved, and spiritualism was paramount to all. Christianity was fanatical, and Jesus had risen from the dead. Viviane, the Lady of the Lake, was real to the king, and her words had to be heard.

"Is there anyone else who wishes to speak before I ask the sheriff to answer the accusations?" the king said.

Friar Tuck stood up. "Sire, I am a man of the cloth, and as such, I can confirm everything that has been told this morning."

"Thank you, Father. That means a lot to me," the king replied. "In that case, I will ask the sheriff if he has anything to say."

The sheriff got up, getting ready to plead for his life. He bowed deeply and said, "Some of the things said today, I cannot deny, but my actions have been at the behest of your brother. He made me do the things that I did, on peril of my life. Your brother is a vicious man. I am merely his servant, and I place myself at your mercy."

The king said, "You admit by your own mouth that the accusations are true and, therefore, you are guilty. I take your point as to pressure from above, and one day I am sure these things will be written down so your actions cannot be repeated. I will spare your life on this occasion, but you are excluded from this town, and your personal finances will be taken from you other than a stipend to see that you and your wife have a meager existence in the future"

The sheriff was relieved with the outcome; he had expected death. He duly left the castle that day, never to be seen or heard of again. His money was taken, and a proportion was given to the poor of the district by way of housing to be built in the next months under the supervision of Friar Tuck. Tuck said, "The houses will be called almshouses, and only certain types of people can live in them, the poor."

The sheriff thought that although he had lost his personal fortune, he still had his wife's fortune at the Devon Estate. Little did he know, but that estate was in debt. He would find that out the hard way.

The king had to appoint a new sheriff; he offered the job to Merlin.

"Thank you, sire. I appreciate your confidence, but I think my time in this era is finished, and I will be leaving soon, but there is one thing I'd like to discuss with you, if I may."

The king said, "Certainly. Once we are finished here, let's have a chat." One of the other dignitaries of the town took over the role of sheriff, and the townspeople were happy with that appointment.

Robin Hood was given a royal pardon. Merlin, on the other hand, knew his role had been performed and was ready to head back to the Lady of The Lake, but before he did so, he went to see the king.

"Sire, a question, if you please. I know your ancestor King William built a castle at Windsor. Do you have any knowledge of the building?"

"Oh yes, Merlin. Windsor is a palace of mine and every king of England. As you say, King William built it. I'm not sure why he chose that position, but I do know there was a former building of importance there. Maybe that was the reason."

Merlin was getting hopeful. "I understood that, too, sire, but do you know who occupied the former building, and if there had been any artifacts there then, where would they be now? I am particularly interested in a bust of King Arthur."

"I don't know who occupied it; I believe it has been empty for many years and is a ruin. As to the rest, I always thought Arthur was a legend, but had there been any artifacts, they would have been retained for prosperity. I can tell you there is no bust of King Arthur on the property. I visited there on my way up to Nottingham."

"Did you, by any chance, see any cannons?"

"Cannons?" said the interpreter.

Merlin realized now that the cannon had still not been invented yet, which meant that his cannons must have gone, but he said, "A cannon is a tube seven feet long from which iron balls can be fired."

The king said, "So, that's what those pipes are. There are four pipes of that description lying at the back of the Windsor Castle. No one knew what they were for, and they are now corroding away."

"Thank you, sire," said Merlin.

He left the building, thinking, *Well, my attempt to alter the course of history didn't work, did it? I won't trouble with that again.* He was annoyed with himself; he had so wanted to make Arthur a real person to future generations.

Behind Merlin stood Viviane, looking full of herself. Gleefully she said to herself, "I've done it. My mother would be proud. It's time to move Merlin on." Unbeknownst to him, she flew around him and sprinkled stardust on him.

The proceedings being over, Robin went to Marion and her father and said, "Let me take you both home."

He drove the buggy back to the manor house and was invited in for a drink. Lord Howarth said, "There's something I would like to discuss with you, Robin." Robin went inside the house, wondering what this was about.

"I am getting timeworn now," said Lord Howarth. "I would like to see Marion settled before I go, which won't be long now. My hope is that you will marry her, but if you don't feel that way, then I would like to offer you the job of estate manager, thereby securing Marion's future."

"Oh, Dad," said Marion, going red in the face.

Robin chipped in immediately, saying, "If Marion would have me, nothing would give me more pleasure than to be married to her. I would never have dreamt such a thing because of our differing status. I have always loved you ever since our childhood," he added, turning to Marion.

Marion moved nearer to Robin and said, "I feel the same. I'm not interested in status. Actions are much more important, and we will make a wonderful home here."

They kissed, and Lord Howarth shook Robin's hand. "We have to make the wedding arrangements. There's no point in waiting. I want to see this before I die."

"I would like Friar Tuck to marry us, if that's all right, sir," said Robin.

"Wonderful! My choice exactly. He is a good man," said Howarth.

Robin left shortly after and went back to his camp. He gave the good news to Merlin, who wasn't at all surprised. Robin said he would be moving into the manor house in three days' time, during which they had to organize the wedding with Friar Tuck.

Merlin said to Robin, "I am so pleased for you, and I wish you every happiness for the future. By the way, what is the name of the area where the manor house is?"

"Oh, I think it is called Loxley, but no one uses the name."

"They will in the future," said Merlin, realizing that the legend had gotten the house name in the wrong order, but so what?

The next few days were used to organize the wedding of Robin Hood to Marion Howarth. Friar Tuck was delighted to be asked to marry them at the priory. Both Robin and Marion wanted a simple affair, not like the sheriff's. The service took place one sunny morning, just Lord Howarth, Merlin, and a few family friends, and many of the Merry Old Men were present.

Lord Howarth arranged for a feast to be at the priory, but there were no oil lamps this time. Robin had arranged to disbanded the outlaws. Little John moved up the country, and most of the other men sank into the background. Robin now worked all his energies into running Marion's estate as, sadly the day after the wedding, Lord Howarth died. He had a good passing; he knew it was coming and just hung on to see his daughter get married.

Merlin realized his task was over, and he said goodbye to Friar Tuck. After the Camelot trip, he had become very close to Tuck, and he told him, "I will be leaving soon. I am sure my task is done, but I have to thank you for your friendship and understanding. To be frank, I don't think I could have done it without you. I will treasure my abacus; I can now keep track of my age. Strangely, that worried me, getting old but not knowing my real age, but now, thanks to you, I will."

"Now, stop that, or you'll have me crying," said Tuck. "I am glad to have been able to help you. I knew those many years ago that my task was something like this. I will make sure your change in Robin will be continued so that the legend will mature as you want. I have fulfilled my vocation now. God bless you, my son." They hugged, and Merlin left.

Merlin set off a few days later from the priory; he had moved in there when the outlaws had abandoned their camp. Leaving at sunrise, he left quietly, not liking goodbyes.

He took one of the horses and rode it to London, his abacus in its pouch. He had nothing to fear now, traveling down that road. Merlin found the lake easily and released the horse. There was no one at the lake, which surprised him, so he walked up to it, found the tree where he had carved Viviane's name, and rubbed his finger over the word "Help."

Viviane rose slowly from the water. She was alone. Merlin thought she looked beautiful this time. She said to him, "Well done, Merlin. You have done well. Robin Hood will now be the legend you know. King Richard will also be one of those kings who will never be forgotten; he will be called the Lionheart. He won't get back to Jerusalem, but others will. You have learned much from these experiences and will be a better man for them. Always remember your need for a family. That will come again in time. Be patient. Your mind still needs time to heal for now."

"I never did thank you for saving me in the bank raid, did I?" said Merlin. "I realized I was being dragged into things that were against my nature, and I do thank you for guiding me in the right direction. I promise not to make that mistake again."

"It is now time for you to leave. Are you ready?"

"Yes, I am, but can I go back to Gwen before she was killed? That way, we could restart our lives together."

"I'm sorry, Merlin, but that would not be a good idea. Remember, you cannot alter history; you can only make sure it happens in the way you know from the twenty-first century. Gwen is already dead, and you cannot alter that. Just remember that she is watching you and is happy, but she wants you to live your life and start a new family. She knows how important that is to you."

"So, where am I going?" asked Merlin.

"You'll have to wait and see. I have other tasks for you that will build upon your character." She had now moved across the lake towards him, and she said, "Just walk into me again."

Merlin, or Robert, walked forward, clutching his abacus tightly. Viviane turned into the bright light once again, and he entered her, and…

To be Continued

HISTORICAL NOTE

In the year 55 BC, Julius Caesar invaded the southeastern corner of Britain. His army moved north toward what would eventually become Londinium in the year 43AD. He set up a camp in the woods of Keston, which is today in the London borough of Bromley, a suburb in South London. He chose Keston because it had a natural spring, which is the source of the River Pool. The spring was named after him, becoming Caesar's Well. The River Pool feeds into the River Thames.

The escarpment of Caesar's camp can clearly be seen to this day. Caesar installed a friendly king to rule the locality and then left a year later for higher things in Gaul and Rome.

Subsequently, in the year 43AD, Emperor Claudius ordered further attacks on Britannia, as the Romans called it. Within a few years, they were in control of all land south of a diagonal line called the Fosse Way, a road from Exeter to Lincoln, despite the rebellion of Queen Boudicca from Essex. She decided to take poison rather than be captured, having lost the battle with the Romans.

Soon afterward, the Romans controlled all of Britannia south of Caledonia, modern-day Scotland, which had been cut off with Hadrian's Wall. That was built by another famous general, Hadrian, who would also become Caesar in due course of time. The Romans set up their capital at Colchester in Essex and built a bridge over the River Thames in Londinium, near the site of the present-day London Bridge.

The Roman occupation of Britain was undoubtedly the first traumatic start to the success of this nation, which one day was to outstrip the prowess and size of its founders.

The Roman rule of the country continued until 410 AD. At that time, the Roman Empire had already split up into the Eastern and Western Empires. The Western Empire was in turmoil; the barbarians in Northern Europe were pressing down south, fighting their way toward Rome.

Consequently, the legions in Britain were ordered to return home with all haste to protect the fatherland. The Eastern Empire, centered at Constantinople, would continue in strength for many centuries. The Western Empire was shrinking back to Rome and changed its name to The Holy Roman Empire.

Britain was left on its own to fend for itself at that time. Hadrian's Wall, erected to keep the Scots out, fell into disrepair, and the sentries were gone. Anarchy set in all over the Isles. Warlords sprung up, setting up many small kingdoms, one of which was said to be ruled by the King Arthur of legend.

King Arthur is probably the most famous of England's legends. For centuries, the actual Round Table was thought to be the one housed at Winchester Castle in Hampshire, but through carbon dating, this table has recently been found to date back to about 1290. It is on view at the castle, hanging on the wall of the Great Hall, and is as described in this book.

It is now believed to have been made for the betrothal of one of the daughters of King Edward I.

A Tudor rose was added in the center of the table by King Henry VIII, the implication being that Henry was the reincarnation of Arthur. Part of the legend is that Arthur will return when England needs him.

There are several claims to the actual site of Camelot, ranging from Cornwall to Wales, but I suspect it rotted away as described and sunk into the countryside like Sarum, although it is accepted to have been in the west country of Britain.

Some think that Arthur was King Alfred the Great (or Aelfred, as the name really was). He was probably the king who unified the country of England and ousted the Vikings to the south of the country. The main Viking settlement was in the north at York, where road names are still in the Viking language, Old Norse. The word for road is a gate.

As for the settlers, initially, I was working on the Vikings, but the dates did not fit. The Vikings didn't arrive in Britain until 793 with the attack on Lindisfarne. The reader can choose between Jutes, Saxons, or Angles for the settlers, all from the Germanic regions of Europe.

When we come to Robin Hood, the forests of England were full of highwaymen in the Middle Ages, as the nooses at Tyburn in London testified. The site of the tree at Tyburn is at Marble Arch at the beginning of the Edgware Road; a stone marks the spot where hangings were carried out. The term "hood" referred to all these highwaymen at that period, probably derived from the hoods they wore, not for privacy but for warmth when living outside year round; it was just as cold then!

There is no record of our Robin Hood other than in all the literature that has been written over the centuries.

Originally, all these legends were all passed on in song by roaming minstrels. No doubt, Chinese whispers would have taken place, and the stories became exaggerated as they went on.

King Richard the Lionheart is, of course, factual. He did not speak English and was only in the country for about six months of his whole reign, and he is the only king to have been crowned twice. The kidnapping and ransom were as stated and are well documented. The method of capture is not fully known, so I have adopted the one that best fit this plot.

King Henry VI, the Holy Roman Emperor, and the Duke of Austria were subsequently excommunicated by the pope for not complying with his decree, that returning Crusaders be allowed free passage through all countries they passed on the way home. The Holy Roman Empire was what was left of the old Western Roman Empire after its downfall. The Eastern Empire was ruled from Constantinople and became known as the Byzantine Empire, and it continued until 1453 when the Ottomans won Constantinople in battle and the Ottoman Empire began. The town now is called Istanbul.

Richard's brother Prince John did eventually succeed him to the throne of England on Richard's death in 1199 following a battle at Limoges Castle in France, when Richard was injured and, after twelve days, died of what is now thought to have been septicemia.

King John was, of course, famous for the signing of the Magna Carta in 1215, although he was forced into it. The document was prepared by the barons at the time on the basis that he sign or they would not provide troops for his battles in France. Subsequently, he denied it and dissolved it, but of course, it was later reinstated. One of the original Magna Cartas, and there were two hundred of them written by hand at the time, is housed in Salisbury Cathedral, England. Only four of the original documents exist today.

The quality of the one in Salisbury Cathedral is outstanding, and I highly recommend that everyone see it. It looks as though it was written yesterday – in Latin, of course. The quality of the ink used was outstanding for its time. The Magna Carta has been amended several times over the centuries. It is a living document.

The building of Salisbury Cathedral did eventually get started in 1220 and was completed a century later; it does, indeed, have the tallest spire in England to this day. Stonehenge is a short distance from Salisbury and Sarum. The description given for Stonehenge in 1200 is as I remember it in the early 1950s when, as a child, I climbed over the stones. It was restored in 1958, and since then, visitors are not allowed onto the site. Now the grandeur of the area must be viewed from a distance, which is a shame, as stones of this antiquity need to be touched to obtain their energy.

The other thing that King John is famous for is losing the crown jewels. In 1216, King John and his entourage were traveling through the Wash and Fen country of eastern England. As always, he carried his jewels with him, being frightened of them being stolen if he left them in London.

In those days, the countryside in that area was very marshy, and the coach carrying the jewels sank into the marsh, never to be seen again. The value of the loss today is suggested at £50 million. There have been many modern-day attempts to find the jewels using modern electronic devices, but to date, they have not been successful. One day, someone will come up with the answer. I wonder who the treasure will belong to then.

The first cannon recorded was in 1260 and used in a war in China. Windsor is, of course, the personal home of the Royal Family to this day. The castle was built by William the Conquer and has been in the Royal Family's occupation ever since. The current Royal Family adopted the name of Windsor as their surname on July 17, 1917, when King George V disassociated the family from all its German origins during the First World War.

The first recorded cold was in 1611, when John Common caught one – from where, no one knows, but he did give it to William Shakespeare – hence the name "common cold." To this day, doctors are still trying to work out where it came from.

The plague, or Black Death, occurred every twenty years or so. It was so contagious that towns were sealed off. No one was allowed in or out until the epidemic was over. The very limited medics in those days did not know what caused it. The main pandemic episode, which devastated all of Europe and Asia, was from 1346 to 1353, when between 75 and 200 million people died, around one-third of the total population. The other major incidence, which affected Britain, was in 1664, when London was sealed off, huge pits were dug all around the city, and the bodies were buried in mass graves. These pits today are parks and cannot be built upon for a thousand years.

The 1664 epidemic ended with the Great Fire of London, which started in Pudding Lane. We know now the disease was carried by fleas on rats from Asia that came over on ships. The fire killed the rats. The very cruel children's nursery rhyme resulted from the disease:

- *Ring a ring of roses* – First signs were large red welts all over the body.
- *A pocket full of poses* – People put flower petals in pockets to fight off the disease.
- *Atishoo, atishoo* – Sneezing, as with the flu, followed.
- *We all fall down* – death in about two weeks.

This book has been a change of direction for me; I would be interested to hear the reader's views by email at malcolm@malcolmjohnbaker.com.

www.ingramcontent.com/pod-product-compliance
Lightning Source LLC
Chambersburg PA
CBHW051215190726
48288CB00006B/1975